Soul Mate

AUDREY ENNIS

ISBN 978-1-63630-051-1 (Paperback)
ISBN 978-1-63630-052-8 (Digital)

Covenant Books, Inc.
11661 Hwy 707
Murrells Inlet, SC 29576
www.covenantbooks.com

Chapter 1

❦

Today at 10:00 a.m., Edward Moore and I, Brittney Bentley, were married in the First Baptist Church in Van Nuys, California. We are having the Van Nuys Country Club cater our wedding reception for us. Edwards's idea. I'm not sure if this reception is just for us or just Edward's alone. I feel so left out and alone but still am not sure where I belong in Edward's world. There are times leading up to this moment when I still felt that it was all a huge mistake. Am I just lonely for company, or is this his way of really loving me? I'm not even sure how I made it this far, moving to California and not really knowing this person that I married. Maybe this is all a big mistake. It wouldn't be the first mistake that I have ever made in my life. My life had many ups and downs before all this happened. I have always been hated so much. Hate is such a nasty word, but even growing up in my hometown, I never created any friends.

Edward is a medical doctor to the stars; all the top actresses and actors go to him. He is surrounded at all times, it seems, by all the females you can imagine. It is as if I don't exist even at my own wedding. I pray that it is not always going to be this way, but I have a feeling that wherever he goes, the ladies will be attracted to him, like flies to molasses, and I will always be left behind as it was when a teenager.

I didn't realize he was so popular or why when I first met him that I was attracted to him. Don't get me wrong, I love Edward so much, and I love the way that he hovers over me all the time when we are together.

But now the time has come, and here we are at the reception. I have never seen such a banquet that was spread for us: lobster, clams and oysters, all the most favorites of Edward, never mentioning his now wife, me. These are also the foods that I grew up with in Canada, where I have lived my entire life. Rivers of alcohol was flowing in a crystal fountain. I have never seen anything like this in my life, but I am really getting ahead of myself.

This may seem like the start of a fairytale and that I will wake up at any time now, which I wish, was true. But before that, let us go back to how this all started only a short time ago and how we ended up here.

Chapter 2

This is how it all started with the two of us, just a short time ago, back in July, on a warm summer day.

I grew up in the province of Newfoundland, Canada. I guess I was known to many as a Newfoundlander and to others as a Goofy Newfie, and that's where I met Edward on a slightly warm, windy day on the edge of a high cliff looking out over the Atlantic Ocean from the top of Signal Hill, St John's, which is the capital of the province of Newfoundland.

Newfoundland is an island off the east coast of Canada. It can be mesmerizing as you look around at the beauty of the mountains and the surrounding ocean. I was stretched out on the top of the cliff listening to the crashing of the waves taking me away to another world far from here. I spend most of my free time here thinking how my life has been and how I ended up having a career that I hate. I need to change, and I come here to be closer to my Heavenly Father and to talk with Him.

It was at this very site in 1901 that there was a major international breakthrough. Guglielmo Marconi, using an antenna suspended five hundred feet by kite, received the first transatlantic wireless signal, the letter *S* in Morse code. Many people visit this spot every year, but I always count it as mine. I only visit here when there aren't any visitors, which is at least once a week. I'm sort of a loner. I don't have any friends, and I really never did. Signal Hill was the perfect spot to look over the city and to think, and I had lots to think about, especially how my life was straying from the straight and narrow. It was the perfect place to come and cry my eyes out, feeling sorry for myself.

I am always mesmerized by the fury of the waves and have always loved the ocean and this particular spot, which I have always counted it as mine. This is where I found to be at my best at all times. I loved it here. The foam here today and most days was as white as the cliffs of Dover in England, although I have never seen them, and today I was so caught up in that particular moment and just putting everything out of my mind. I loved the ocean, and lying there I felt as if I could be part of it. I lay there on the edge of that cliff and leaning over wondering about the majesty of it all, as if it was created for me alone. I had tears in my eyes, as I normally do when I come here thinking of how our Creator adorned this special place, it seemed, just for me alone. But I know our Creator designed it to be loved by one and all, and it was just perfect. What a magnificent sight! God knew what He was doing when He created this place. If only I could save that moment in time and how I wished and prayed for someone in my life that I could share this beauty, but there wasn't anyone and probably never would. The weather was beautiful this day, a refreshing breeze and the sun high in the brightest blue sky with a few puffy white clouds in a variety of shapes that sometimes looked like animals. The pure white seagulls soaring far above seemed endless in their flight. I could barely see, as the tears were coming more and more, and I was sobbing uncontrollably. To anyone there, seeing me, I looked a mess, my eyes all red and my cheeks covered in tears.

As I was being swept away by the moment in time, I noticed a man walking along the path coming toward me at a very fast gait, with a cigarette in his hand. As I looked at him, I started to get slightly scared. Never before had I ever seen anyone come to this part of the cliff, my secret spot; normally, they just walk to the tower and then gaze at the ocean. Why was this tall man coming toward me, especially this fast? I didn't recognize him; he was a complete stranger. I had never seen him before, at least not that I could remember. Maybe it was someone I had hurt in my job as an investigative reporter, and now he was out to get revenge. He could have been stalking me for days and now had me all alone on the edge of the cliff. I was scared. What should I do? What could I do? I started to shake. There wasn't any place to run. If I screamed, no one could hear me over the sound of the waves. I could jump in the ocean, but that was committing suicide, killing myself upon impact. I made up my mind that I would face him and endure the consequences. If it was my time to die, then that would be it, and I wouldn't have to ever think about anything else in the world and would be in a far better place.

He came up behind me and grasped me around the waist. Now I was really scared, and he was overbearingly strong. I couldn't fight this man. I tried to get away from his grasp, but it was useless. I wanted to scream, but I was too scared. I opened my mouth, but nothing came forth from my mouth.

He spoke and with the gentleness of voices. "Nothing is worth doing what you are thinking," he spoke as he still grasped a hold on me. He saw the tears that were flowing down my cheeks. Finally, I found my voice again and yelled at him.

I finally found my voice. "What do you think you are doing and who you think you are, sir, coming here bothering a person? Sir, just leave me alone. I don't know you, and you do not know me. I have nothing on me if you are looking to rob me." I was still squirming trying to get his hands from around my waist. He was too overpowering for me to get away from him as I tried to wipe my tears away. My tears were flowing now like stream down my cheeks, and his features were very gentle as I looked at him. I was sobbing so hard, and he was trying to console me like no other person that I knew. Here was a complete stranger who had such a gentle voice and took the time to care so much.

"Please stop squirming. I am trying to help you. Nothing is as bad that you need to throw your life away by jumping in the ocean. I'm a medical doctor, and I would never turn my back on someone in need, especially as beautiful as you. What would your husband or boyfriend think? Excuse me, please don't be scared of me, so let me introduce myself. My name is Edward Moore, originally from England, but now I live in California. And may I enquire of your name? I will release you of my grasp if you promise to just talk to me."

Between the sobs, I finally spoke, "My name is Brittney Bentley, and I didn't intend to throw myself into the waves. You would have to be crazy to commit suicide, and it is a sin to do it. I was just enjoying the moment. I love the ocean and the freedom that it represents to me. The smell of the salt air and the fury of the ocean take me away to another place and another time that was less hectic and more serene and where I had a better life. It is so alive here and makes me feel the same. I come here to make sure that I am still alive in mind, not just body. But never mind that. You didn't stop here to hear my sordid story, so now that you know that I am not going to jump, you may leave. I thank you for your concern." I started to wipe my tears with the back of my hands when he produced a handkerchief and did it for me with such tenderness.

"I would love to hear your sordid story, if your boyfriend or husband wouldn't mind." At that moment, he took the handkerchief that was still in his hand and started to wipe away more tears that I couldn't seem to stop from flowing. What a gentle act!

"I am not married, and no man would be caught taking me anywhere. I haven't any boyfriend. People stay away from me as if I had the plague, which is why I don't understand your desire to be even near me." As I said all these things to him, I kept wondering why I was telling him, a total stranger, all these things. I never did anything like this in my life. It was as if there was a spell put on me.

"I can't believe that, and to reassure you that you are a gorgeous woman, I would love to take you to the most elegant restaurant in the city tonight, not just because I tried to save your life that didn't need saving, but also I love talking to you and would like to get to know you better. You have a beautiful voice. I really didn't mean to intrude on your alone time or scare you. I really, really didn't mean to scare you. I didn't mean to do anything of the kind. I hope you don't think that I am being too forward. I'm a stranger here on vacation and don't know anyone, except you now. Someone I know in California, a patient, recommended that since I needed a vacation so bad that I should come here to Newfoundland, and I would get all the rest I needed and to enjoy the beautiful surroundings, especially the ocean. I also love the ocean and grew up next to it in England. I miss it every day. That's why I live near the ocean in California, just to see it every day. Would you be so kind and consider going out to dinner with me tonight? I'm here for a short time before I have to return back home. I want to ask you before some other man sweep you off your feet. Don't be scared because there will be people in the restaurant, and we will not be alone."

I started to laugh out loud. "That would be a miracle for someone to ask me out. What about your girlfriend or wife? I know a doctor must be married or have plenty of other girls on your arm every night. You must have met other girls since you came here."

"Not me. I'm a bachelor. I just haven't found the right girl."

"Are you sure you want to dine with me? Not one man around here even likes me enough to invite me to dinner or would even consider it, and I don't think you would want to take me to dinner if you really knew me. They would rather hurt me before they would invite me anywhere. Why would such a sophisticated and educated man as a doctor want to take out someone like me? I'm sure I'm not a person up to your high standards of being a doctor, and I would probably embarrass you at the restaurant, not knowing even which fork to use. Also, I never go out with a person who smokes, and since you say that you are a doctor, I would think that you know all the bad effects smoking has on the body, also it is definitely not a good sign to be seen around town with me. You will start to get a bad reputation. I'm just a down-to-earth girl who has grown up on the shores of Newfoundland in a quaint little village. I have never been out to dinner where I would be invited to a lavish restaurant. Are you absolutely sure that you want to go or be seen with me? You really don't know anything about me. You don't need to pay me back for scaring me."

"Yes, my dear, I really do want to go out to dinner with you, now more than ever, since you really have gotten my curiosity going. I will pick you up at 8PM. Just to let you know, I smoke for something to do with my hands, but I don't inhale. Mostly the cigarette just burns down, and since I perform surgery all the time with my hands, they are never idle, and not for the effects of the nicotine. Tonight when you accompany me, I'll not need to smoke with having such a beautiful lady by my side. I will hold your hand instead. Could you give me your address please, and I will pick you up on time. Can I give you a ride home now since I scared you so much?"

"No, I am fine. I will walk home after I spend a little more time here taking in all this beauty. Here is my address. Do you think that you will be able to locate it? Also, you are really being forward-thinking that I will let you hold my hand after just meeting you."

"No problem, but I don't like leaving you here all alone. Are you sure that you wouldn't like for me to stay and keep you company? There is something that draws me to you, and I'm not sure what it is. If you're sure that you will be okay, then I will pick you up at 8:00 p.m. at this address that you wrote down. Just be ready for a dazzling time and a luxurious meal."

"Don't worry about me. I come here quite a lot for the peace and quiet and when I need to think about where my life is going and if I require a change. I will be ready on time and looking forward to dinner, I think."

I stayed on that cliff about another hour, and all these weird thoughts kept running through my head. What was I thinking saying yes to a total stranger to accompany him to dinner, but he stated that he was a doctor, but was he really? Now I couldn't even call him and say forget it because I didn't get his telephone number, and he didn't say where he was staying. He can't call me since I didn't give him mine. He did seem like a decent person, but what was I thinking giving him my address. He was dressed very neat and groomed perfectly. He probably wouldn't show up anyway, but I guess I should look presentable just in case he did show.

I had already decided on what I should wear. I would dress in my best dress, which was my only dress: short, but not too short, black, low-cut, but not too low and strapless. I didn't want him to get any ideas. I wanted to make a great impression on him especially after the circumstances of how we had met. I kept thinking that maybe this could be mister right instead of all the one-night stands that I decided I was never going out with again. I then thought about it and realized that he would be flying back to California in a few days, and that would be the last I saw of him also. Another one-night stand. I have such horrible luck where men are concerned. I guess I am destined to forever be single.

Chapter 3

I was very careful putting on my makeup for my dinner date with Edward. I waited until the last minute to put on my dress as not to wrinkle it. Also, I was as nervous as a teenager on my first date. My hair was long and so I put it up on my head. I was trembling wondering what this date would be like and who this doctor really was, also where would he be taking me this evening, probably some sleazy out-of-the-way place down on Water Street where all the ships from different ports of call in the world assemble with their exported goods.

Edward arrived exactly on time that evening, not one minute late or early. Very prompt! I was very impressed so far, and I was ready for whatever. The way he looked, I thought I was in heaven. He was so suave-looking, debonair, elegantly dressed in a black suit. He was tall, muscular, and very handsome, and I just loved hearing him talk with that wonderful British accent. He was driving a black convertible Mercedes, top-down. He rang the bell to my apartment, and when I answered, he actually bowed to me. "Your coach awaits, my lady."

I stood there in awe of what was happening. I kept staring at him. He made me feel like I was a grand lady, and this was my royal coach. I felt as if I was in a fairy tale, and I was Cinderella. I guessed that in a few minutes, I would awaken from a dream.

He walked me to the car, holding my arm and opened the car door for me. No man has ever done that for me in my life. He had such manners. He then walked around the car and slid in beside me. "Would you prefer the top up, or should I leave it down, your preference?"

"Would you mind leaving it down, please? The wind feels wonderful."

The wind was rushing through our hair. Everything up to this point was perfect, almost too perfect. Something was sure to go wrong; I just knew it, especially if you happened to be me. I just never had a perfect date in my entire life. Nothing as wonderful as this ever happened to me. We went to the Country Club restaurant in St. John's. I just knew that this was a mistake from the very beginning, but I didn't want to spoil Edward's evening that he had planned, and I wanted a great evening out for once in my life and some decent food. I didn't say anything to him about what might happen here, so I kept my mouth shut.

We walked into the restaurant arm-in-arm, and as we entered there were some people there that I recognized, and they recognized me. I tried to keep my head down as much as possible. They looked at me as if I had two heads, seeing me with this very outstanding debonair-looking gentleman and drive up in this luxurious car. One man, Mr. Owen, approached us as we entered. "Well, if it isn't Brittney Bentley. What are you doing here tonight? I told you to never ever set your face around this door. I barred you from this restaurant. You usually only come here when you are reporting something happening where you can stretch the truth. We don't need any investigative reporting for that rag newspaper, *the Weekly Telegram*, which you work for, done here tonight. We have had enough of your reports for a lifetime. We shouldn't even allow you to enter the club, but we can't stop you from eating dinner here, especially when you are with a stranger. We need all the customers we can get."

I felt so embarrassed with my face turning red as a beet. My eyes were starting to well up with tears, and Edward stared to notice as well. "Good sir, this lady is with me tonight, and we are here to eat dinner and nothing else. I am Dr. Edward Moore, and we have reservations for dinner. There will be no working tonight. Miss Bentley is my grand lady tonight, not an investigative reporter. Could you please seat us at our table, and I would prefer that you look on her as a lady tonight, else I can create rumors around here that I don't think you want to hear."

"I am so sorry, sir! Please, come this way. Your table is waiting, and everything has been prepared just as you requested."

Edward linked our hands together, and we walked to a table that was secluded and that when you are seated, you stare at each other. There was no other way to sit. Very romantic. I could see out of the corner of my eye that many of the patrons were gossiping among themselves as to who this man was that I seemed to know and that they hadn't yet met. It bothered them for this reason. The people that usually came to this restaurant were oftentimes the snobbish, rich people of the city. I also noticed that they called over to their table Mr. Owen as soon as we were seated. They just had to know who Edward was and how come they didn't know him and hadn't met him. Many of them wanted him to introduce them to him. In their eyes, you could see that they were altogether out of my league and wanted to be with Edward.

"Edward, I think you should take me home. I'm not wanted here." My eyes were still misty, and Edward reached out and took my hand.

"That's nonsense! I want you here with me, isn't that enough? We are going to enjoy a wonderful dinner with you as my date, and I'm proud to have you here with me, especially that you said yes in dining with me. Hold my hand, please." I placed my fingers inter-twined with his. "You are so beautiful tonight, and I want to make sure that this is not a fairytale that I will wake up to tomorrow. I hope you don't mind, but I wanted the table away from everyone to be alone with you. I think you are blushing. I pray that isn't tears that I see in your eyes. I'm praying that they are twinkling stars."

I felt myself turning red. I also thought that he wanted to put me in the back where no one would ever see me, but maybe I should have more confidence in what he was saying than on my thinking. I wouldn't try to think about it for now. Edward had preordered champagne and caviar, which I had never tasted before in my life. It seemed to be a romantic gesture on his part. I couldn't help myself, but I kept looking at him. I couldn't take my eyes off him. He was so handsome. It was like I was in a dream world and would wake up at any minute and realize that I had been in a dream and back at my apartment eating a TV dinner, something that I usually did while watching television each night. I really couldn't afford any luxuries on my salary.

"Why are you staring at me? Is there something wrong? Is something out of place?"

"I'm sorry, Edward. Something is definitely out of place here. You are here with me when you could meet any gorgeous girl and have them seated here with you. Instead, you are seated here with me, a miss nobody. I still can't figure out why you want to be here with me of all the girls you could have, especially with your looks and elegance. I'm not used to being with someone like you. I feel so out of place."

Our waiter brought the champagne and caviar, and we sipped and put the caviar on tips of toast.

"Are you sorry that you are here with me because I'm happy to be here with you? I don't want to be with anyone else. I want to be with you. Please stop putting yourself down. You are a beautiful woman and great company. Do you mind if I give you a nickname instead of Brittney? I think you should be called Britt, but only by me. It suits you."

"I don't mind you calling me that. I have been called many other names that I won't mention. It will be only for a short while, and then you will be heading back to California. You will then have only stories to tell the other doctors about the girl you renamed Britt and how funny and amusing it was to actually have her eat with you."

He sighed and looked so sad. I felt so awful for saying what I did. I really regretted it but kept my mouth closed.

"We will talk later about how you keep putting yourself down. How about a nice green tossed salad to start the evening? Do you mind if I order for both of us? Waiter, the lady and I will order the lobster with butter sauce and potatoes au gratin. For dessert, we will have cherries jubilee. You may bring us our salads now. Does that sound good to you?"

"It sounds just wonderful. I have never eaten like this in my life. I could never afford such extravagances. Edward, I'm not rich. I wanted to let you know that I'm dirt poor, but that is not the reason that I accepted this dinner date with you. I really don't know why. I have never done something like this in my life, but something kept pushing me to take you up on your offer of dinner. Reporters don't make much money. Is that why you invited me to dinner because you felt sorry for me?"

"No, that's not the reason I asked you out. Something strange kept nagging at me as we were on that cliff. I tried to think about what it was that was nagging at me, up until I picked you up tonight. I will tell you later what it was. Britt, I was poor once also. I wasn't always a well-known surgeon. I had to work to get where I am today. Britt, I only want to be with you tonight. You have made me very happy by accepting my invitation to dine. I may be a doctor, but that doesn't mean that I have to eat with the rich and famous or with other doctors. Here comes the waiter with our food. Let's eat and then we'll talk."

We enjoyed the best meal that I had eaten in months. Normally I just go home and curl up in front of the television with a good book and a TV dinner and then fall to sleep on the sofa. We ate slowly, savoring each morsel, and drinking champagne while I just kept staring at him.

The evening went so beautifully; we sat there and talked about everything that we could think of, from his life in Great Britain and then how he went to California to earn more money so he could have his family brought to the States to live with him, but sadly his mother passed away before that could happen, so he stayed in California after that. Then we talked about my life here in Newfoundland, with the rag paper that I worked for and all the people that I have hurt along the way. I regretted it all, but I didn't know what else to do. Reporting was all I knew, but I didn't know it was going to get me a bad reputation. I hated my job. He listened attentively, holding on to every word that I spoke. He held my hand while we talked, and he knew how sad I was getting since the tears started welling up in my eyes. I excused myself and went to the ladies' room.

"Please excuse me for a minute, Edward."

He arose from his seat as I got up just like any gentleman would, and I headed for the ladies' room to dash water on my face.

"Are you okay? Is there anything I can do? Did I say the incorrect thing? I hope I haven't offended you in some way."

"I will be fine. I just need to splash cold water on my face."

"Hurry back. I'll miss you." He stood up as I stood to go to the ladies' room. Today, men here do not allow themselves manners as Edward.

I started to return to the table after a few minutes, but as I was coming out of the ladies' room, there were a large group of ladies that were in the club eating that decided they should come over to our table and introduce their daughters to Edward, asking him if he was married. What a bunch of nosy busybodies! This was after they somehow found out that he was a famous doctor to the stars of Hollywood. I found this to be rather distasteful and decided to give Edward the slip and leave. I would get a cab since there were always cabs waiting out front. Edward didn't seem to be enjoying himself with all these ladies, but he was a gentleman and remained calm. I started to walk to the door to leave when Edward caught a glimpse of me leaving and quickly excused himself from the ladies and ran after me. I almost made it to the door. I was actually just about to open the door and disappear into the dark night when I felt his hand on my arm.

"Excuse me, ladies, but I need to go get my date."

"She can find her own way home, we don't need her kind here."

"Maybe you don't, but I do."

"She is not one of us, the elite here in the city. We think you are one of us, and we all have daughters that you should get to know. If you want to meet all the rich and famous, you will need to sit with us, and then you can get to know us better."

"I need her, not your daughters who would have the same ideals as you do, and these are people that I despise. I absolutely hate these people who think that they are better than others."

I stood up and ran after Britt. The ladies just stood there with their mouths wide open, not realizing that someone had just put them in their place.

"Britt, where are you going? I know these people somehow don't like you, but I do very much. Come back inside and let's go out on the balcony and have a nonalcoholic dinner cocktail. I really want to get to know you better."

"I don't think I'm the person that you need to be seen with here at the country club. I'm not really welcome here to even eat dinner, but tonight I was allowed to eat here because of you. Please take me home, Edward. These people that were talking to you are important in this city and are more your kind."

"What do you mean by my kind? Do you mean because they have money? I don't care who they are, they mean nothing to me, but you mean a great deal to me, and I want to show you how much you are really meaning to me. I have never felt this way before."

I had tears in my eyes, and Edward noticed them. He drew me close to his chest and wrapped his strong arms around my back. The people that had been talking to him noticed this, and he excused himself with a smile. They were starting to follow him, but he said that he wanted to be alone with his beautiful girl. We went back inside, ordered drinks to be brought out to the balcony overlooking the ocean, and talked for about an hour. We talked of everything about our lives, and then he hit me with both barrels, so to speak.

Chapter 4

"Britt, do you believe in true love at first sight? I have never in my entire life been married and have waited all my life for the right person to enter, my soul mate to come along. I think I may have found her, you my dear. You are everything that I have looked for in a woman, beautiful, kind, wholesome, gentle, tenderhearted, funny, and very feminine. Love is the essence of life, and I have been missing that. Nothing else matters if you don't have love. It usually only happens once in a lifetime, and you need to grab it with both barrels when you find it, and I have definitely found it. This is the strange feeling that I had on the cliff about asking you out to dinner, only I didn't know it then, but I do now. I know this is so soon since I just met you this afternoon."

My mouth was open, and I didn't know what to say. "Edward, you say the most wonderful things. You can sweep a girl off her feet. I'm not very popular around here, more like a case of scurvy which, of course, nobody wants or needs. I am an investigative reporter, and the people here don't like how I report certain things that are happening around the city. You hardly know me. I am thirty-eight years old and was married at one time for about six months. I think I am too old to give you a family. Do you mind if I ask you how old you are, Edward? I thought it was just me that fell for you, and I was going to tell you later that we should not see each other anymore because it would hurt me to keep seeing you up and return to California. Even now, I will be very sad when you return to California next week. Just seeing these ladies all talking to you before at the table made me want to throw fiery darts at their hearts. I shouldn't talk like this. I'm sorry. That is not very Christian-like to talk this way."

"Why are you sorry? I love you, Britt. I don't understand it, but I can't help myself. I'm overjoyed that you can reciprocate that love. I have never been so happy. I feel that I'm turning red now. You asked how old I am, well, I'm forty-five years old. Does that make a difference?"

"Never, but you saw all the people around here that seem to be overwhelmed with you and who you are, a very important doctor, who they will think that I am making a ploy for and somehow probably report on some malpractice suit that they can dream up. They always think the worse of me, and most of them have never taken the time to get to know me, but yet they always like to see their name in print."

"Let them be! They are a group of busy-bodies who have nothing better to do than to go around and gossip. I know that I love you, and I was hoping that you felt the same. I am so excited that you spoke to me of how you feel in your heart."

"Oh, I do, Edward, yes I do. I know it is rather sudden, but I can't seem to control my emotions concerning you."

It was at that moment when the tears starting flowing again. He leaned in toward me and kissed me for the very first time and what sweet kisses, ever so gentle. He kissed each tear away. We left the balcony overlooking the ocean hand in hand. Edward paid the bill, and we walked out the door. The valet brought us our car, and Edward opened the door for me, and then we drove to the Newfoundland Hotel where he was staying for a night cap at the lounge before he drove me home. We needed to talk more about what was transpiring between us.

We arrived at the hotel, went to a secluded table in the corner of the lounge, sipped on a night cap (nonalcoholic), and talked. We talked about where we grew up and how he came to the United States to study medicine, then returned home and got his mother and brought her back, but sad to say, that wasn't how life played out.

He was now in Canada just to get away from the ladies in California, his patients, and the Hollywood groupies, who were always throwing themselves at him and trying to set him up with the movie stars and get him married. As he spoke, I thought that maybe if we got married, it would be the same. I couldn't put up with that. I had to say something.

"Edward, if I do marry you, it may be still the same with people throwing themselves at you. From what I hear about movie stars, they don't care if you are married or not. I couldn't take that. I would be so jealous knowing that other ladies out there want you as much as I do. I am a one-husband wife forevermore."

"I am so happy to hear you say that. I want someone like you, a soul mate to spend all my days and nights with, when I am not working. I want to come home to a loving wife, you, my love, someone who when I am home, we can put up our feet in front of the fireplace and relax or take long walks on the beach. Please don't worry about the plastic people. So, Britt, will you consider becoming my wife forevermore?"

"Yes, I will marry you. I love you." It was then he gave me the gentlest kiss. "We are too old to act like teenagers, even though I have only known you for one day. I never thought that I would find another person that I could love or who would love me, just for me."

"Britt, you have made me the happiest man alive. If I love someone, it is with my whole heart and soul. You are the one who have made this come true. I have searched for years, and now I have found my perfect mate, my soul mate, you."

We talked and talked for hours, and then Edward drove me back to my apartment and kissed me good night. What a night! I had a difficult time getting to sleep after all that had transpired. Was it all true? Did it really happen? I was so in love with him.

Before I drove Britt home that night, I returned to the bar to pay the bill for our drinks. Ray, the bartender, looked at me so strangely, and I asked if there was something wrong.

"I see you are with Brittney tonight. She usually comes in here every night and sits at that same table, orders one drink, and cries continually all night until closing and then I call her a cab to take her home. I'm not sure if someone really hurt her while they were maybe sitting at that same table. It's so wonderful to see her with a smile on her face."

"Are you sure it's the same girl? Why does she do that every night?"

"I think that she's been hurt so many times. We just leave her alone, and if someone starts to bother her, we tell them to leave her alone. To me, she is a special lady, no matter what the elite people of the city think of her."

"I truly thank you for telling me all this. I really appreciate it. As long as she is with me, she will never be hurt again."

"Goodnight, Dr. Moore."

Chapter 5

The remaining time here in Newfoundland passed very quickly, and we spent the entire next week together, with Edward picking me up every morning, taking me to a different restaurant for breakfast every day, then skipping lunch, and for dinner we would find some out-of-the-way quaint restaurant or have a picnic in some secluded cove or some out-of-the-way meadow where we would find ourselves talking about our lives and what it would be like for me to be a doctor's wife and also the transition from living in Newfoundland to living in California. I was a little scared to say the least. Edward had already applied for a passport for me in order for me to travel to California with him. He called me every night before I fell to sleep after having dropped me at my apartment. While we were still in Newfoundland, we traveled on long drives together out and around the countryside, and of course we spent long hours on the cliffs where we first met. We ate out at many different restaurants. Sometimes we would order out and take the food to the cliffs since we counted them as ours, and sometimes we went to my apartment with our food for a quiet meal together.

The cliffs were a very special place and held special meaning for us. It was a pleasure to be with someone who appreciated me for who I was and not what I do for a living, although I still wondered deep down in my soul why he picked me to marry instead of any of the Hollywood beauties. I kept thinking in my mind that I was doing the correct thing by saying that I would marry him, but everything was happening so fast. Was there some meaning for him to get married so fast? To me I was no great beauty, just really plain. All these things kept flowing through my mind until I had to do what my heart was telling me. I would marry him.

Edward wanted me to fly back to California with him the coming week, but I wanted to drive back toward the end of the month. It would only take a few weeks. That was the only thing that I hadn't told him. I had a secret. I think he was nervous that if he left me here, then I would change my mind and not go at all. I was scared to death of flying. I had to tell him. I just had a very hard time thinking that I would be flying thousands of feet above the earth. I couldn't do it, or could I?

"Edward, please let me come later in the month by driving to California. I will need my car eventually."

"Britt, is there a problem with traveling with me now? Are you having doubts concerning marrying me? Also, you don't need your car in California. I will buy you the perfect car for you to drive."

"I didn't want to tell you this, but I am scared to death of flying. I can't even get on the plane. My heart starts to race." He smiled and kissed me on my nose.

"My beautiful Britt. I love you. By having a doctor for a husband, I will always take care of you. I will never let anything or anybody ever hurt you. I will give you a strong sedative, and you can sleep completely through the entire flight."

"Edward, what would I do without you by my side? I love you." I wanted to go so much with him that I quit my job immediately so I could travel with him. He would take care of me on the flight. I cancelled my apartment, and the last night in Newfoundland, I stayed at the Newfoundland Hotel with him in an adjoining suite to Edward. No hanky-panky until after we were married.

We ate the last night at the Country Club again, and what a reception. We were welcomed with open arms. The club members had heard of our engagement and now were as sweet as could be. People were walking up to me and actually talking. They were probably glad that I was leaving the country, but there was always someone else to take my place. Little did they know that the toughest reporter in St. John's was taking that place. I couldn't wait for them to read his articles in the coming columns. I actually smiled when I thought of what he would include. What hypocrites! We ate this dinner in peace and talked about our future together, especially me being a doctor's wife. I just had a hard time swallowing that.

"My friends are going to love you, just as I do."

"I'm not so sure about that. They will think that I am marrying you because you are a doctor and rich. How do I act as a doctor's wife? I'm not a sophisticated lady by any means and never go to big dinner parties, as I'm sure you must be invited to often in your line of work or even throw-dinner parties. I'm just a down-to-earth person."

"That's what I love about you the most. You're honest with me and not one of the plastic girls of Hollywood. I can be myself around you and not have to pretend. I never grew up in a big city, and like you, I am just a country person at heart. Most of the people that know me do not know where I came from, except the doctors I work with, who, like me, are from every walk of life."

Chapter 6

The last week in Newfoundland went very quickly. We were all packed, and Edward hired a limousine to take us to the airport. We arrived the next day at the airport for an early-morning flight. I didn't have much luggage, as according to Edward, he was going to buy me all the clothes I needed, which wouldn't be much living in California in the heat. Edward said that most clothes would be cocktail gowns for the fancy parties. I had just packed some jeans and sweaters that I love and a few essentials. It seemed already into this relationship that Edward was invited to quite a few parties, and as his wife, I would be obligated to go also. I never went to any parties, especially "elite dress to the hilt" parties. I wouldn't know how to act. I would be laughed at. I was thinking that this was going to be all a big mistake, but I loved him so much. It was days like this when my mind starting to think of things, that maybe I regretted doing all of this and that I shouldn't marry him but stay in Newfoundland where I knew people, even though they weren't my friends.

In my heart, I prayed to my Heavenly Father. "Dear Heavenly Father, I have always looked to you for guidance and knowledge for my life. I'm not sure now if I am making the biggest mistake of my life or is this from your hand. Protect me and guide me in all that I am about to do. Thank you for always being beside me. Amen."

We walked arm in arm up the steps to the plane, and I started to weave back and forth. I felt as if I would collapse at any moment. Each step was a milestone for me. Edward held me close and guided me to our seats. As soon as we were seated, and in first class no less, I started to get agitated and hyperventilating, so Edward administered a mild sedative to me that would last the entire flight to Toronto, Ontario. From there, we had to change planes for the last leg of the journey to California. The flight to California was a longer flight, so he administered me another sedative, a little stronger, and I dozed off. It seemed as soon as I sat in my seat on the plane, I was rising from it. Edward was whispering in my ear to awaken. We had arrived in California.

"We are here, sweetheart. Time to wake up."

"Are we here already? Didn't I just go to sleep? I missed the entire flight."

"That's perfectly okay. This way you weren't scared of flying and didn't get sick. Let's depart from here. I want to get you to our house. Herbert will be waiting for us."

I couldn't believe it had worked. I flew to California. There was a chauffeur waiting for us with a limousine, which I thought Edward had hired. He was so considerate to do that for me. He even called him by name, Herbert. We drove to Edward's home, not knowing that he owned it, and now it would be my home also. I was still so tired from the flight and the drugs, also with the four-and-a-half-hour time difference, I still needed time to sleep. Edward showed me to my suite in the house and told me to sleep a little while he checked in with the other doctors to let them know that he had returned from his trip and with a huge surprise for all of them. I fell into a deep sleep and awoke, not remembering where I was at that moment. I sat up screaming. "Help, somebody help me. Where am I?" Edward heard me and came running to comfort me, thinking that something was completely wrong.

"Darling, are you okay? I heard you screaming. What scared you? Let me hold you."

"I'm sorry if I disturbed you. I awoke and for a few minutes felt disoriented, never realizing where I was. I'm fine now. Just seeing your face makes me warm and tinkling all over."

He held me for the longest time and kissed my face and neck. I was thinking that in about a month, he would be all mine. Just being in Edward's arms made everything in my life so perfect, but was it and would it ever be? Everything was happening just too fast.

"I can't wait to do this all the time. By the way, I hung all your clothes in the closet, and this suite will be yours until we get married, and then you will join me in my suite which is larger and fit for a couple."

"Edward, you are making me blush even at my age. I haven't blushed since I was a teenager. I love having you near me all the time. At my age, I don't know if I can wait a month to get married, but if you can, then I can. I never realized how alone I was back in Newfoundland, and now that I have you, I will never feel alone again."

"I can hardly wait to take myself the most beautiful bride where we will be joined as one, the pure soul mates. I will never dishonor you now, not before we are married, although you are driving me crazy every time I look at you and realize that in a few weeks, you will be all mine and I yours. I have never known a woman who could do to me what I feel for myself, my darling. I was thinking that if I hadn't gone to Newfoundland for a vacation, I never would have met you and fell in love. I will always be grateful to the patient who suggested that I go to Newfoundland and relax near the cliffs and ocean air. That happened to be the most important day of my life, finding you on that cliff that day. I had been praying for months for someone to share my life with, and something was calling me that day up to the cliffs, and I only thought that it was because I missed the ocean and being near the cliffs where I grew up. Newfoundland is a little like parts of England. I have now found you and will never, never let you go, ever. You are all mine."

Chapter 7

We had planned to get married within the next three weeks to a month if we could get all the arrangements made, but it seemed that Edward was making all the preparations since this was his city, and everyone seemed to know him. I wanted to help, but I was more hindrance than getting anything accomplished. I felt so left out, but he stated that I should just sit back and relax until after the wedding, and Edward still had a few days' vacation left. I felt like I wasn't needed at all. Was this the way it was always going to be, that he needed someone to go to parties with and to be seen in public, but then he should have gotten someone not so plain who knew how to handle themselves at medical affairs?

I didn't know what I was going to do after he returned to the hospital. I hadn't mentioned it to him because I didn't want to upset him, but I felt so alone here in this huge house and in the city where I hadn't any friends or acquaintance that I could talk to about these things. How was I ever going to cope with life here, especially since I wasn't a very outgoing person to begin with, which made it all the more lonesome? This was the start of a nightmare that I hadn't thought of when Edward asked me to marry him. What was I ever thinking? Was it just to get married or that he could support me for the remainder of my life? I had to stop thinking like this.

The following day, Edward went to his study where he had been busy calling the church, the caterers, and the Van Nuys Country Club for the reception. He had arranged everything, except for the wedding invitations, which were to be printed overnight and sent out by the printer. Edward gave the printer all the names of his friends that were to be invited and whom I hadn't even met yet. I was so scared and nervous. They probably would all hate me as all the people in Newfoundland that I met hated me. Why do I always think so negatively?

Behind my back, he had secretly had Herbert arrange a small informal party the next evening to introduce me to his friends. He mentioned it to me that evening at dinner. I finally realized that Herbert was his butler, chauffeur, and all-around helper for anything and everything that he needed. He had been with Edward for years and was also a great friend.

"Britt, I have arranged to have a very informal dinner party here at the house to introduce you to the doctors and their wives and a few other people that I work with at the hospital. I want you to get to know them."

"Edward, I'm not good around other people. You remember what happened at the Country Club in Newfoundland. I usually just get scared and run away."

"I will be by your side the entire evening, never leaving you for a moment. Would you be okay if I am by your side?"

"You promise!"

"I promise, darling."

The party consisted of about 120 people. Small indeed! Small to me was about twelve people. His butler Herbert and housekeeper Monica, who was just so wonderful to me, had arranged all the food, drinks, and music. I was not accustomed to housekeepers and butlers taking care of things. Here, it was different, and I would have to get it through my head that I didn't need to cook anymore, although I loved to cook whenever I had a chance, and I would have loved to cook in Edward's kitchen. It was fully stocked and tremendous in size. He had two enormous refrigerators that were completely stocked at all times with everything that you could ever need in the way of meats and vegetables.

The next afternoon before the party, Edward took me shopping at some fancy boutique called Madeline's, and I bought some new clothes, matching shoes and perfumes that he loved, and other small accessories. He had me model all the dresses for him before buying.

He looked at me in awe. Every dress I tried on, he would say that we would take it. I had a hard time buying items that, as I glanced at the price tags, were outrageously priced, but Edward told me that he could afford them and that he wanted me to have the best of everything. Just the car alone that he was driving was so fabulous and comfortable.

"Edward, I don't need all these expensive clothes. They are too much. You bought too many, just one or two would have been enough. But a dozen." I started to get tears in my eyes, and he looked at me with such love.

"Britt, you are going to have the best of everything. You will never be neglected while being with me. I never before had anyone to spend money on, and now I have you. Please allow me to do this. I don't ever want you to look at prices. You are going to look spectacular at this party, and there will be many more parties for you to attend and wear these other dresses."

"Okay, if you say so. By the way, what kind of car are you driving? I have never seen it before."

"It's a Maserati Gran Turismo Convertible. Do you like it? I ordered it for us as a wedding gift. I thought that you would love the black. You look wonderful there sitting next to me. My friends will be jealous of you."

"It's just perfect, too perfect. I am not used to all this pomp and glory. You don't have to buy me expensive gifts to show your love for me and make me love you. I can get along without all the luxury. I am ecstatically happy being with you. You have made me the happiest girl in the world. Edward, I love you so much. What will your friends and colleagues say when a confirmed bachelor is finally getting married? What will they think? That I married you for your money, which is what people usually think."

"Don't you worry about my friends. They haven't any idea what this party is about. Any true friend wouldn't even think those thoughts, and I would like for you to forget about things like that. Okay?"

"Okay, if you say so, but it is so different from how I am used to living." I kissed him on the cheek, and he looked toward me and smiled with a smile that would light up all of California.

"Aren't your friends going to be astonished when you tell them that you have a fiancée and are getting married soon?"

"I want to see how their faces will look when I announce this and then see you walk down the staircase."

"I don't have any close family here in the States. They are all overseas in Britain. I'll call my brother and sister, John and Joanne. Neither one of them is married either. They will definitely be surprised, but I don't think they will be able to make it to the wedding, although it would be great to see them after all these years. We still keep in touch, but they have never had the time to come here and visit."

Chapter 8

The next evening came very quickly, and as I was getting ready for the informal party, I was very careful with my makeup and wardrobe. I wanted to look my best for Edward and his friends. I didn't want to embarrass him. I spent a little longer than necessary with my makeup as Edward didn't like too much, so I wore just a very minute that he wouldn't notice. I wasn't used to wearing any makeup at any time. Normally I would wash my face, and that was the entire routine before going out. I just wasn't used to all this high-society dress up. I was so scared that I would embarrass Edward at this party, and I thought that maybe I would feign being sick, and that way I could stay upstairs. What would I say to these people? As soon as they heard me speak, they would know that I was an unsophisticated nobody. Then I didn't want to hurt Edward since this party was to introduce me to his friends and colleagues. I guess I would try to be happy just for him.

My dress was a long black gown. Edward's idea, low-cut, but not too low, as he said that he didn't want the other men staring at me, undressing me with their eyes, is exactly what he said. All this was then accentuated with a diamond necklace that Edward had surprised me with that afternoon, also buying me a 3-carat diamond engagement ring, which I could have done without. I thought it too extravagant, but he said that he wanted to show me off as he was so proud to be with me and also that he could afford it. He said that he never spent much money because he had no one to spend it on. I thought that if he kept spending the way he had spent in the last few days, he would be broke sooner than he thought. He knocked on my suite door as I was finishing getting ready.

"Britt, are you ready for your grand entrance? Is it okay if I enter?"

"Yes. Just coming, darling! I hope your friends approve of me." I opened the door, and Edward was standing there with his mouth open and just staring at me.

"Britt, my darling, you are a vision of loveliness. Words cannot describe how you look to me at this moment. I love you more with each passing day."

"This is all too much, sweetheart. I love you from the bottom of my heart, but like I told you before, all these luxuries are not necessary. You don't have to buy my love for you. I'm just not accustomed to all these luxuries and great finery. You make me feel like a queen."

"To me, that is exactly what you are and will always be." And then he kissed me.

We walked down the staircase and entered the grand living room where the guests were now assembled with glasses of champagne in their hands. All his friends were gathered around as Edward and I walked into the elegant living room, decorated beautifully by decorators that he had hired, holding hands with our fingers intertwined together, and he introduced me to his friends who didn't seem to be very friendly toward me, especially their ladies.

"Friends and coworkers, I would like for you all to meet the soon-to-be, Brittney Bentley, soon-to-be Moore. I have finally found the girl of my dream, my soul mate. Please lift your glasses and toast my future happiness as I never thought that I would ever receive, but if you trust in the Lord, everything works out. Thank you all for coming to celebrate with us. I know this must be a shocker to you all. Please enjoy yourselves."

The women just seemed to turn their backs to me and whispered together. The doctors came up to us and congratulated us both and wished us well. As the evening progressed and I walked around, I heard many comments such as: "She must be after Edward's money, and she isn't glamorous. How could he want her?" Another was saying, "I heard that he felt sorry for her, but that he doesn't love her. I guess we will still have a chance with him if we play our cards right. Another was saying that she guesses she wants him to buy her things that she never could afford before, and that she was just a hillbilly from a backwater town in Canada. She is not our kind of people, and by having her here, she is intruding in our lives. We have to find a way, without Edward knowing, to get her to return from where she came, but then allowing her to think that it was her own idea. How could he entertain by sneaking behind our backs and disappearing for two weeks and then showing up here with such a plain girl? I just don't like her, and we need not to include her in any of our functions, thus Edward will be back in our grasp, and we will set him up with our own kind of woman who can accentuate him at parties. Having her walking in this room on his arm makes him look cheap, and we can't have our top-ranking surgeon and confirmed bachelor with an outsider from another country that we have no idea what her status is in life, but she has gotten her claws in him and corrupted his way of living the romantic life with all of us."

I had a hard time just staying in the same room with everyone. The men were very friendly and asked me to dance until their lady friends and wives noticed and then decided to interfere. I'm sure that most of the ladies were Edward's patients and seemed to be very jealous. They all crowded around him. They were combing their fingers through his hair, gently rubbing their hands over his back and hugging him. I actually started to feel jealous. He was my man, at least I thought he was, and the one that I would be marrying in a couple of weeks. I now started to have doubts about him wanting me for a wife. I started to believe what they said was true. If only I could be sure of everything.

I overheard one woman say, her name was Ashley Drew, wife of one of Edward's best friends and colleagues, Greg Drew; "that if Edward wanted to get married, then she could have found him a wife, since she had lots of connections here in California. He needed to marry a glamourous girl who knew the California scene, instead of him going to some backwoods town in the boondocks of a town that no one ever heard of and finding a little nobody that he didn't know anything about. How could he do this to us? We are the people who have to spend time with him, and I'm surely not going to spend any time getting to know her. Maybe we can convince her to go back where she came from. We just have to be very cautious at how we approach this nobody and get her to return where she came from."

I had heard enough and ran to my bedroom suite and sat there crying my eyes out. She was absolutely correct. I was just a nobody, and why was he marrying me? Why had he come so far to find a wife? Was it a game that maybe someone put him up to, to see if he could actually find someone who was willing to marry him, and when he got married, then he would divorce me? Tears were flowing as I was running up the staircase, and Edward saw them. He ran to the bedroom after me. "Darling, did I do something to make you cry? Please tell me what's the matter? Are you not feeling well?"

I was sobbing so much, and Edward was holding me so tight, and I was actually shaking. He buried his face in my neck and kissed me. Between sobs, I tried to talk and tell Edward what was wrong. "Edward, can't we just go away and get married? Let's elope. I just want to marry you. I don't need a big wedding to be happy, not with you by my side. That woman, Ashley Drew, said I was from the backwoods and that you could have done better. You know, she is correct. You could have had any girl in Hollywood or anywhere in the world. Why me?"

"Darling, you ran out of the room and didn't hear what I said to her. I heard what she said to the other women. You ran before you heard the entire conversation. I told her that you were so fresh, not make-believe like the Hollywood people, and that you are my soul mate, although she had no idea what a soul mate was. You are all I need and love and pray that you will remember that no matter what anyone else has to say about us. I would do anything for you. I have never been in love before or been as happy as I am at this very moment. Now I know what other people mean when they say that they have found their better half. You are my better half, and it will keep us on track and keep us going through thick and thin."

"Oh, I will, my dearest love. I love you with all my heart and soul. No one is better for me than you. I should have known that you would never take advantage of me. I'm so sorry, Edward, for thinking the worst and doubting you. I just haven't any self-confidence. Will you please forgive me?"

"There is nothing to forgive. Just always remember that I love you more than life and always will, and that will keep us on the correct path of life. Also, with our Heavenly Father by our side, always."

We kissed long and passionate. You never would have guessed that he had never been married. It was times like this that I felt like I really didn't belong and that I should leave.

"We should get back to our guests. Please refresh yourself, my darling, and meet me back downstairs." His kisses lingered long after he left the room.

I splashed water on my face, applied a little more makeup, and went back downstairs to the party. We ate and drank long into the night. The only female person that really talked to me was Edward's secretary, Alicia Fortune, a lady about Edward's age who was there with her husband, Cliff. She had been his secretary for about twenty years now. She must love her work. She was a very refreshing woman to talk to and very down-to-earth. I could see why Edward had her as his secretary. She and her husband seemed to love each other tremendously just from the way they danced and the way he kissed her. They must be soul mates. I was thinking that maybe Edward and I would be still like them after remaining many years together.

About 1:00 a.m. after the last of the guests had left and Edward adjourned to his study for a few more hours, I entered in the room to say goodnight. He lavished kisses and hugged me until I thought that I would lose my breath.

"I am going to bed, my sweet. Please don't stay up too late. You need your rest. You will have to go back to work on Monday, and I am going to miss you."

"I will go to bed in about another hour. I need to answer a few e-mails."

I went to my suite, took a long hot shower, and then went to bed. I went to sleep almost immediately, and so without thinking that I wasn't at my apartment, I just stretched out on the bed, half-dressed. I didn't think anything about it until I was awakened by Edward covering me with a blanket and kissing me good night. I was half nude and so embarrassed. He pulled at the blanket to cover me when I woke up startled and began screaming.

"Darling, I found you in a state of disarray, not covered and half out of bed. Is this how you usually sleep? I'm sorry if I startled you, but I was just going to kiss you goodnight, not meaning to wake you. I should have called out to you first. Please forgive me. I will let you go back to sleep now and dream sweet dreams of us being on our honeymoon."

"This is usually what happens. I am so tired when I retire that I usually plop myself on the bed and wake up the next morning like this. I didn't mean for you to see me like this. When we get married, I promise that I will sleep under the blankets."

Things were going just great. During the weeks before the wedding, Edward would take me for long walks along the beach and extra-long drives up the coast where sometimes we would find an inn, isolated by the sea, and spend the night, always in separate rooms. Somehow, there was always an overnight bag for each of us in the car for these random trips, like Edward had it all planned ahead of time. I never questioned him about it because it was very romantic to be led on such an excursion not knowing where I would spend the night. He even packed bathing suits for us, and we would swim in the ocean. I truly felt at times like this that I belonged here, but then other times, I felt left out and wanted to return home to Newfoundland. At least there I knew what I was up against.

One afternoon, Edward took me to the hospital to show me where he worked. I was very impressed with the hospital. It was small but with all the modern technology and up-to-date medical equipment. I was thinking to myself that if I ever fell sick, this is the hospital where I would like to be treated.

Chapter 9

I had been in California for almost a month now. The wedding was to be held the following Saturday, and according to the information that Edward was telling me, I was to be treated to a glorious honeymoon. He wouldn't tell me where we were traveling to for our honeymoon, only to say that it was near water, as much as I harassed him about it.

I thought about his position at the hospital. How could he take so much time off? Wouldn't the other doctors get annoyed with him? But I refused to say anything. He had just returned from an extended vacation to Newfoundland, Canada, only a month before. He must know what he was doing, at least I hoped he did. I prayed that this was not going to affect his position of doctor at the hospital and that he would lose his job, especially on account of me.

It was to be a small and informal wedding, but small here in California meant anything over 120 guests. Three days before the wedding, Edward was working, and according to Alicia (who called and talked to me at least every day to ensure that I wasn't lonely), he was getting all types of Hollywood stars running to him for every little line in their neck or face. He called them the "plastic girls," as it seemed they were all phony from their head to their toes. He was having more appointments than he had at any other week and ended up staying late every night to catch up on the paperwork. I knew it was because they all wanted him. Besides being a plastic surgeon, he was also a medical doctor performing other surgeries on these patients and taking care of all their other ills.

One morning when Edward came home after a long overnight at the hospital, he had another surprise for me. He looked so tired, but wouldn't go to bed until I heard his glorious news.

Chapter 10

"Britt, I have the greatest surprise for you and greater even for myself." He had a huge smile on his face.

"What is it? I can't stand the suspense. Have you changed the location of where you are taking us on our honeymoon?"

"No, that remains the same. Not that. You will never guess in a million years. Okay, I can't hold it in anymore. I'm so overjoyed that I don't know what to think. I'm just flabbergasted."

"Well! Let me in on this glorious news that has you so overwhelmed. I've never seen you like this. You are grinning from ear to ear. It must be something special to have you in such a state. Please tell me or I am going to just burst with excitement. I love surprises. Tell me so I can join in your excitement."

"Okay, here goes! I heard from my family in England. My brother and sister, John and Joanne, are flying in for the wedding. I received an e-mail this morning, and they will be on the flight tomorrow afternoon. They want to meet the girl who finally caught the confirmed bachelor. They said that you must be something special for me to fall head over heels in love and to get married so fast. They even wanted to know if we had to get married."

"Is your brother as handsome as you? I can't wait to meet them. You must be so excited to see them after all these years. How long has it been since you saw them?"

"You can wait and see his looks, although he was always the more handsome of the two of us. I haven't seen them in about fifteen years. We were both still young. I will be so restless until I get to meet them at the airport. This is so special for both of us, my love."

Edward had a hard time sleeping that night. I heard him up walking around in the middle of the night. I decided to join him and maybe get a cup of tea to soothe us down. Together we sat and drank tea at the kitchen counter and talked about his family, and he said he would really miss his mom on their most special day. After an hour or so, we both were so tired that we went to bed knowing that the next day we would probably stay up late talking with John and Joanne.

After a night's rest, the day had arrived, and Edward was so excited. I was almost as excited as him.

Chapter 11

The afternoon couldn't get here fast enough for Edward. He was on pins and needles and couldn't sit still. He was constantly smiling from ear to ear. I was so happy for him.

Finally, it was time to drive to the airport. Herbert drove the limousine to the airport to meet his family, with Edward still being on pins and needles and fidgeting. We took the limousine, so there would be plenty of room for the entire luggage without being cramped. We arrived a little early, and it was like looking at Edward when his brother exited the plane. I couldn't believe that they looked so much alike. I couldn't have missed him. It was as if they were a twin. The same tall, suave, and handsome figure of a man. Their features were almost identical. As soon as they saw each other, they ran to each other, hugged and were very teary eyed after all these years to make up.

"Britt, forgive me, please meet my brother John and my sister Joanne. John and Joanne, this is my fiancée, the love of my life, Brittney Bentley, soon-to-be Moore."

"Edward! Where did you find this beautiful girl? She is so gorgeous yet looks as if she is so down-to-earth. Point me in the right direction, will you? I need to get started looking in the same place."

He hugged me as if he knew me all his life. They were both such wonderful people, and I was so happy to have a sister now.

"I met her in Newfoundland, Canada, while I was up there on vacation about a month ago."

"Brittney, you must have some special qualities to catch Edward, a forever confirmed bachelor. He promised me years ago that he would never get married because all the girls out here are phony. I think I remember you calling them 'plastic girls.' Do you have any sisters that I could marry or at least meet?"

"Well, thank you, John, for that beautiful compliment. I have a brother only. Sorry, but maybe you can find someone who is truly just for you with Edward's help. Edward and I are truly soul mates, and that was his main concern in finding a wife. Someone who had the same qualities, values, ideals, and beliefs that he has, and I have those same ones. I am not concerned about Edward being a doctor, as some people think I am marrying him because of that. I love him for himself. I will not concern myself with all these other hypocrites that think otherwise. Joanne, you are absolutely gorgeous. You must be a knockout with the guys. You must have more than your share of men waiting on your doorstep."

"Instead of standing around here and talking, let's go home. We can talk better with a nice hot meal."

Edward's sister and I got along perfectly from the moment we met. We picked up their luggage at the carousel and headed to the car in the parking lot. Herbert was waiting by the car for us. We had brought the limousine that Edward kept in the four-car garage driven by Herbert. We had stocked up on champagne in the back to toast their being here and having Edward and his siblings being together once again.

"Edward, my brother! Where did you get this luxury car? You must be doing very well. Maybe I should be working here with you. Are you and Brittney living together, Edward? I just can't imagine you sleeping with someone until you are married, unless you have changed since having lost your senses being in California."

"John, you know me better than that, even with not seeing each other all these years. I am still and always will be a gentleman. We live in the same house, separate bedroom suites, but that is it. I would never do anything to jeopardize Britt. That is the one thing that I truly thank our parents for, that they instilled in us growing up, and that is, that we were raised correctly, and I have always held to those rules and beliefs and would never compromise them, no matter what."

"I didn't think you had changed that much by moving to California, but when I hear of all the things that take place in California, you have to wonder. I'm happy you haven't changed. I'm sorry, Edward, for even bringing it up."

"Don't be sorry. Lots of women, mostly my patients, have tried by inviting me on their yachts or to dinner and then think that I will just want to run and jump into their beds. Never did happen, and never will. I love Britt, my soul mate."

Herbert drove us home, and as we approached the house, John was gazing at its size. He almost choked as he tried to speak. His jaw seemed to just drop open, and he looked from Edward to Joanne. I wondered what could be going through his mind at that moment. "Is this all yours, Edward? You bought a mansion. Now I know that you are doing very well indeed. America must be a wonderful country."

"It is just an ordinary home, just that the rooms are very large. Let's go inside, shall we?"

We showed them to their separate suites which were overwhelmed with when they saw the size. Herbert carried their luggage to each individual suite. We stayed up late and talked for hours with John and Joanne, and during that time, Herbert had prepared a seafood extravaganza for dinner. We talked and ate. John and Joanne were the most wonderful people, and I counted them as being my brother and sister. They already were treating me as family, and I loved them for that. John was a medical doctor also, and Joanne was his nurse and secretary. No problem if someone gets ill around here. I was so happy for Edward that his only remaining family could be here to celebrate his wedding day. You could just see the love in his eyes that he had for them. I was just sorry that my brother and sister-in-law couldn't make it, but they just couldn't afford to fly to California.

"All this food is so delicious. I have never had such tasteful food. You must eat like this every day, but you haven't gained an ounce, it seems, since the last night we were together fifteen years ago. You know how to entertain your guests."

"You are not guests but family who needed to be together."

I started to think how wonderful it would be if John could stay and join Edward here at the hospital. Maybe I would hint about it to Edward and John. They hadn't seen each other in years, and none of us were getting any younger, also they hadn't any ties to England, except their patients that other doctors could take on as part of their practice. Maybe I would mention it later to them.

Edward and I spent every minute together when he was at home, but he was so tired. I would feign tiredness just so he could get some rest. I wanted to help him but was unsure of what to do to help. I would cuddle him on the living room sofa and massage his temples, but then he felt he needed to stay awake for me, so I gave in and went to bed and read the Good Book, God's Word. Some nights, he was so tired that he would fall asleep in the study and would be there in the morning. He had too many patients depending on him these last few days.

Chapter 12

Our wedding day was here at last, and I didn't see Edward at all that day. Monica said it was bad luck for the bride to see the groom before the wedding. I thought that we were too old to be thinking of old wives' tales. But to appease her, and it sounded like fun, I stayed in my room until it was time to leave for the church. I wasn't wearing a white wedding dress; instead, I had bought a cream-colored, slightly tight-fitting suit that I knew Edward would love, also matching high heels. Joanne helped me get dressed, also fixed my hair, did my nails and makeup. She was great at it, and I loved her as the sister that I never had.

"Brittney, you are looking gorgeous. I can see why Edward loves you so much. This is your special day, and Edward's love for you is the genuine thing. I am sure of that. He would never lie to us. He was always incapable of lying, even as we were growing up. If he was lying at any time, he would always have to hesitate about what to say, and I haven't heard that in his voice since we have arrived. Edward will just beam like the stars of heaven when he sees you walk down that aisle to meet him. You look breathtaking."

"Thank you, Joanne. I love him with all my whole being. He is such a wonderful man. I never ever thought in my entire life that I could find a special someone like Edward has been to me."

"I would be so ever thankful to be able to find someone just, as you have found Edward. I need to meet my soul mate, and that's so hard to do, to find the right man. I have morals as high as Edward's. Look at Edward, he had to wait until he was forty-five. I'm thirty-eight, and I really need someone to love. I get so lonely at times, especially when I am alone and sitting at home. I feel like I'm missing out on life. Do you think you can help me after you are married and back from your honeymoon, that is to find someone?"

"Joanne, I will help you as much as possible. I really love you like a sister. I never had a sister or someone to confide in and talk to about girl things. Now I do! You are not too old because you see, I am also thirty-eight. We are the same age."

"Well! We better get you married then as soon as possible so we can start looking."

We rode to the church in the limousine with Herbert driving. As I entered the church, I felt like a young nervous bride, and my hands were starting to feel damp, but then I thought that there was Edward waiting for me. Greg Drew was standing beside him as his best man. He has asked him to be his best man before he knew that John was arriving from England. I was having Joanne as my maid of honor since I still didn't really know anyone here.

The music started. Everyone stood, and I walked down the aisle that Edward had arranged beautifully just for me, with red roses and beautiful red bows on all the pews. I wanted to cry, but I realized that I had to control my emotions, at least this one time. I was being married today to the most wonderful man that I had ever met. How could I be so lucky? We stood there in front of Pastor Steve Corrigan. I was smiling and never felt as happy as I did at that very moment.

"Edward Moore, please hold your bride's hands. Do you, Edward Moore, take Brittney Bentley to be your wife? Do you promise to love, honor, cherish, and protect her, forsaking all others and holding only unto her as long as you both shall live?"

"I, Edward Moore, take thee, Brittney Bentley, to be my wife. To have and to hold from this day forward, in sickness and in health, for richer or for poorer, to love and to cherish, till death do us part, according to God's holy ordinance, and thereto I pledge thee my faith and abiding love. With this ring, I thee wed. All my love, I do thee give."

"Brittney Bentley, please hold your groom's hands. Do you, Brittney Bentley, take Edward Moore to be your husband? Do you promise to love, honor, cherish, and protect him, forsaking all others and holding only unto him as long as you both shall live?"

"I, Brittney Bentley, take thee, Edward Moore, to be my husband. To have and to hold from this day forward, in sickness and in health, for richer or for poorer, to love and to cherish, till death do us part, according to God's holy ordinance, and thereto I pledge thee my faith and abiding love. With this ring, I thee wed, all my love, I do thee give."

"By the power invested in me by the state of California, I pronounce you husband and wife. Edward, you may now kiss your bride."

He took me in his arms and planted a wonderful lingering kiss on my lips. All the people at the church stood up and applauded. We had exchanged our vows before a packed church, and I took these vows very seriously, and I prayed Edward did the same. I never saw so many people in the church, and I hardly knew any of the faces, except the people that I had met already, but at that moment in my life, I really didn't care who was there, even if they weren't invited.

I was there, arms linked with Edward, my husband. I was finally married to Edward, and now on to the reception at the Country Club and our final destination tonight, the undisclosed place for our honeymoon. I was so happy that I didn't think anybody or anything could hurt me ever again.

Chapter 13

Brittney Bentley Moore

I am finally married to the man of my dreams and am so happy to know that Edward is my true love and soul mate. I finally have a husband that I have dreamed of for years. We drove to the reception in the limousine, and now at the reception, there are hundreds of guests. The only time I have seen Edward since we said "I do" was in the limousine driving to the reception. He was so excited, holding hands in the limousine, and we were both looking forward to our wedding night as husband and wife.

"Well, my love. Are you happy?"

"Oh, Edward. I am the happiest person on this earth today, unless you are even happier."

"My darling, Britt. I can't believe that I am finally married, and to the most beautiful woman on this planet. I will love you forever, and now we will look forward to a most glorious two-week honeymoon which I'm still keeping a secret from you, as least for now."

We arrived at the reception in style, entering together, and then Edward seemed to disappear. Now I am on my own, so to speak, with all these people, especially the ladies, crowding around Edward mingling around here at the club. The club was also filled with dozens of roses. They must have cost Edward a fortune. I felt so left out at my own wedding. I didn't know anyone, really. No one to talk with here except maybe Alicia, Edward's secretary.

The caterer had a variety of food flown in from Maine at Edward's request—lobsters, clams, shrimp, and oysters. There was also a variety of steaks, cold cuts, and salads to enjoy to your heart's desire. These were all the favorites of Edward and me, although I wasn't really interested in eating at the moment. What a smorgasbord! There was French champagne flowing like rivers; actually, it was flowing from a fountain which Edward had imported.

Well, it looks as if Ashley Drew, Greg Drew's wife, is coming over to talk with me; maybe she has decided that she wants to become friends and to congratulate me on my marriage. I am so happy that I don't think she could say anything that would make me angry today or hurt me, but was I ever wrong. She did it again.

"Brittney, may I speak to you for a minute in private? I'll meet you in the ladies' room in the foyer. I need to talk to you about something if you have a minute."

"Absolutely. No problem. I'll be right there." I walked in the ladies' room and waved and smiled to Edward on the way.

"I have something to tell you that I think you should know about Edward, especially now since you're married to him. You had better sit down. I hate to hurt you, especially on your wedding day, but the sooner you know, the better it will be for both of us."

"Yes, what is it?"

"Well, here goes. Edward and I have been lovers for about two years now, and the only reason he married you was because my husband Greg was becoming very suspicious of me going out, and we needed a diversion when I go out almost every night to meet Edward. It was Edward's idea. I thought you should know because he didn't want to tell you himself, so I told him that I would do the dreadful deed, but I didn't tell him when I would talk to you. He told me before he left on his trip to Canada that he would find some girl that didn't stack up to me and bring her back here. He wanted some girl that was beautiful, but was a backwoods type, that would just fall in love with him and want to return and marry him.

"Sorry about this, but I love him with all my heart, and he loves me. He didn't want me to divorce my husband because he is Edward's best friend and colleague. We wanted to get married but realized that it would be out of the question, at least for now. If he is late some night getting home and smelling of perfume, you will know where he has been, always with me. No other woman can stack up against me is how he put it. There may be many nights like this. We meet about three nights a week. So sorry, Brittney, but that's the way it is here in California. Everyone sleeps with other people's husbands and vice versa.

"Maybe it would be in your interest to leave him now and go back where you came from, that backwoods town in Canada. No one around here will ever be your friend, especially if they are Edward's friend, because that means they are my friend also. I sort of rule our little group of doctors and the ladies that they hang out with, and you will never be part of that group. Don't mention this to my husband Greg because he doesn't know, and I will deny everything even if you say anything to Edward."

She turned and walked out the door with a smile on her face, and I just sat there angry and stunted with rivers of tears flowing down my face and my mouth hanging open at the words that I had just heard. I couldn't even answer her. What a wedding day! I was so happy, and now I might have guessed that it was too good to be true. I felt that I was choking on my tears. Edward and I together, it was definitely too good to be true. We never did run in the same circle of friends. Well! It started out happy, and I guess I was never meant to be happy. Edward was so convincing. Things like marrying a doctor just do not belong to a girl from the backwoods of Newfoundland. No wonder that he wanted a down-to-earth girl, since he already had his plastic girl. I would not want him ever touching me again, especially realizing that he had already been with another woman before me on the same night. Now he just wanted someone to go to parties and to be seen on the great doctor's arm. What a crock of lies! He was just so deceitful. What was there left to do but to leave? He even deceived his brother and sister.

I had to escape, get out of there. I couldn't breathe. I would not be humiliated any further, and now I needed to get away and get a divorce as soon as possible. Married for less than half a day would probably go down in history books as the shortest marriage ever. Edward and Ashley must be having a great laugh at my expense. What a fool I've been to think that someone like Edward could really love me. I had nowhere to go, and I had no friends here. What was I to do? But it definitely was not to stay here another minute. I would return to the house, change my clothes from my beautiful suit, and put on jeans and a sweater with a coat over them, which I was going to wear for later when we would be leaving on our honeymoon. What a crock of lies that was. I couldn't stop crying. I looked like an evil witch with all my mascara running down my face, but I didn't care who saw me now. Nothing mattered anymore to me. I was running away from here forever.

I was going back to the house, pack a small suitcase, take my credit cards with my maiden name, and money, and write a goodbye note to Edward and leave it on his pillow. I would sneak out now before the party ends, even though I'm not sure where I'm going. I will not stay where I'm not wanted. No one will ever make a fool of me again.

I arrived at the house and started to write the note to Edward. I was never a nasty person, but now everything starting to spill out on the paper, my entire heart and soul.

> *Dearest Edward or Dearest Cheater, whichever suits you at the particular moment that you are reading this;*
>
> *I loved you with all my heart and soul and still do, thinking that you were my soul mate and vice versa. What a fool I have been. You must be having a great laugh at getting away with this, and me being the backwoods girl from Newfoundland. Your great find for this great scheme and all at my expense, but that surely didn't bother you since I was never loved by you. Ashley Drew told me all about the two of you being lovers and that was why you got married so that you could fool her husband. According to her, you had to marry someone beautiful, but with no brains, very stupid with the brains of a jackass and from some place in the backwoods.*
>
> *Boy! Was I ever stupid and a total jackass? An idiot! I guess both Greg Drew and I are the biggest*

fools. No wonder you didn't care whom you married, just a backwoods girl would do fine. What a sap that I've been. You must be having a great laugh tonight at getting married, and no one the wiser about the two of you, especially putting off such a glamorous wedding and the big reception following. I know I wasn't wise to it. You put on quite an act for me.

By the time you read this, I will be long gone, not sure where, who cares, not you for sure, but just that I get away, maybe a shack in the woods somewhere, but don't fret yourself about it. I am no longer your responsibility anymore. I think I need to go back to my backwoods island, for I am only a girl without any manners and could never make it as a doctor's wife. I am leaving everything you ever bought me, including the diamond necklace, which maybe you would like to give to Ashley, also both the engagement ring and my new Celtic Love Knots wedding band. They are all on the dressing table in what would have been our bedroom. Who am I kidding? I never want to step foot in that bedroom or that bed seeing that Ashley laid there. I will get an annulment as soon as possible since we never consummated our wedding and never will. Hope you don't get too lonely there now, but why would you, with Ashley to keep you company in your king-size bed. You better snuggle up close to her tonight so you can both celebrate the accomplishment of the wedding that you pulled off without a hitch and have a great laugh at my expense. I guess she will have a great honeymoon with you wherever you take her.

I didn't think you would be the person to treat me in such a manner. I trusted you explicitly and believed everything you ever told me. I loved you as never had I loved before, and I thought you felt the same, especially the way you acted with me, but I guess that now it was all an act. I guess being a doctor to the stars, the acting comes naturally. I thought that you were my soul mate, but I guess that means nothing to you at all. You have ripped my heart out and stamped it to shreds. There is nothing left to it. You tore me away from my native home to have me humiliated in this way. I guess you really don't love me as Ashley said. Why did you lie to me, Edward?

If you find this hard to read because of water marks, they are the tears that you have put on my face flowing down like rivers and can't seem to stop and also the makeup mixed together. I really don't care what I look like at this moment because you won't see me ever again, and you will never find me. Don't even try to find me. I will be long gone before you read this.

Maybe I will get robbed out there, or maybe I will just walk in the ocean, especially since I love it so much. It is always calling to me, and this time I may just answer the call. Maybe now I will listen. It is the one true thing that I can depend on, since it never changes, always true and free. I will be free now, also.

Good luck with Ashley! I hope you find love with her that you could never find with me, especially since you weren't looking for love from me, just someone to humiliate.

Goodbye forever.

Don't bother looking for me. You'll never find me. I have been long gone even before the reception ended, and you never even noticed. That shows me just how much you really cared. You left me unattended all evening, knowing that I didn't know anyone there. I felt so much alone at my own wedding. I'm sorry that this is such a truthful note, but it's the

*way I'm feeling tonight. I have cried so much that I
barely have strength to walk away, but I will.*

Brittney Bentley, not ever Brit Moore

I dressed in my old clothes and went down the back staircase to
the kitchen carrying the small suitcase. Monica stopped me on the
way, since she had returned to the mansion earlier to clean up, and
I told her that I was putting my bag in the limousine for later. She
believed me, except for what I looked like with the mascara all over
my face.

"Your face is all black, Mrs. Moore."

"Sorry, I forgot. I will run a cloth over it." I did and left the
house looking behind me to make sure she wasn't watching me, and
so I left to never return. I felt rotten lying to Monica, with her being
so wonderful to me since I arrived, but she would have called Edward
and told him. I could not confront him about this tonight or ever. I
couldn't handle it.

Chapter 14

Edward Moore

Edward was busy scurrying around the reception hall looking for Britt.

"I can't seem to find Britt, John. Have you seen her around the reception hall or back at the house?"

"I saw her go into the ladies' room earlier with one of your colleagues' wives. I think it was the one named Ashley Drew, but I never watched to see her come out, and I never saw her after. What is it, Edward? I figured she would be getting ready to go on that fabulous honeymoon to the tropics. I heard her talking about it earlier, and I know she was excited to go. It's time that both of you get started soon."

"We will, as soon as I locate her, but I'm afraid Ashley may have upset her again as she did before, but this time she may have confronted her in person instead of talking behind her back."

The guests were all departed for their homes now, and I needed to find Britt and get us started on our great honeymoon. I had returned to the house to locate Britt, seeing she had gone from the reception hall according to a few people who saw her leave. I knew Britt was looking forward to two weeks at the beach, even if she didn't know where I was taking her, but why didn't she wait for me? It was to be a surprise. I went upstairs to our bedroom, and there on the pillow lay a handwritten note from Britt. I had never read such heartbreaking words in my life. I felt numb all over after reading the words. What kind of state must she be in, and where had she disappeared in the dark night? How long had she been gone? Where would she go? Nothing else mattered now but finding her and bringing her home. I had so many questions about what was happening. Tears started to flow like rivers.

"Noooooooooooooooooooooo!" I screamed. "It can't be. What lies? Ashley has ruined our marriage and has told lies about me to Britt for the very last time. What must Britt think of me, and now she is out there in the unknown surroundings not knowing where to go and nobody to trust or turn to."

When John heard me scream, he came running. I gave him the note to read, but he didn't read it at that moment, realizing it was private. I then gave him Greg's telephone number and told him to call and have both him and Ashley come over immediately as it was an emergency. Don't tell them anything else about Britt. I was so angry and upset, I couldn't see straight; also, I wanted to cry, but the tears wouldn't come. How could I have found my soul mate, only to have her taken away from me through deceit and lies? I was shaking, knowing that the love of my life was wandering around outside alone.

"John, please tell Herbert to tell Greg as soon as he arrives to come immediately to my study." It seemed like only a few minutes, and Greg and Ashley were at the house and wondering about an emergency. Herbert showed them to my study.

"Ashley, I think you know what this emergency is concerning, and you will communicate to Greg the lies that you have told about the two of us."

"Edward, my friend, what is this about? Where is your beautiful wife, and why aren't you on your way to the tropics on your honeymoon? You look as if you have been crying. What is the emergency? Is Brittney injured?"

"She may be by the time we find her. I don't know where Britt is, but I think Ashley can tell you what this is about, Greg. Go ahead, Ashley, tell Greg what you've done to both me and him."

"Well, Ashley, what have you done this time? I'm almost afraid to ask. You have done so much to people in the past that we barely have any friends left."

"I was afraid that our dear Edward was making a mistake in this marriage by hardly knowing anything about the person he was marrying, and so I told Brittney that Edward and I were lovers, and the only reason he married her was so you wouldn't find out because you had become suspicious. I thought maybe she would think it was all a big joke. I guess I was wrong. I didn't want her after your money, as Greg and myself are your heirs if something happens to you. I thought she might try to do away with you and grab the money and run."

Greg was fuming. His face was turning red, and if looks could kill, Ashley would have been dead from his anger. He started to pace the room, and at one point, I thought he was reaching out to hit her. I'm not a vicious man, but at that point, if he tried to hit her, I wouldn't have stopped him.

"Ashley, you have done some pretty stupid and bizarre things since we have been married, but this takes the cake. What did you think she would do? Did you think she would think it a big joke? This is her wedding day. Of all the insensitive, outrageous, idiotic thinks you have done. This day will go down in history, and you will always remember it. I am saying it here in front of my friends. Today will be the day that I will get a divorce from you. I can't and will not put up with your involvement in other people's lives any longer. These are things that are none of your business. Did you not think of how Edward would feel? This is his wife, and he loves her. You should have kept your nasty nose out of other people's business where it is none of your concern."

"But, Greg, I did it for us. I love you."

"Ashley, you haven't any idea what true love is, and someday I will find that same true love that Edward found with Brittney. Maybe I will have to go to Newfoundland so I can find my perfect soul mate. At this moment, I despise you, and I do not want to see your face ever again. Do you think that I really want Edward's money because that seems like it is your sole purpose in life, money? Go home, Ashley, and pack your things. I want you out of my house tonight before I get back there since it is my house, not yours. Ashley, I had stopped loving you a long time ago, and this just makes it all so real and permanent and also helps me put an end to our so-called marriage. Don't forget, Ashley, our prenuptial agreement so you will not get a thing that is in the house or any money from our accounts. You will leave as you did when you walked into my life. With absolutely nothing! Now, leave under your own power, or I will throw you out. As of this moment, you have no right to be near Edward or myself."

"Edward, what can I do to help find her? Do you know where she went? Did anyone see her depart? I'll stay and help as long as you need me."

"I haven't had time to think about anything except my wife being out there all alone. I love my wife with all my heart and soul. Now it looks as if I may never get to tell her how much. And by the way, Ashley, before you go, Britt has no knowledge of my wealth or where it comes from, but she will know if I ever get her back. Also, your name will be removed from my will immediately tonight, and Britt's put in your place. I hate to be so cruel, being a Christian, but, Ashley, after what you've done tonight, I'm sorry I ever put your name on my will or that I ever knew you. You are a conniving woman who needs help. Please leave my house immediately, and I never want to speak to you or see your face again ever. Never step in this house ever. I'm sorry, Greg, for having to say these nasty things, but they needed to be said."

"Don't be sorry, Edward, you spoke the truth. I should have done something about this a long time ago when she started doing strange things to other people. I feel so responsible for Brittney out there."

Ashley ran to the door and disappeared into the night, and Herbert made sure she left the premises. After the fiasco with Ashley, I finally broke down, and the tears that were there just below the surface started pouring. I am all man, but I've never cried like this in my life. I'm crying for my lost soul mate, my reason for living and carrying on each day. It took me a lifetime to find someone that I wanted to love and marry. I just can't lose her now.

Herbert and Monica heard me crying and came into the study. "Excuse me, sir, but I think Monica may know something about Mrs. Moore."

"Yes, Monica. What can you tell me?"

"I'm not sure if any of this can help, and I'm not sure if this means anything, but during the reception, Mrs. Moore came back to the house, and I saw her as she came downstairs carrying a small piece of luggage. She told me that she was going to put it in the car for later when you left on your honeymoon. I should have thought something about it was all wrong because it seemed as if she had been crying, but not just sobbing, but outright big tears. Her face was all black from her mascara running, but she didn't seem to really care what she looked like at that moment. She was also wearing her warm coat. That should have stood out because why would she need a warm coat in the tropics? I didn't think of it because I knew that you were planning to leave immediately after the reception. I say that it was a little before 1:00 a.m. when I saw her, which was about two hours ago. I should have noticed something wasn't right because as she went out into the dark night, she really started to cry, as if her whole world had just ended, but she didn't see me looking at her. She was trying to conceal her face from me in the collar of her coat. Sir, is there anything we can do? I just feel like it was my fault."

"Thank you, Monica, you may have already helped some. You didn't know what was happening. Herbert, please call the police for me. I just can't speak to them on the phone right now. Have them come here immediately or as soon as possible."

Greg spoke up at that moment and said whatever the cost, he was going to pay to get Brittney back to the loving family who needed her, and in the meantime, he would stay and help if that was okay, he would stay there until she was found.

"Thank you, Greg. You are a true friend."

I was so happy to have my brother and sister staying there with me. They were a great comfort. They had never seen me cry before, and now here I was blabbering like a baby, but I didn't care who saw me.

"Edward, I haven't seen you cry since we were kids. Brittney will be found. Now I truly know that you are over your heels in love with Brittney with all your heart and soul. I've never seen you like this. I always knew that you were the sentimental brother, but I love you more at this moment, brother, than ever in our entire lives. I pray that I can eventually find someone as you have found Brittney."

"You will, John. I found out that it is never too late as far as love is concerned, but now I am not so sure about me. John. You need to read her note. It is heart-wrenching, and I can't imagine what Britt must be going through out there all alone."

"Here!"

"Let me read what she said. I now felt that it was okay to read Brittney's heartfelt words that took her into the dark night."

As he read it, he understood more of the magnitude of their love. He started to show signs of tears flowing down his cheeks, and he didn't even try to wipe them away. John and I hugged, and he tried as a brother would to comfort me as never before. This meant more to me than anything else anyone did.

"We will get her back, Edward, so help me. No matter what the cost."

At that point on my wedding night, I had no more hope or strength left in my body. I had lost my wife on our wedding day to travel the streets all alone. All the lies that she heard were, to her, real. She had been hurt so many times back in Newfoundland because of her job as a reporter, and now to end up here with almost the same type of hurt, except now she is blaming me, and I wasn't with her to take the hurt away. At this point, I was hurting along with her, but I could take it. I didn't care anymore what happened to me or how I looked at this point. All I wanted was to get Britt back.

"Edward, are you okay? Would you like to lie down until the police arrive? You are going to need all your strength to get through this."

"I need to be up and helping." With tears in his eyes and streaming down his cheeks, he looked at me. "John, I can't go on without Britt. She is my life. I have never known what it was to have so much love to give another person. I can't accept what has happened without a fight. I have lost my soul mate on our biggest day."

Chapter 15

Brittney Bentley, not Moore

Where am I going? I'm walking and sometimes running along the shore somewhere up the coast following the coastal road where Edward and I traveled in the days preceding the wedding. It was the only road that I had memorized because it was so scenic and beautiful, but at this particular moment, I didn't care what it looked like. I had mascara and makeup running down my face mixed in with the tears that I had shed. I cried so hard that I finally didn't have any left.

I was getting tired from carrying the small suitcase. It wasn't really heavy, but it was annoying to be switching it from hand to hand. I decided to leave it on the beach near the water's edge. There wasn't anything in it that I really needed. I had more clothes in Newfoundland, and I couldn't wait to get back there, at least the people there hated me, but actually spilled their words out in the open to you. I just had to find a way to get to the airport because with Edward's brain, he would know that was the first place I would think of traveling to. I had taken all the cash I had and took my credit cards that were in my maiden name. I had left behind the credit cards with my married name. I didn't want to be indebted to Edward for anything. I now had probably traveled about five or six miles, and I was so tired and hungry. I didn't even know what time of night it was. I wanted Edward so much, but then my mind would go back to the complete fool I had been, trusting him. I needed to find a hotel for the night. I could hardly walk another step, but I was so happy that I had worn my great walking shoes.

After dropping my luggage on the beach, I left there and did some walking along the coastal road. It was so scary being out here in the dark with all this traffic. People are beeping their horns at me. I guess it is strange to see a woman walking along at night by herself dressed in a really heavy coat for this time of the season. They probably thought that I was just another bum. I was hoping that I wouldn't see any police cars because they would definitely have pulled over and stopped me from walking along the highway, and then they would have transported me back to Edward or jail.

After about three or four hours of walking along the highway, a car pulled over. Inside were two guys and a girl. She told me her name was Cinnamon, short for Cynthia Beam. They asked if I needed a ride somewhere and could they help. I accepted the ride without even thinking of what the consequences could be, but at that moment, I didn't care anymore about what happened to me. They could kill me for all I cared after the day that I had. They drove along roads that I didn't know and had never been on before. I said I was hungry, and if they were hungry, I would buy us all some food. They knew of a fast food restaurant where we stopped, and I bought food. I never realized it, but the two guys were watching as I pulled out the cash in my pocket, and they even saw my credit cards that were folded in the bills.

After eating the food in the car, we drove for about three more hours, and then they seemed to drive onto a side road that was very bumpy. They said that they knew of a cabin where we could spend the night. We arrived at the cabin, and after that, everything seemed to be a blur. I seemed to go into a twilight zone, another dimension. I tried to move, but couldn't seem to get my arms or legs to move. What was happening?

The next morning, I awoke not realizing where I was and then started to remember the night before. I couldn't figure out why I had such a headache. The three travelers were gone. I reached into my pocket to check on my cash, and it was gone and also my credit cards. All they had left me was enough coins for a telephone call. There wasn't a telephone in the cabin; really, there wasn't much of anything worth mentioning in the cabin except a couple of cots and a bathroom.

I was alone. I didn't know where to turn. I felt so dirty, not having any extra clothes now, as I left them on the beach hundreds of miles back. I had no idea how to get back to the main road, but I would have to try. I hadn't watched for any signs from the night before.

What was I to do, or where should I go from here? The only thought was that maybe I should locate tire tracks and see which way would take me back following the tracks from the previous night. I wouldn't and couldn't go back and beg Edward to take me back. He was far better off without me. I wonder if he was even thinking of me or maybe he was on my honeymoon with Ashley at the fabulous tropical beach. I wonder what John and Joanne Moore, Edward's siblings, thought of all this. They must hate me for running away, but what must they think of Edward and his lies to me?

Chapter 16

Cinnamon first saw the girl walking along the highway, and all three agreed that they should see if she needed a ride.

"Bart, Odie, someone is walking along on the highway. Do you think we should stop and pick her up?

They both spoke together. "Great idea."

"Maybe she has some money that we could get some food. I'm starving."

"You're always thinking about food, Odie."

"That's because Bart is always the person thinking about stealing money for drugs. Maybe we can get money for both, and we can take her to that abandoned cabin that we sometimes go to spend the night."

"You two guys are pathetic. She may be in trouble and maybe we can help her, at least get her someplace where she is out of the weather. She could be tired."

They pulled the car over and spoke to the girl. "Hi, we are Odie, Bart, and Cinnamon. Would you like a ride somewhere?"

"Hi, I'm Brittney Bentley. I'm so tired and hungry. Do you know anywhere to get some fast food, like a hamburger? I'll even spring for buying everyone dinner."

Cinnamon spoke up, "There's a restaurant about twenty miles up the highway. We can take you there, and then we can take you to our cabin where you will be warm and comfortable. It's about a couple hundred miles away, if you don't mind traveling."

"I'm trying to get as far away as possible from here and never look back."

"Okay. Get in and let's go."

She opened the door of the car and hopped inside. She was so happy to be sitting.

They arrived at the restaurant, and Brittney paid in cash for the food. Lots of hamburgers and fries with sodas, then they proceeded to the cabin. After about a couple hundred miles, they turned off onto another road that was mainly a narrow road through some fields. They all entered in the house, and Brittney went to the bathroom. While she was in the bathroom, Bart drugged Brittney's soda, and Odie stole her credit cards and her money, leaving only coins, and soon after all this and having eaten, they all fell asleep.

Chapter 17

Edward Moore

The police patrol arrived within half an hour of being called, and I tried to explain what had happened to Detective Sgt. Martin and then showed him the note that Britt had written to me before she left. He explained that they usually do not start looking for a runaway until after twenty-four hours had passed, but this was a special circumstance, and they knew my reputation as a doctor.

Greg was great support, and he explained it much better telling them how his soon-to-be ex-wife had manipulated Britt into thinking that they were having an affair. This had caused her so much grief, not just to me, but to Greg also, and this being our wedding day. Britt had believed everything in the note and had taken to running away to be free of all the lies that she thought I had told her.

I was still a mere basket case, still sobbing and thinking about Britt out there all alone. My eyes were all red and swollen. I must have looked a sight for a man, but at that moment, I didn't care. This was my wife, and I needed to get her back and care for her.

"Edward, are you up to answering a few questions so we can get started on this investigation?"

"Yes! Please ask away anything that can help with her return."

"Do you have a recent photo that we can distribute to other officers?"

"John, can you get the photo upstairs on the dresser?"

"Sure, immediately, Edward."

"What about height and weight?"

"She is five feet and seven inches and weighs approximately a hundred and forty-seven pounds. She was last seen wearing blue jeans and a beige coat. No jewelry of any kind. She left her wedding band and engagement rings here. I'm not sure if she has any cash or credit cards in her maiden name, which would be Brittney Bentley, because she left her credit cards with her married name here."

John returned with the photograph and gave it to the officer, telling them that it was the perfect likeness of her. The police left after receiving all the information needed to start searching and said that they would keep in touch with any happenings as they were received. The police had been out searching and combing the surrounding area for about two hours now when Police Officer Hardy put his head in the door and asked for Detective Sergeant Martin. They started talking and whispering and looking at me as if someone knew something and didn't want me to know. I knew something was up at that point.

"Please! What have you found? Don't keep anything from me. I need to know absolutely everything, no matter how much it hurts."

"Edward, Police Officer Hardy has found a piece of luggage along the beach, next to the water's edge. We will need you to identify it, if possible, if you are up to it. It is beat-up quite a lot and full of water."

"Can I see the luggage now, please?"

"Bring in the luggage, Hardy."

I looked at it and knew immediately that it was Britt's. I broke down again. Greg and John were there to help me through this. I was not alone. They both held me, one on one side and one on the other. I never felt so loved by friends as at that moment.

"Edward, I hate to say this, but we are combing the beach and the ocean for a body, just in case. I know it's not what you want to hear, but we have to investigate all aspects of what might have happened to her. We don't think that she went into the water, but normally no one would leave a piece of luggage on the beach to find unless they were going into the water. We are looking for any recent footprints around that area."

"I really don't want to hear any of this, but I want to know everything you find. I know you have to think of every aspect of what may have been going through her mind at the time. She has to be alive. We have to find her. Britt is a great swimmer, but she loved the water enough to just wade in and disappear or make us think that she did. I was thinking that she may have rented a car and drove to the airport to take a flight back to Newfoundland, Canada. In her note, she did mention being torn away from her homeland. I know there were times when she was homesick, and going back there is where she would feel safe from anyone who she felt threatened by. She hasn't made any friends here, and I think Ashley Drew made sure that none of her friends talked to Britt."

"Edward, do you think we can search her bedroom?"

"Absolutely, whatever you need. It is at your disposal."

"John, could you direct them to Britt's bedroom suite?"

"We definitely will be looking for her credit cards being used by her or someone else. We are hoping that she wasn't so upset that she went swimming and got caught in the undertow. Do you know if she knew about the undertows here?"

"I don't think she did. I pray that she didn't do that. Since I brought her here, some people have always been mean to her, and she doesn't have much confidence in herself. She doesn't deserve any of this."

John wanted me to rest, as it was probably going to be a long night. I couldn't sleep at all thinking of Britt and where she could have ended up out there; this would have been our wedding night. I paced the floor all night. I looked a wreck, but I really didn't care. Even my clothes were all wrinkled from having been in them all night. I was more concerned with Britt's safety. We should have been on our flight to the oceanfront honeymoon suite that I had reserved for two weeks in Hawaii. I started sobbing again. I prayed out loud for my beautiful wife. "Dear Heavenly Father, please protect Britt out there all alone, and wrap your loving arms around her and envelop her with your everlasting love. She loves you and knows that you answer prayer. Bring Britt back home to us where we can wrap her in our love. I never knew what true love could be like until I met you, Britt.

All these years, I have been so lonely, and I had been waiting to meet you. It was you, dear Lord, that brought us together and put us in the place where we could meet each other. Britt loves you with her heart and soul. Please keep her safe tonight in your loving arms wherever she may be and hold her in your heart, amen!"

John heard me and came into the bedroom. He came over to the bed where I was sitting and just put his arm around me for comfort. It was so wonderful to have my family near at a time like this.

"Edward, we will find her and bring her home to you to be by your side. She deserves all the happiness you can bestow upon her as your loving and eternal soul mate. I have never known what I've been missing in not having someone to share my life and dreams with like you. I am definitely going to be looking now after seeing you both together. I need the closeness and the happiness that I saw the two of you share in the past week together. By the way, the police didn't find anything in her suite, not even a hair."

"You will find your soul mate, brother. After all this is over and Britt is back, we will concentrate on your love life."

Chapter 18

The night passed without any sightings, and now Police Officer Hardy checked into the house the next morning, which is where the police had set up their headquarters for this search. The search stakeout for finding the credit card that was used belonging to Britt had been a success. It had been used in a couple of bars the night before, and it was in the name of Brittney Bentley. One of the bars was named Quiet Time, quite a distance up the coast, approximately five hundred miles north. Britt could never have walked that distance alone. I kept thinking of all the malcontents out there, and they could have taken Britt for a joy ride somewhere along that route, robbed and killed her. My mind was working overtime thinking of all the scenarios that she could have gone through just to get away from me. The card was traced to the bar, and according to the bartender, there were two guys and a girl, but the description for the girl was all wrong comparing her to Britt. The girl at the bar was about five feet and two inches and about hundred seventy-five pounds. This wasn't even close to Britt, and there definitely was only one girl. I was praying Britt was still alive.

Detective Sergeant Martin entered the house. "Police Officer Hardy will be going back to the bar Quiet Time later tonight and stake it out, dressed in plain clothes and try to arrest the credit card thief and see where they got hold of the cards. We may be able to trace Brittney from there. It may take a couple of nights for them to return, if they do return."

Police Officer Hardy explained to the bartender what had happened. The bartender had definitely agreed to the surveillance. He didn't want any ne'er do wells in his establishment. He was running a good, clean family bar and wanted to keep it that way. The bartender remembered the trio very well. He would nod when they entered and tried using the same card.

Police Officer Hardy didn't have to wait long. He had sat there by himself dressed in jeans and a sweat shirt and drank soda. After about an hour of sitting, there was a trio that came in and ordered drinks. He waited until they paid, and the bartender nodded his head, then Police Officer Hardy advanced to the bar nonchalantly. "Good evening, you three. Nice evening outside."

The bartender then spoke, "They are using Brittney Bentley's credit cards again."

"Of course, I am. I'm Brittney Bentley. I wouldn't use someone else's credit card."

"You just did. Brittney Bentley does not look like you. We are looking for her. I am arresting all three of you for possession of stolen credit cards and whatever else we can come up with when we get you back to headquarters. Backup is on the way."

I had them sit in the booth until the backup police walked in the door and apprehended them to escort them back to headquarters for questioning. I read them their Miranda rights and arrested them on sight. Then I drove back to headquarters alone where they would be interrogated about where these credit cards were found or stolen from.

We arrived at headquarters and went about the usual interrogation of the suspects. "I am Police Officer Hardy, and what are your names?"

The tall guy spoke up, but wouldn't tell us his name. "Why are we here? And neither one of us will tell you our names. You have no reason to arrest us. We were having a drink, minding our own business. Why did you take my girlfriend's credit cards?"

"You are in possession of stolen credit cards of a missing person. Where did you get these cards?"

"We found them."

"Why did you say that it was your girlfriend's card and now are saying that you found them? Which is it? Do you have any knowledge of the whereabouts of the said woman? Have you seen her?"

"No."

"Then where did you find the credit cards? I hope you are telling the truth because lying to me will only make it harder on you."

"They were lying on the beach."

"That's a lie. Do you want to try for another lie?"

"I think you may have picked her up as she was walking along the highway and taken her somewhere and robbed her."

The girl then interrupted and said that she wanted to tell the truth. "I am not going to lie for these two anymore. I will tell you the truth about what happened and who did it. I am Cynthia Beam, but I go by the name of Cinnamon, and these two are Bart Carlen and Odie Pyre."

"Keep your mouth shut, Cinnamon, or we will shut it for you."

"Officer Morgan, can you take these two and lock them up until we know what to do with them. No one is going to shut her mouth for her."

"Come on, guys. We have lovely accommodations for you back here."

"Cinnamon, you keep that pretty little mouth quiet, or we will quiet it permanently."

"Do not threaten anyone here. We have witnesses here if something happens to her."

"I will not, Bart. We picked up some woman. I am telling you the truth. We didn't know that she was missing. She looked like she had been crying and so tired and lonely. We took her to a vacant cabin that we know about, that is, after she bought everyone food at a local fast food restaurant. She went to the bathroom at the cabin, and that was when Bart put a drug in her soda, and then she was out like a light. We didn't abuse her in any way. We don't know where she is now, but she was still at the cabin when we left the next morning. As we were leaving the cabin, Bart said he had to go back in the cabin, and when he came back, he had her credit cards and some money. I told him he should have left her some coins, so he did. I don't think he abused her in there when he went back to the cabin. He was only in there a short time. Then we drove away leaving her in the cabin, still asleep."

"Do you think you could find that cabin again if we drove there?"

"I really think I could."

"We need to find her. She may be wandering around in the hills, maybe getting even more lost than what she already is and high on whatever Bart gave her. We need to find her as soon as possible. You are coming with me, and you are going to guide me to the cabin."

"I will definitely try."

"Let's go."

Chapter 19

Edward was home trying to make some sense of the way his marriage started out. He was so unhappy, and every so often, he would pray that Britt was fine. He would start crying whenever he read her note, keeping it in his hand continually. He had never cried so much in all his life as he had done since last night. If he ever got Britt back home, he would take her to the ends of the earth to try to make up for what she had been through. At least Ashley was going to pay for what she had done. Greg would see to that.

How could I have been so wrong about Ashley? Greg and I were my best friends as I thought, but not anymore, although Greg still was. All she wanted was to see me dead so she could have my money. Greg would always be my best friend. I felt so compassionate for Greg that he was so taken in also with Ashley, and he never knew she was so inconsiderate over other people's feelings to have done something this outrageous.

It was at that moment that Detective Sergeant Martin entered and told everyone of the arrest of the trio who stole the credit cards from Britt, and more than likely, she had been drugged, from what they can figure from the girl. Police Officer Hardy and the girl were now in the process of trying to locate the cabin where Britt was held overnight.

I was praying that she would have stayed there until someone would come and locate her, but she still thinks that I am in love with Ashley and not worried about her.

Chapter 20

Brittney Bentley, not Moore

Waking up in an unfamiliar cabin somewhere in California, I put my hands over my head to stop the throbbing and to try to remember what had happened to me and how I arrived at this place. After about an hour, I started to remember the three people that had picked me up the night before. What was happening to my mind? I couldn't remember much of anything and couldn't seem to focus my thoughts on any part of the evening. The throbbing in my head seems to be worse, and it was hard to see straight. I was scared. I screamed out. "Edward, what have you done to me?" How did I remember him, the one person that I wanted to forget?

I eventually got the strength to stand up and started to walk toward the door. I was like a drunken person, stumbling everywhere. I couldn't walk a straight line. I didn't want anyone to see me, especially the three from the night before. I put my hands in my pockets for warmth, and it was then that I realized that my credit cards were missing and most of my cash. They had robbed me. I am too trustworthy. Now what am I to do? I needed to get back to the main road, as I thought that would be a safer place than out here in the woods all alone. Who knew what kind of riff-faff would be here, and there would be more traffic on the highway? And if I saw a police car, I would stop them to ask for help. No, I couldn't do that, what I was thinking? I'm sure that Edward would have called the police by now, although I'm not sure why. My head was throbbing so much. I was hungry and thirsty. I walked and walked, it seemed like hours, and

I was sure that I could smell the ocean and the calling of the waves to me. My nose was always sensitive to the smell of the salt air from the ocean. I stumbled as I walked as if I was drunk from too much alcohol. What did I drink? I must have been drugged. How could I have been so naïve? I realized that now that I was to be on my own that I needed to be more cautious and not to be so trustworthy. I was not in Newfoundland anymore.

Even though Edward had done me wrong, I still was in love with him. I just couldn't go back to him, though, after what he had done to me. I was still walking and thinking and wishing that I had at least one friend, not one of the "plastic girls," but a true friend. Then I remembered Alicia, Edward's secretary. I didn't have my cell phone, as I had threw that in the ocean, but I did have some change in my pocket, and now all I needed was to find a phone booth. I was starting to get excited about calling Alicia. I knew that she would help me.

A couple of times, I saw a car coming and going, a police car with the siren blasting. I hid in the bushes until it disappeared down the road. That was close! After about a half an hour, it came back, and I jumped in the bushes again. I couldn't keep doing this. This time is was going very slow and without the siren, it seemed as if they were looking for someone.

It seemed like maybe it wasn't coming back, so I started to walk again. I could see the highway now ahead, and walking faster made it to the highway. I crossed the highway without getting hit and found a phone booth at the Fisherman's Restaurant. I called directory assistance and got Alicia's phone number. I called, and she answered on the first ring. It was so great to hear her voice, and I was thinking that maybe she could get me a plane ticket back to Newfoundland and help me get my luggage back. I would pay her back later. I was hoping that if I could make it to her, she wouldn't tell Edward where I was staying.

"Alicia, do you think you can help me get back to Newfoundland? Edward has done me wrong, and I loved him so much."

"Brittney, my husband and I will come and get you and take you back to Edward."

"No, I can't go back. I need rest, I am so tired, and I think I was drugged. Can you help me?" I told her where I was, and she knew the place. I started to cry into the phone. It would take them a couple of hours to drive there, but she promised not to tell Edward that she had found me.

Within three hours, I was sitting in the car with Alicia and her husband. I cried most of the way especially after she told me that it was all a lie that Ashley had told me, that Edward had the police searching for me, and that he hasn't slept since I left, also that he has been crying constantly knowing that his soul mate was gone.

"Alicia, how can I go back? I said such awful things to him in that note and accused him of infidelity with Ashley. He must think that I am a child to run away when I should have stayed and fought for my husband, but Ashley was so convincing and told me that it was his idea. She made it so real when she told me all these things as if they really happened. I would think about why Edward would want me for his wife, a backwoods down-to-earth girl with hardly any manners, when he could have any girl in Hollywood."

"He loves you so very much, Brittney, he would forgive you for anything as long as you come home to him. He has been so miserable the last two days. I'm not just telling you this to get you to go home, but you are his soul mate, I can tell, after seeing the two of you together."

"I just can't face him at this moment, maybe later tomorrow. Is there any way that you can help me get a motel on the beach where I can stay for a few days while I think? I am so tired and need the rest just to think and get rid of this headache. My credit cards were stolen, so I am destitute at the moment."

"Of course, we'll help you. I know the perfect hotel, the Paradise Resort. I am friends with the owners, and they also owe me a favor. I also bought you a few things thinking that you wouldn't want to go back immediately."

"Thank you, Alicia. I am so grateful. You are a great friend."

Alicia took me to the Paradise Resort, a very luxurious place, and I slept for twenty-four hours straight. I was so tired and felt so dirty. I relaxed under a hot shower and then decided that the next day, I would love to hike on the cliffs overlooking the ocean. Back in Newfoundland, the cliffs always cleared my mind and made me relax. I had changed into the clothes that Alicia had bought for me, all a perfect fit. I walked about two miles over the crevices in the cliff, being very careful especially not having my hiking shoes with me. I realized that it was beginning to get dusk, and I didn't want to be caught on the cliffs after dark. I turned around to start back when suddenly my foot slipped and down I fell, screaming as I realized that this was the end. I tried to grab onto anything, a shrub or bush, that might be on the cliff, but nothing but emptiness.

All I could think about as I was falling was that this was the end and that I would never be a wife to Edward or ever see him again. Goodbye, my love. I'm sorry for what I have put you through. I hit the ledge hard, and my mind entered total darkness.

Chapter 21

Alicia and Cliff Fortune

Alicia went back home feeling great that they had Brittney settled in a hotel room but wondering if she should keep her promise about calling Edward. She asked her husband what he thought.

"Cliff, what should I do? I gave my promise to Brittney, but I know that Edward has been so worried, and he would definitely feel better if he knew that she was in a safe place. I don't want to let Brittney down as a friend, seeing right now I am her only friend, but I also owe Edward all the gratitude and love that I can give him and that he deserves."

"Alicia. They are soul mates together, but put it this way, if it was you out there wandering around, I would go to the ends of the earth to find you and return you to the love of family."

"Thank you. I love you, sweetheart, and now I know what to do. I am going to call Edward. He deserves to know where Brittney is at this moment. He truly loves her and is so worried."

The phone started to ring, and John picked it up. He handed Edward the receiver with a smile on his face. "Is it Britt?"

"Hello, this is Edward Moore. May I help you?"

"It's Alicia, Edward, and I know where Brittney is, and she is safe for now. She told me not to call you. She doesn't trust anyone right now, but she thought about calling me since I was the only person that spoke to her at the wedding. I felt so sorry for her, Edward. She can't face you at the moment. She looks just awful, dirty, tired, and ragged. She actually was like a drunken person. She said that she thinks that the people who picked her up drugged her. I promised her I would not call you, but she needs more help than I can give her. She is worn out and needs rest. She has been through so much in the last day."

"Alicia, I need her home with me. I want to take care of her. I can't think of her suffering in the cold out there all alone. She may need to be in the hospital for a few days. Please tell me where she is, please, Alicia. I will be so ever grateful and am already."

"Okay, Edward, but please don't tell her that I ratted on her. She will never speak to me again. She is at a resort and in a warm place. I took care of it because she had her credit cards and money stolen after she was drugged. She had a tremendous headache. She won't come home at the moment because she is at the phase where she doesn't trust your word. They are empty and cold to hear them at this time."

"What do you mean by drugged? Is she lucent or staggering around? It sounds as if she needs medical treatment and to be examined by a medical doctor, maybe John or Greg? We need to find out what drug she was given?"

"Didn't the police tell you she was drugged? All right, boss, but don't tell her that I told you where she is. I want to stay friends with her. I love talking with her. She is at the Paradise Resort, Room 435. Do you know where that is located?"

"Yes, thank you Alicia. I will be always ever so grateful to you and Cliff."

Edward called the police and told Detective Sergeant Martin what Alicia had told him. Edward, his brother, John and Greg with the police made their way to the Paradise Resort only to find that Britt not there in her room.

"Do you have a Brittney Bentley Moore registered here in Room 435? I'm her husband."

"We have a Brittney Bentley registered here in that room. She said that she was going cliff climbing around the crevices, but that was over four hours ago. She should have been back by now. It gets dark fast here around the cliffs."

81

They went down to where she was going climbing and walked the beach to start checking along the cliffs to see if they could see her up there. They were afraid that there may have been an accident, but didn't correspond that back to Edward. Everyone went in different directions with flashlights, but they didn't seem to be powerful enough to shine upward on the cliffs.

"Edward, we need searchlights brought in here. I'm placing a call for searchlights, also an ambulance standing by just in case."

Then Greg spoke up, "Police Officer Hardy, please do not say anything to Edward, but I have a bad feeling that this is not going to end the way that Edward would like."

In about fifteen minutes, the searchlights, ambulance, and a firetruck with a ladder appeared on the beach. The lights were placed strategically along the cliffs where Britt was supposed to have been climbing. At the base of one cliff, Police Officer Hardy found a fairly new shoe. He handed it over to Detective Sergeant Martin.

Edward saw the transaction between them and ran over to where they were talking. "Detective Sergeant Martin, did you find something?"

"Yes, a shoe. Can you identify it?"

"That's Britt's shoe. She has to be here somewhere. Keep looking. She must have fallen. Please, no. It can't end like this, not now when we are so close to finding her."

The lights were brought closer and shining over the face of the cliff where underneath the shoe was found. They scanned the lights up and up until about halfway up the cliff there was what looked like a person straddled over the outcropping of rocks. It was impossible to reach without the help of the ladder on the fire truck. The truck was brought closer, and the firemen and paramedics were all geared up to climb the ladder to retrieve the person, if it was Brittney or whoever it was now on that ledge.

"Detective Sergeant Martin, is it possible that I can go up there to help? If it is Britt, she's my wife, and I'm also a medical doctor. She may need attention, which I'm sure she needs. I pray that she is still alive after a fall from any height."

"Not this time, Edward. These paramedics are especially trained for accidents like this. Edward, I know you want to help, but you are too close to the victim to give your expertise medical knowledge on cliff falls. When she is back on the beach, we will then need all of your, John's, and Greg's help with a diagnosis. You may ride in the ambulance with them."

"As you wish, but we will need to get to the hospital as soon as possible, stat. We may get her checked out in the ambulance on the way, not here on the beach. Just that she may have been on that cliff for any number of hours and the fastest we can get her to the hospital, the better a chance she will have, if she is still alive." I was starting to ramble like a crazy person.

Chapter 22

Edward Moore

With the paramedics climbing up the ladder straight up the side of the cliff, it seemed like an eternity, but it was a very treacherous climb even with the ladder, due to other rocks falling and crumbling around them. Edward knew they were risking their lives and trained for such a task as this. He knew he could never do this. They finally reached the ledge which was hardly wide enough for one person. They confirmed that it was Britt from what they could tell by looking at her, but she was so battered and bruised and many cuts, but the clothes were Britt's. She was badly injured and almost beyond recognition, her face being swollen. They communicated down that they couldn't help her on the cliff due to the amount of room to work, but would strap her to the backboard and get her down as fast and carefully as they could. She was unconscious and never made a sound during all of the procedures to lift her off the cliff. Edward was wishing that she would just moan a little, but nothing.

Inch by inch, they descended to the beach below. John ran to check her out but immediately looked at her and then at Edward and decided that they needed to get to the hospital as fast as possible. Edward stood there like in a daze staring at her beautiful face, all battered and bruised. She was unconscious and had a huge bump on the left side of her head. She was bleeding from cuts all over her body. At least, she was still breathing, but barely. They immediately hooked her up to oxygen.

"Please, God, protect her from everything that she will be going through in the next couple of hours. You have kept her alive while up on the cliff, and I know you are watching over her now. Thank you for being with us and guiding us to her. Amen."

I would never be able to thank all these men who were devoted in their work and involved in the rescue operation that took place on that cliff that night, with Britt, their care and the smoothness of their handling of her. She was lifted into the ambulance and rushed to the Van Nuys Medical Center where I am a doctor, with sirens screaming into the night. John checked her out more in the ambulance, not exactly knowing about any internal injuries. He could tell that she had a broken right tibia and a broken right radius in two places that would require surgery. Her stomach was distended, and John noticed an exuberant amount of swelling.

"It looks as if she is bleeding on the inside, Edward. We need to get her to the hospital and surgery as soon as possible."

The ambulance arrived at the hospital in short-order time. Greg had gone on ahead, and they were all set up for when the ambulance arrived. The emergency team knew it was my wife, and Greg was the Chief of Surgery, and John was Chief of Internal Medicine in England, and I trusted them both explicitly. Britt was still unconscious. I wanted to be there with her, but Greg and John suggested that I stay away until they knew what they were up against. He would only be in the way.

Greg came to me and said that they were all ready to start on Britt. I was sobbing again, especially wondering if she would be able to survive the surgery. She was so weak.

"Greg, please keep me informed about what's happening?"

"They have examined her, so let me just check, and I'll be back immediately with the prognosis."

Greg went to the ER, and it seemed almost hours later returned and told me to stop pacing and sit down. "Edward, you need to remain calm, and I know that it's going to be hard for you to do right now, but you have to try for Brittney's sake. She is banged up quite a bit, but those will heal over time. She has internal injuries that we need to check with surgery. John was correct, and she is bleeding on the inside, and that is our main concern at the moment. Possibly, we can try to operate on her spleen and sew the damaged part, or if we can't do that, we may have to do a partial splenectomy. We noticed this with a CT scan. She is still unconscious, which I was hopeful that she would wake while we were examining her, but she didn't move. I am very concerned about that and especially the head injuries, but not as much as first getting the bleeding stopped. We need for you to sign all the necessary papers for permission for surgery as soon as possible to save her. I would also like your permission for John to assist me in surgery. I could really depend on him and his expertise at this time. This is going to be a long, hard night."

"I know that it's too much to ask you to go home and get some rest, but please go to your office and try to sleep. She is going to need you wide awake when she wakes up. You won't do her any good if you are falling apart yourself. You haven't slept in over twenty-four hours. I'll call you when the surgery is over. I estimate at least six or eight hours or more of repairs. The minute we finish, I will call."

"I hate to leave her, but I could use a shower. Please call me the minute you finish. I'm worried about her being unconscious for so long and not moving."

I took a cab home, only because if I stayed at the hospital, I would be in the way of what was happening in the ER, and I needed to be refreshed for Britt after the surgery, and it was then that she would need me the most; at least, I pray that she still needed me as much as I needed her. I was in a daze as the cab drove me home, probably from lack of sleep. Joanne was still waiting up for me when I arrived home and was waiting to hear all the news concerning Britt. I explained to her what was happening at the moment, and if she would pray for Britt and the surgical team for their God-given skill.

"We both wanted to stay until you found Brittney, dear brother. We have a flight back home tomorrow night, which is actually today now, but we are returning here. John and I talked it over a few days ago, and we decided that we need to be near to each other as a family should. We're going to move here. We're thinking in about six months after John has everything settled at the hospital in London, especially finding another surgeon to take his place. I am so glad that he has the chance to help operate on Brittney, helping you as siblings should.

"I love you both so much, and I appreciate you being here for Britt and myself. John will have a position here at the hospital when you return and also you, Joanne, can still work for him. John's diagnosis was correct about the internal bleeding, possibly her spleen, according to Greg. It'll be wonderful having you both here. As soon as I take a shower and freshen up, I will be returning to the hospital, but have a safe flight, and if I don't see John, tell him I will see him in a couple of months. We may miss each other when I return to the hospital. I love you, sis."

I hugged her and kissed her and went upstairs to the bedroom.

Chapter 23

B ritt needed all the prayers she could get right now. I also called Alicia at the office in the hospital to tell her to cancel all my appointments, but she had already done so. She had arranged them for a month or two with a couple of other doctors on staff. I thanked her for breaking her promise with Britt because if she hadn't, I hesitated to think what the consequences would have been. I also asked her to pray for Britt as I knew she was a great warrior for prayers, and also if she could get the hospital prayer chain up and running. I ran upstairs, took a long hot shower, shaved and dressed, and looking in the closet, saw all Britt's clothes that I had transferred to the huge walk in closet in the master suite from her suite. I walked over to them and held them against my face, smelling her fragrance. It was at that moment that I finally broke down and started crying like a baby.

"I love you, Britt, you are my soul mate. Please don't leave me. Fight, Britt, with all that you have within you, with all your strength. Come back home to me. We need to be together. After you are feeling better, we'll go away from here for as long as it takes you to recuperate."

I splashed water on my face and went downstairs, kissed Joanne goodbye, and left the house. I drove in the Maserati and returned to the hospital. I couldn't bear to be away from Britt longer than was absolutely necessary. I parked in my assigned parking spot in the underground garage and entered the hospital. By now, all the employees at the hospital knew that my wife was in surgery and in critical condition. Most of the doctors that were at our wedding came up to me, hugged me, and let me know that they had all been at the chapel praying for about half an hour. There were still some down there praying. All the doctors at the hospital were Christians, but I never imagined that they were this close, although nothing like this had ever happened to either one of them, so we had never tried out the prayer chain.

"I truly appreciate all the prayers that are being lifted up today for Britt. Thank you everyone for being there."

I went to my office on the top floor of the hospital thinking that I could get some work accomplished, but knowing that Britt was five floors below me in surgery, I just sat there with my head in my hands staring at the phone willing it to ring with good news from the ER. Alicia entered with a cup of piping hot tea, just the way I enjoyed it, which I was grateful for and to let me know that Greg had just sent word that everything was going along smoothly and that they should be through in surgery in about thirty minutes pending any complications. I thanked her, hugged her, and would wait for Greg to contact me. I didn't want to be in anyone's way by going down there.

I must have dozed off as I was reminiscing about how I met Britt and the times that we had spent together before moving her to California to spend the remainder of her life married to me. Back in Newfoundland, she was so happy, and now I was regretting having taken her away from everything that she loved and ever knew. This was all new to her, and she hadn't made any friends here, except for Alicia. She was such a joyful person to be around. What had I done to her? I wanted to give her such a joyous wedding since this would be the only one she would have. She was married before, but it never worked out. I never asked her the reason, and I didn't care. That was over, and I never intended to bring long-ago pains back to Britt. She was my soul mate now, and that's the only thing that mattered to me. I loved her with all my heart and soul. As I was deep in thought about all these things, Greg was there shaking me awake.

"Edward, the surgery is over, and now only time will heal all her cuts and bruises. She had a broken right radius in two places and a broken right tibia. She has casts on both. I also had to repair her spleen by doing a partial splenectomy. She is extremely bruised inside and out, but these should heal rather quickly with rest. She hit her head fairly hard. I had to operate and relieve some of the pressure, but she may need to have more surgery there. Her eyes are swollen shut at the moment. Just to let you know before you see her that she is not a pretty sight to look at with all the tubes and bandages. It may be a few days before she wakes up. John suggested that we keep her sedated so as she may heal faster but continue to talk to her. I think that she will hear you, although she may not want to after all the things that she has heard, so talk to her about the truth. She may remember what Alicia told her at the hotel and believe you. I'll be back in a couple of hours. I'm going to lie down in my office for a while. I want to stay around the hospital just in case. By the way, John was a great help and a fantastic internal surgeon. Maybe he would like to relocate here and come to work for us. He was going back to your home for some sleep and then on to merry old England later tonight."

"Thank you, Greg, for everything. You are a great doctor and a true friend. Also, I have some great news concerning my brother and sister. John and Joanne are returning back here in about six months to live and work with us at the hospital. John will be Chief of Internal Medicine, and Joanne will be his nurse, just as they are in England."

"Edward, I feel so responsible after what Ashley did to Brittney, but never again will she hurt Brittney or you, my friend. Why don't you go down and sit with Brittney in Intensive Care? I have left word that you can be with her anytime. She will be in Intensive Care for a couple of weeks. If she heals faster, we will get her out quicker, but I don't want to push her."

I almost ran down to Intensive Care, just to be with my beautiful wife. As I walked in, I just stood there staring. It was as if she had been beaten up by thugs and left for dead. I was aghast looking at her. Being a doctor, I have seen much worse, but it was my wife that I was looking at, and if I hadn't known it was Britt, I wouldn't have known that it was her in that hospital bed. All of that beautiful body was beaten, and I had a tremendous time trying to adjust myself to look at her without breaking down in tears.

"O my darling, Britt, I love you so much. I know that you may be hurting now, and you probably don't believe anything that I tell you about my love for you, but I'll make it up to you, even if it takes me the remainder of my lifetime to do it. I have never had an affair with anyone. I have never been unfaithful to you. I have never been to bed with another woman and don't intend to unless it is with you. You are my true love and will be my first and last. I would never do anything that would cause pain to you, especially on our wedding day, which would have been cruel for any person to do, although I'm sure there are those who do it, but, Britt, that is not my style. I can actually admit to you now, Britt, that I have cried my eyes out thinking about where you could have gone. Please come back to me, hear my voice and know that I am lost without you."

I stayed every day with Britt and part of every night for almost two weeks. After a week, the bruises were turning lighter and lighter, but she was still in a state of unconsciousness with the help of drugs prescribed by Greg. She would soon be able to open her eyes as the swelling was going down. Her bones were healing fast. We kept turning her from side to side to not permit any bed sores from appearing. I asked Greg about her not waking up since two weeks had gone by.

I walked into the ICU one morning, as was my usual beginning of every day before I returned to my office and was very surprised at what I heard. I heard singing coming from Britt's room and thought that she must be awake, but not as I thought. She was singing a song from her native Newfoundland. I didn't want to disturb anything, especially Britt, so I immediately picked up the phone and called Greg and told him to get down to the ICU immediately. She was still unconscious but singing. All the ICU nurses had already gathered there listening to the beautiful yet sad words coming from this comatose woman, especially the way she was singing them.

"See the coast of our dear island/Rising from the troubled seas/ And a peace and rugged beauty/Where my soul has longed to be/I have heard her softly calling/ Heard her voice on every hand/ Bless this rock, this dear old island/Bless my homeland, Newfoundland."

She stopped for a few minutes, and Greg and I stared at each other and listened, and she just kept singing.

"I can see her visual harbors/Mighty cliffs that tests the tides/ See the snowcap homers rolling/Cross the ocean wild and wide/In the tiny towns and hamlets/Nestled 'neath the rolling hills/There's a bred of happy people/Steadfast hearts which freedom fills.

"From her sandy western beaches/To her rugged eastern face/ From the icy winters beauty/And the sunny summers grand/Where the timeless ageless calling/Beats the heart of Newfoundland.

"Bless this rock, this dear old island/Bless this rock and misty seas/For her ways are in my bloodstream/And her hills are calling me/Bless this rock, this dear old island/Bless my homeland, Newfoundland."

I stood there, weeping, and I could see tears flowing down her face, and even Greg had tears in his eyes.

"I'm coming home. You are my rock, my Newfoundland."

"Is Newfoundland really this beautiful, Edward? It sounds like the most spectacular place on this earth and the people as well?"

"Yes. It is the perfect place to grow up, and the people are spectacular. Why is she singing and talking, but still unconscious?"

Greg couldn't believe what he was hearing.

"Greg, have you done an MRI on her head? When will she wake up? She must miss her native homeland so much that her brain is conjuring up all the most beautiful things that she remembers before the accident. What have I done to her, bringing her here to California? She never complained about moving, but that is her way. She wanted to make me happy."

"Edward, you're an MD. You know the answer to that question. Now that I know she is starting to come out of the unconscious state, we will stop the medication and allow her to reawaken on her own. The medication should wear off in a couple of days or even sooner. The singing is a sign that she is slowly on her way back to us."

I returned to my office to take a shower and get some sleep. I felt much more optimistic knowing that she may wake up soon, and I wanted to be alert and rested when she did. I had so much to tell her, but tonight my brain was telling me, please don't go home. Stay here tonight, Britt may need you. I started to get scared thinking that tonight was the night that she was going to be taken from me for eternity. That was the hardest idea in my head to think about. I just couldn't lose her now. I called Greg and told him that I would be sleeping in my office tonight and to call me on my cell phone if there were any changes in Britt, even the most minute.

Chapter 24

I was in a deep sleep dreaming about Britt and how we met on Signal Hill when around 2:00 a.m. my cell phone rang. I jumped up and, not realizing where I was, stumbled and fell across the coffee table. I reached across the table and grabbed my phone. It was Greg. "Edward, Brittney just woke up, and as you can hear, she is screaming. Please come down at once and try to calm her down. I hesitate to give her a sedative as I would like to keep her awake. You need to talk to her."

"Greg, thank you. I'll be there as fast as I can get dressed."

I stumbled across my office trying to dress at the same time. I dressed in a hurry and took the elevator down to the Intensive Care unit, where there was an immense amount of screaming. I walked over to her bedside to give her a hug to calm her down, but instead, she started screaming louder. She looked at me and asked Greg who I was. I was dumbfounded.

"Britt, I'm your husband, Edward. My darling, we were only married three weeks ago, and we haven't gone on our honeymoon yet because you got injured on the cliffs as you were hiking. Do you remember any of what happened?"

"I don't know who you are, sir, but claiming to be my husband is not funny to me. I definitely would not be married to someone as handsome as you. I think that I would remember if I was married recently. I'm not wearing a wedding band, but you are, so that proves that you are a married man. Get away from me and go back to your wife. I'm sure she will be missing you. Where am I anyway? What happened to me? I don't remember a hospital in St. John's that looks like this, and I don't remember any of these doctors here, and I know most of the doctors that practice in the hospitals."

"Britt, you are in the Van Nuys Medical Center in California. We were married here. I was in Newfoundland on vacation, met you there on Signal Hill where I saw you staring into the ocean. We spent the next week together, and then you flew to California with me where we were married three weeks ago. Do you remember any of that, darling?"

She started crying, and I wanted to hug her to take away some of the pain and to let her know that I loved her. Every time that I went near her, she would start screaming. "Please tell this man to leave, Doctor. Get him away from me. Why is he here with us? I don't allow strange men to just come up to me and give me hugs and call me darling. I'm not that kind of girl. He doesn't need to be here, does he?"

"Your name is Brittney Bentley Moore, and this is Edward Moore. Brittney, he really is your husband and also a great doctor. I know because I was at your wedding, and I also work with Edward here at the hospital."

"How can I have a husband that looks as handsome as him? All my friends hate me because of the stories that I report in the newspapers, which sometimes hurt people. Why do I keep hurting people? Is that what happened to me, someone hurt me?"

I looked at Greg, and at that moment, I couldn't bear to tell her that someone had actually hurt her yet again. She was always getting hurt by someone, and I wanted to make all the pain over the years to be forgotten, but now here, Britt lay with all these bandages and bruises because someone hurt her again. How could I protect her? The tears were starting to form underneath my eyes.

"Britt, you are living in California now, not in Newfoundland. You don't work on a newspaper anymore. Darling, please try to remember. Your wedding rings are back at our house where you took them off before you ran away on our wedding night. If you want to wear them, I will bring them to you."

"What is the last thing that you remember, Brittney?"

"I remember being at a very lavish house, surrounded by lots of people, and I was dressed in a fancy black dress with diamond jewelry around my neck and fingers. Now I remember, you were there, holding my hand and kissing me. After that, I remember nothing. Did that really happen? What was that party? Was it our wedding? Did I get married in black?"

"That house was our home, and the party was our engagement party. It really did happen, and I have adorned you with all kinds of diamonds. We met in Newfoundland while I was there on vacation. We met on the cliffs overlooking the city, and you agreed to accompany me to dinner at the Country Club. After that, we spent almost every day together, and you agreed to marry me and return to California with me, which is where you are today. That all happened back in July, it is now September."

"You haven't violated my body before we were married, did you?"

"No. I am a gentleman and never touched you. You had your own suite in the house until we were married, but even now, you ran away on our wedding night, so we have never slept together, ever. I always told you that I would never do that to you, and only by God's grace could we have never been intimate with each other. I love you too much to hurt you, Britt."

She started to weep because she couldn't remember anything else and wanted so desperately to remember everything. "I can't remember anything after that night. Will I ever remember you again?"

"I pray that you do, but you have had a head injury, so give it time to heal, and it may all come back."

Greg then spoke up. "She has blocked out all the things associated with her hearing what Ashley told her. She only remembers the good things."

"Even our wedding day also, Greg?"

"Yes, because it was at the wedding that it all happened. I'm so sorry, Edward. Brittney, you and Edward were married a week after that party, and it was on your wedding day that everything happened to you. But rest assured, you are definitely married to this wonderful man, who is really a great doctor and will be a great husband to you."

"I believe you, Dr. Greg, but I can't seem to remember him as much as I try. I don't have any rings on my fingers. He is too handsome to have married someone that looks like me. I'm just a very plain girl, from a very small community, not even a town. I'm a very down-to-earth girl. Edward, you are so muscular, handsome, and very suave. Wow! What made me say all these things?"

"Because you said all these things to me the first night we went to dinner, and that was when we starting dating."

"I'll let you and Edward talk for a while, and he can explain what happened to you. Just don't overdo it. You still need plenty of rest to heal."

"Britt, before you awoke an hour ago, you were singing a song about Newfoundland."

"Was it about Bless this Rock?"

"Yes, is it special to you?"

"That is my favorite song of Newfoundland. I guess I miss it. The song tells all the things about Newfoundland that is so special, at least to me."

Greg walked out and left us together in Intensive Care after that and told us not to talk too long and get Britt overexhausted.

"Britt, Ashley Drew, Greg's wife, soon-to-be ex-wife, told you some awful things about her and me that were not true, just plain lies. You decided to run away, and so you left a note that broke my heart when I read it. You also removed your beautiful jewelry and your rings that I put on your finger just hours before by me, your husband. You left them with the note that you wrote. I have cried for you the last couple of weeks as no man has ever cried before. I cannot live without you. We are soul mates, sweetheart."

I continued talking and looking out the window. When I turned around from the window, Britt was asleep as I thought, but when I examined her, she was in a coma. I contacted Greg immediately, and he came running.

"Greg, what about the bump on her head? Do you think that the coma has anything to do with brain damage?"

"It has to be the pressure on her brain. I thought I just might have to go back in and look for a blood clot. I was hoping when she woke up that I wouldn't because she was acting normal except for the memory lost, but that was normal considering what she had gone through. We'll keep a watch on her for the next few hours and look for any changes. Her blood pressure and heart beat are normal. I'll check on her in an hour."

Greg informed the Intensive Care Unit nurses to really keep a watch on Britt for the next hour, and if there were any changes, no matter how small, to call him immediately. If he had to operate during the night, he would. We both walked out and went to other parts of the hospital. I went back to my office to think.

Chapter 25

I was back in my office to check any messages and maybe catch a few winks so I could be refreshed when Britt woke up. Before I went to sleep, I got on my knees and prayed that Britt would be fine and would wake up and remember everything, and that she wouldn't require anymore surgery. Greg was keeping watch in case of any blood clots.

"Lord, I know that you are in control, always there in control of everything in this world. I don't talk to you as much or as often as I should. Please forgive me of all my sins and things that I have done that I shouldn't, for I am sure there may be many. I am not asking this of myself, but for my wife who is in Intensive Care and struggling to survive. I know that you are the great physician, greater than any human doctor today, but you do give us the knowledge to help those in peril and who are suffering. They need to turn to you, if they can, but at the moment my wife cannot speak for herself, so I am speaking for her. Britt really needs your power of healing and your comfort to survive. I ask all this in your holy name. Thank you, amen."

I flopped on the lounger in my office and fell asleep almost instantly. In my sleep, I could hear Britt screaming out my name. I woke suddenly and realized that my phone was ringing. I jumped up and answered it, thinking that maybe Britt had woken up. It was Greg.

"Hello, Greg. What's up? Is Britt awake?"

"Yes, Edward. Brittney is awake, but you had better come quickly. We are getting prepared to go back into surgery."

"If she is awake, why the surgery?"

"Just get dressed and come as fast as you can. We can't wait another minute."

I was so upset by Greg's call that I started sobbing again and trying to get my pants on at the same time. I made it to the Intensive Care unit, and Britt was definitely awake, screaming as I heard in my dream, wanting someone to help her and turn the lights back on, so she could see. She was crying her eyes out as if she had lost her best friend.

"Can't you turn the lights back on? I don't like the dark, it's scary. I can't see anything. Where is everyone? Someone, please, help me. Please talk to me because I hear you talking among yourselves. I'm scared, Edward, are you here? What is happening to me? I can't see. Edward, please come near so I can feel you next to me."

"Edward, Brittney is blind in both eyes. It has to be a blood clot or just the pressure from the bump building up behind her eyes. We won't know until we operate. We will relieve the pressure or remove the blood clot, whichever it may be or both. I have the neurosurgery team personnel standing by, just waiting for the call."

"Edward. I'm so scared. I want you to perform the surgery. I trust you to do this surgery to save me."

"I'm sorry, sweetheart, but it is against any hospital to perform surgery on any member of their family unless there isn't any other doctor nearby, plus I'm not a neurosurgeon. Greg and the neuro team are the greatest team anyone could want."

I hugged and kissed her and held her close until it was time for her to be wheeled into surgery. She at last remembered me. It was so good having her body next to me after almost losing her, but now she was in more danger than ever. Operating on the brain is a very complicated surgery and very tedious. I signed all the paperwork, and they were ready. Stat."

"Just remember, Britt, that our honeymoon still awaits us when you are all well. I love you, sweetheart. You are my soul mate for life. Please take her to surgery, Greg."

As they wheeled her down the corridor into surgery, she called out. "I love you also, my dearest."

And as quick as a wink, they turned the corner and went through the big double doors into surgery that would either make her well or not at all. It wasn't a sure thing that this surgery would work. However it turned out, I would always love her so much. Britt was my whole life. I couldn't imagine what my life was like before I met her. She was my life, and if it was destined for her not to come out of this, she would always be my only love.

Chapter 26

The time passed so very slowly.

The minutes turned into hours and still no word from Greg. It had been approximately seven hours since they wheeled Britt into surgery. Finally, after about another hour, Greg sent word to my office through an assistant that it probably would be about another hour, but everything was going along very smoothly and as planned. I was so curious about what was happening. I decided to go to the observation balcony and watch the procedure unfolding before my eyes. I sat in the back of the balcony and did not turn on the lights so the surgical team would not know that anyone was up here observing. I didn't want to place any unforeseen interruptions in their way, but I felt so helpless, for here was my wife lying on the cold operating table in a cold operating room. I whispered to myself, I love you, my darling. Please keep fighting.

It had now been eight hours since the surgery started. The time was going so slowly. I knew Greg was tired, but he kept going. He felt so responsible, but he was my best friend, and when Britt pulls out of this, he will still be my best friend. I know for a fact that he hadn't slept in the past twenty-four hours, but he was just that kind of surgeon that he could go for a whole day if there was an emergency that required his expertise and knowledge.

I left the observation balcony after about another hour and returned to my office, and then word came to me to meet Greg in Intensive Care in Britt's room. I left my office and almost ran to Britt's room. I was so anxious to know how everything went during the surgery, for I knew that Greg would tell me the truth about her condition.

It seemed that the elevator was so slow this evening, but it was me, not having any patience waiting for it. It came and was too crowded. I left the bank of elevators and took the stairs to the fourth floor, meeting Greg at the nurse's station. "Greg, how did everything go, and how is Britt?"

"Edward, she had a massive blood clot on her brain, a thrombus. I was scared that it may have been an embolism. We threaded a catheter through an artery in her groin, and the rest you know what happens. You don't need me to give you each detail. I was just scared that she would end up having a stroke. But either way, if we hadn't gone in when we did, we may have had very different results. Also, there was a fair amount of pressure built-up behind her eyes which we relieved. It may be quite a while before she is conscious again. I want to keep her sedated for a few days to help her healing process. She has had so many injuries to her body that I need her to really heal completely, At least this time, she is not in a coma, but sleeping normally with a little help from a sedative. Edward, I feel so horrible about all that she has gone through, between having all these surgeries and all the pain inflicted on her. Sometimes, I think that it is my entire fault, and she will hate me."

"Greg, you are a true friend! I don't know how to thank you for all your help. You have been by my side this whole time and also Britt's. Britt will never hate you. She has always thought of you as her friend. Please go home now and get some sleep. I'll stay with her the remainder of the night. I will see you tomorrow."

"I just find it hard to sometimes face Brittney, knowing what Ashley did to her."

"Just don't even think about that part of your life anymore. You can have a new beginning, and let it start now."

"Edward, another question I need to ask you. I hate asking this one, but would it be okay if I stayed at your house until I can find another place to live. I'll be selling my home now after everything that has happened. I don't want any part of that house as a reminder of my past life with Ashley. I want to start over anew."

"I would be delighted for you to stay at our house as my special guest. Use the guest room, Greg. I also placed my house on the market to sell a few days ago. You have always loved and admired that house when you have been there for parties, and you are looking for a new start. How about buying mine if it is something that you would like? I don't want to push it onto you, but I would be honored if you would think about it. No forcing of hand, but just think about it. I've bought a huge home in Monterey Bay. I have watched this house for years, trying every month wishing for it to be for sale, but it never came on the market, until recently, so I grabbed it before I lost it to someone else. We will be moving there as soon as Britt is well enough to come home. I will not take her back to my house. I want her to start fresh also with no reminders of what happened in the old house. It is still not much farther to drive for the hospital."

"I've always loved your house and envied you having such a luxurious home, but isn't it a little big for just me?"

"Who said that you would always be alone? You are still a young and vibrant man, and women love to be seen on the arm of a great doctor. Just ask Britt."

"I would love to buy it, Edward. Thank you for your offer. I'll call the real estate agency in the morning. Thank you. Call me immediately if you need anything, but I think you can handle Brittney if she wakes up. Sometimes patients will just come out of the sleep when we don't want them waking. I need Brittney to stay asleep to give her time to heal. She should sleep through the entire night and maybe a couple more days."

"Thank you again, Greg. You are a most gracious friend."

I returned back to Intensive Care, and I sat by Britt's bedside for the next couple of nights and dozed off once or twice until she woke up about six the next morning after two days. She was sore and had a terrible headache. Her head was bandaged, also her eyes to protect them from the light for a day or two, and then Greg would remove the bandages. Greg had prescribed pain medication on her chart, to take as needed, I signed off on them, and the nurse on duty went to the floor dispensary to get them. I helped her sit up, and she took two.

"Edward, is that you? I still can't see. What is happening to me now, and my head is throbbing?"

"Your eyes are bandaged to protect them from the light, but only for the next couple of hours, and then Greg will remove them. The pills I just gave you are for your headache. Try to go to sleep, and that will alleviate the pain."

She lay back on the pillow, and before I knew it, she was asleep. I sat on the bed and held her with my arms around her. It was so great to feel her near to me again. She put her head on my chest and went to sleep. This time, it was a natural sleep. She was so exhausted and the headache so bad that she was sobbing in her sleep with tears running down her cheeks until the pain medication cut in, and she relaxed. I massaged her temples for her, what I could through the bandages on her eyes, to try and sooth away the pain. After she fell asleep, I spoke to the doctor on duty to check on her headache when she woke up and to give pain medication as needed, and that also I was going home for a few hours and to call if there was an emergency.

I spoke to the nursing supervisor on duty that Britt was asleep, and I was going home and get refreshed and would return later.

"Mrs. Sparks, if there are any problems or if Britt needs me, please call me at home or on my cell, also Dr. Drew will be at my home, and you may reach him there. I will be back as soon as possible."

"Dr. Moore, we will take great care of your wife. I will check on her personally during the night."

I realized that I had not eaten all day, so as I was leaving the hospital, I called Monica, my housekeeper, at home, and asked her if she could make me a sandwich, nothing fancy, because I was on my way home for a couple of hours. When I arrived at the house, there was a big spread laid out for Greg and myself.

Chapter 27

I was so hungry, not having eaten for over twenty-four hours. I didn't even realize it until I saw all the food that Monica had prepared for Greg and me. There were all kinds of cold cuts, salads, and fruit; also, she had prepared a whole cold roasted chicken, my favorite, to munch on while we talked. Monica outdid herself as she usually does when it comes to feeding us.

"I didn't realize I was so hungry, Greg. You must be starved. Just ask Monica if you need anything. By the way, Greg, I gave Britt a couple of pain killers, and she fell asleep on my chest. I have never felt so needed in the last month as I did tonight. It was the greatest feeling knowing that I could be there for my wife. I will never be able to thank you enough for being there for Britt and myself when we needed you the most. You are a most special friend and colleague."

"I still feel so rotten after what Brittney has gone through. I still feel that it is partly my fault. I should have kept an eye on Ashley, after knowing what she was capable of doing, but I never thought she would never do anything to your wife, especially since she didn't even know her or even try to get to know her."

"I don't blame you for anything. It is not your fault. You have always had my best side, and you are like a brother to me. Don't beat yourself up. You are like family."

We ate and talked mostly about hospital work and the advancement of the hospitals services in the years to come, especially the additional wings that I requested that we needed if we were going to be one of the top hospitals in California. We had grown tremendously in just the last few years, and we were receiving more patients every day. Patients wanted our many services, and the doctors that we had on staff were the most top specialists around.

"You and Brittney are more than welcome. I would do anything for you. By the way, I called the real estate agency, and I agreed to your price. I would have paid more. It's worth a lot more than what you are asking. This home is perfect for me and great for any parties that I throw, and maybe a new wife in the near future. Ashley will be getting her own place. She has her own money, and I'll not have to pay her anything due to the prenuptial agreement that she signed when we were first married. I never knew that it would ever be used, and I'm so happy that my lawyer told me about it when we married. She gets absolutely nothing from me, not even the furniture, just the clothes on her back and anything she bought with her own money. Any jewelry which I bought her stays with me. I bet you didn't know this, Edward, but Ashley comes from a very rich family. I always wondered why she ever married me, but that's over now. I realized as I was sitting here that I stopped loving Ashley a long time ago, and I guess we stayed together because we were comfortable with each other. I didn't do anything about it when I guess I should have, and then this wouldn't have happened with Britt."

"I think she really would have come after me then. I am so happy that now you can finally get on with your life. Everything happens for a reason, my friend."

"I know that you may hate me for what I am going to tell you, but I need someone like Brittney, very down-to-earth. I am in love with someone already, and I think that I have been for a while, but never wanted to admit it to myself or talk to anyone about it. You may not like it when I tell you who it is."

"Don't tell me it's Britt. Ha ha. Well, Greg, tell me. Don't keep me in suspense. Who is this wonderful down-to-earth person that has stolen your heart and that you think might make me upset? It has to be someone perfect for you to take a leap of faith after what you have been through with Ashley. I will probably love her also. Okay, friend, no more games, who is it?" We were both smiling as he spoke what was in his heart.

"Here goes. You wanted to know, well, I am in love with Monica, only she doesn't know that I'm alive. I know she's your housekeeper, but I feel so much love for her that when I'm around her, I can hardly breathe. I feel that I can't live without her. Is that how you felt with Brittney?"

"Greg, I'm so happy for you. It seems that you may have found your soul mate, but have you talked to her and told her how you feel? That is exactly how I felt with Britt. It's a wonderful feeling."

"Did you tell Brittney immediately when you realized your love for her?"

"I told Britt the first night we met, and she thought that I was being fresh with her. Now it seems that I was being very forward, but I couldn't help myself, I just blurted it out. I loved her the minute I saw her on the cliffs, and the way that I felt, I wasn't sure what was happening. I had never been in love ever before, so I wasn't sure it was the real thing or just a crush, but the more time I spent with her, the stronger it became, and that was why I couldn't leave Newfoundland and leave her behind but couldn't come back without her.

"I had to tell her even though she may have said no. I had to try. Friend, you need to do the same. I have always wished that Monica would find the right husband that she could settle down and be happy. She always looks so lonely. I definitely wouldn't mind losing her to the right husband and for the absolute right reason. You need to talk to her. Maybe she feels the same, but couldn't say anything because you were already married."

"Suppose she doesn't feel the same as I feel?"

"Greg, your divorce will be finalized in a few months, and you'll be able to get remarried. I can always find another housekeeper, but it is difficult to find your soul mate, and you don't always find the person that loves you beyond what they have to give. They have to be willing to overlook all your faults and little quirks. That was why I never married. I know you wondered if there was something wrong with me, but I needed to find the right person. I have always felt that way with Britt since the moment I met her as she was listening to the sounds of the ocean from the cliffs. You need to talk to her immediately before you lose your nerve."

"Look, I'm shaking so much."

"She's coming in from the kitchen now. Go ahead and tell her."

"Do you really think this is a good time to talk to her while you are here?"

"Sure, go ahead. It won't bother me while I eat, unless it bothers you. If you love her that much, you should be able to say it anywhere and in front of anyone, especially your best friend."

Monica came into the dining room with plates full of assorted pastries and a teapot of tea. She just loved the way Greg looked, always dressed so elegantly, but he was a married man, and she was only a lonely housekeeper. Doctors did not marry below their status, which is what everyone always told her. She tried to hide her feelings, but it was getting so much harder to do especially since he was now living in the same house at the moment. She loved seeing him here every day, but he would be leaving soon, she suspected. She loved everything about Dr. Drew. She found it hard to breathe when he was near to her, which was why she tried to stay away from him as much as possible. What should she do? She had so much love for this man, and she just couldn't allow him to find out, especially with him being a famous surgeon. She couldn't even bear to talk to him without her heart palpitating.

"How about some tea and pastries for you both?"

"Of course, Monica. We would love some."

"Monica, would you join us for dessert and tea? I would like to talk to you a minute. Please."

"That is not my place to sit with the household, Dr. Drew. The household staff does not sit with the guests, and I am the housekeeper."

"Monica, we are all friends here, and it is okay to sit at this table. Greg has something to say to you."

"Well, here goes!"

As soon as he spoke, I interrupted him. "I'm so sorry, Dr. Drew, did I do something to upset you? If I did, I didn't mean to."

"Monica, you didn't do anything." I started to smile and reached across to pat her hand. "Please sit!" She looked at Edward, he nodded, and she sat. "Monica, you know that I am getting a divorce from

Ashley after what happened to Brittney. That is not the main reason, but it gave me the incentive to do what I am to do."

"Dr. Drew, I really don't think this is any of my business. I should go and clean up." She started to push back the chair and stand, but he stopped her.

"Monica, this concerns you completely. For a long time, I have not loved Ashley, but I do love someone else. I have loved you from afar, Monica, for the longest time I have found it hard to breathe when you are near me. I have a feeling deep down that you are my soul mate, whereas Ashley wasn't." I looked deep into her eyes, and it looked as if there were tears about to burst forth. "Monica, do you feel anything for me?"

I sat there just staring at him and not knowing what to say. I thought that I must be dreaming, and at any minute now, I would reawaken, or if it was true, my dreams were coming true. I started to cry, not realizing that I was crying, and these two great surgeons were there looking at each other, but Edward was smiling.

"Greg, I think you have your answer."

"Edward, are you crazy? I made her cry."

"That was exactly what Britt did when I told her."

"Dr. Drew, do you mind if I call you Greg? I am sorry to start crying when you have been so sweet, but I have loved you from afar for the longest time. I knew that I couldn't have you for my husband, but just looking at you and admiring you meant everything to me. I would even brush against you to be able to touch you, until one day Ashley told me to stop looking at you because you were a married man and you were her forever, and no one person will ever have you, except her, especially a lowly housekeeper who would never be in the same class as her. I always remembered that and never again did I brush against you but kept everything to myself from that time until now. I truly think that you are my soul mate."

"I see Ashley even back then had her claws into other people's lives. I'm sorry, Monica, that she was so nasty to you. I wish I had known then how she was manipulating other people."

"Okay, you two. I am returning to the hospital. Monica, why don't you and Greg spend some time together? Get to know each other as Britt and I did. We took long drives and long walks along the beach. I will see you both later. I am so happy that you found each other before it was too late."

I was actually jumping for joy in my heart.

"Edward, thank you, my friend, for telling me to go ahead and speak to her because I may never had done it without your incentive to forge ahead."

Chapter 28

I drove back to the hospital a much happier husband and knowing that my wife was on the way to be her former loving self. It was now November and close to Thanksgiving. She was healing more and more every day, and now that my best friend had finally found his soul mate, I was in a much happier mood even with all the happenings of the past weeks.

I pulled up to the hospital and parked in my assigned parking space. I practically ran up to the Intensive Care unit, where Britt was just starting to wake up. There were tears in her eyes, for Greg had left instructions for the on-call doctor to take the bandages off her eyes. Those beautiful green eyes, to look at them again, and she could at last see me as her husband. She was in a great deal of pain, and I arranged for more medication. She had refused to take any from the nurses on duty until I arrived to visit her. She still didn't want to take any since she wanted to be with me and not sleep for a while, but I explained that sleeping would allow her to heal faster. I explained that I was going to stay for a few hours and not going anywhere until she fell asleep.

"Why don't you climb onto the bed with me so I can lay my head on your chest? It makes me feel so safe."

"I don't think that the staff would approve, and it doesn't look right to the other patients. We might get kicked out of here. As soon as you are released from the hospital, we will be traveling to our honeymoon spot that I had planned. The faster you are well, the faster we can get away from it all. Our first night together will be very special, not a hospital bed. Maybe if you remain stable and take your medications as you should, we can get you transferred to a private room in a couple of days. We can ask Greg about your progress."

"Can I get transferred home instead?"

"Not yet, sweetheart. You need to heal much more before that happens, but at the rate you are going, you won't have to wait much longer."

"Edward, you must hate me that I didn't try to fight for you, but up and ran away like a frightened child. I should have trusted you instead of thinking that Ashley was telling the truth, only she sounded so convincing and sincere, and I wanted to make friends with some of your friends. I think you married a coward. Please forgive me for not relying on you for help when I needed it. I should have run to your strong arms immediately.

"I love you, my darling. You didn't know what Ashley was capable of doing. You are a very trusting person and want all people to be friends when actually most people like Ashley are out to get what they can from you. You will have to try and change. Not all people are bad, but some are and you have to learn to read into what that person wants. I know that may be hard for you to do, but will you try or just come to me to see if I know that person?"

"I have to tell you something that is actually going to make your day just perfect. Greg has not been in love with Ashley for a very long time, and tonight he told me that he has been in love with someone else."

"Is it anyone I know? Please don't keep me in suspense. Please tell me some happy news. Who is it?"

"He has been in love with Monica, our housekeeper, for months. As we speak, he and Monica are talking together over tea and pastries in our dining room, holding hands. It is so wonderful and romantic to see. I am so happy for both of them. They're our best friends, and they have finally realized that they are soul mates. It was love at first sight, just like us. Also, I have the best news of all. I have sold our house, and I've bought another house, actually it is more than a house, a mansion in Monterey Bay. Greg bought our house, and by the time you get out of the hospital, we will go directly to the new house. What do you think of all this news?"

"Edward, thank you for telling me all this great news! It will take me some time to process all this. I'm also so happy that they have found each other. Edward, can we afford a mansion in Monterey Bay? I know that area is very expensive, isn't it?

"I'm so sleepy. I think the medication is finally starting to kick in. Go home now, darling. Sleep and dream of our honeymoon that we'll have at the beach when I get out of here. I know you haven't been getting much sleep, spending your time here with me and then driving back and forth every day. Will I see you in the morning, sweetheart?"

I started to drift off. I wanted to stay awake a little more, but my eyes were not cooperating. I could barely keep them open, but I was forcing myself.

"You will, darling. I can't wait to start our honeymoon and our life together. I will protect you forever from people that want to hurt you. We have been married almost two months and still have not spent a night together as husband and wife. I have lots to tell you about my money and where it comes from, also it allows me to buy a mansion and very expensive cars, which only Greg knows about."

"Edward, you know money means nothing to me, since I grew up poor and have always lived from paycheck to paycheck. Are you saying that you're rich, very rich? How? Edward."

"I'll tell all about it tomorrow when you're fully awake and can comprehend it all and maybe not in so much pain. Good night, darling. Sweet dreams."

I kissed her good night, and Britt kissed me back, closed her eyes, and fell asleep. She looked so beautiful lying there, as now the bruises were diminishing to a dull color every day a little more.

Chapter 29

I drove back home in a much better mood than I had since Britt was injured. I pulled into the garage very late in the night and walked in through the kitchen to acquire a cup of hot tea before retiring for the night. I could rest more comfortable knowing that Britt was on the mend and very well taken care of at the hospital. I wasn't much of a coffee drinker, so as I was getting a cup out of the cabinet, I noticed that Greg and Monica were still up and were still talking, but this time they were holding hands and smiles on their faces showing that they were so much in love. I felt so overjoyed that they had found each other.

"Would you like for me to get you a cup of tea, sir?"

"Monica, if we are to become friends, please do not keep calling me sir. Edward will do fine, starting immediately. Keep talking; I can get my own tea. How are both of you? Did you get everything talked out, although I can tell from the looks on your faces the answer to those questions? I am so happy for both of you. Also, I told Britt about it, and she is ready to help with the wedding. There is going to be a wedding, isn't there? Greg, did you tell Monica the good news that you are buying this house?"

"Edward, you blew the surprise. But the best news of all is that Monica has agreed to marry me as soon as the divorce becomes final, which according to my lawyer should be in about six months, maybe sooner, about three months since there will be no settlement of any kind. Ashley will have nothing to say about the divorce agreement. He said that there shouldn't be any hang-ups with the divorce because Ashley gets absolutely nothing, and there aren't any children involved."

"Sounds like everything will be moving along perfectly."

"I know it was hard with what Ashley did to Brittney, but Monica and I would never have gotten together if it hadn't been for Brittney leaving that night, and myself staying here to help and also kicking Ashley out of the house. If I hadn't found out what happened, everything would have gone along as always. Edward, I think everything happens for a reason. Brittney was kept safe. Someone was watching over her, and we know who that was, because of all her injuries, someone else may have died being on that cliff so long without medical help. She made it through without any real complications and injuries that we took care of, and she will be back to normal soon. Our Creator was there watching and waiting and guided us to that cliff to locate her."

"Greg, you are so true. Monica, Britt, and I will be moving to Monterey Bay as soon as she is released from the hospital. We'll get a new housekeeper, and this way you can stay here in what eventually will be Greg and your home. I'll be off to bed now. Stay up as long as you want. I'll see you in the morning. Good night, lovebirds, or should I say soul mates."

"Good night, Edward. I have always loved this house, and I will definitely try to find you a good housekeeper if you will give me the opportunity to interview them. Since I have been with you for almost fifteen years, I think I know exactly what you will need."

"Thank you, Monica. I would appreciate that. I know that you will find me the perfect match for Britt and myself."

Chapter 30

I went to bed that night, still alone, but not feeling lonely, but for the first time in over two months, I slept soundly. I woke up early the next morning, feeling so refreshed, as I hadn't gotten much needed sleep recently. I was ready to start a new day knowing that Britt was on the mend and that I would have my wife home soon. I went downstairs, and there was Greg already sitting at the table looking very ecstatic about having his future wife cooking for him—a thing that Ashley had no idea how to do. She only knew how to give orders to everyone else and spend money on food that normal people didn't eat unless they were at a banquet. Ashley spent money like water, whereas Monica would not be saving Greg money.

Monica had created a sumptuous breakfast for Greg and me, consisting of homemade French toast, homemade waffles, eggs, bacon, and a variety of fruit, fresh strawberries, raspberries, and blueberries. I would definitely miss this, but I knew that Monica would help me find the right housekeeper. Mainly Herbert cooked the meals, but not usually breakfast, just lunch and dinner, and sometimes not lunch as I wasn't always home for lunch.

"Edward, do you eat like this every morning?"

"I do, Greg. Monica is a great cook when she gets the chance. Usually, Herbert gets ahead of her. Greg, do you feel just great this morning after last night? I can see it in your face, more pleasant and not constraint. I will be moving all this furniture out next week, but some this weekend. I've hired a moving company. I want to be completely moved in Monterey Bay by the time Britt gets home from the hospital. All the financial preparations have been taken care of, and

I outright now own the new home that has always been my dream home. I don't want her to return to this house to live. We will be glad to return for your elegant parties though.

"If she keeps progressing as she has been doing in the last two days, she'll be able to come home next weekend as long as you can stay home and watch her for about a week, or hire a nurse for about a week, otherwise she may try to overdo it. Also, it will be Thanksgiving, and all of us will have much to be thankful for, especially in the last couple of months. If she is doing fine this morning when I return to the hospital and check on her, I will have her transferred out of Intensive Care and into a relaxing room.

"She will definitely not overdo it as long as I am there. I may stay home myself instead of a nurse, as I have missed so much time with Britt that I need to spend as much as I can with her. She will be happy to be getting out of Intensive Care and into her own room. By not having her home until next weekend, it will give me more time to move the entire house furnishings to our new home. Well, I'm off to the hospital to get some work done, which I have been putting off since Britt has been sick. Monica, I want to thank you for a great breakfast, as usual. See you later this evening."

I'm in a much happier mood today as I have been in a while, as I'm driving on the freeway to the hospital, thinking happy thoughts and smiling at the same time. I can't wait to get to the hospital to see Britt. She has been through so much since we have gotten married. I couldn't even imagine how she felt or what went through her mind when Ashley started telling her the story of outrageous lies. That was still eating away at me that I thought Ashley was my friend and would be Britt's also, but that was truly not the case. I'm thinking that I probably would have reacted in a similar fashion if it had been me. How can people be so cruel to other people, especially when they don't even know them or try to know them? Ashley had other things on her mind, like trying to set me up with some of her so-called single friends, alias the "plastic people." This world can be so cruel to some people, and now I have to reassure Britt that my love for her is genuine, and not all people are like Ashley. I will shower love on her forever to prove my love.

My wife was recuperating nicely. I recently had gone to a boutique and bought her a fancy red negligee, and I was carrying it with me so that when she was transferred to a regular hospital room, she wouldn't feel uncomfortable wearing the johnnie jacket that she now wore open at the back.

I parked in my assigned parking spot and went up to the Intensive Care unit. Britt was sitting up. Greg had already called in to check on her and listened to all the reports of her night and how much medications she had taken during the night that now he recommended that she be transferred into a regular hospital room on the tenth floor. She was already sitting in a wheelchair to be moved to the private room as per Greg's orders. Since this specific room was very elaborate, it was the expensive room that all the celebrities used. Since this room was available, they were putting her in there because she was my wife. Britt didn't like the idea of being in the limelight, but this time I didn't say anything because at that very moment, I agreed that she deserved to be in that room and be comfortable. I would pamper her for years to come to try to make up for all the calamities that had befallen Britt.

"Good morning, darling. I see you had a comfortable night since Greg decided you could be moved to a regular room. You will soon be going home in about another week. According to Greg, you are healing fantastically. Those were his words, not mine."

I walked to the room as they wheeled her in a wheelchair and then onto the elevator to the tenth floor, and then into the luxurious room. The nurses put all her belongings away and then left us alone. Britt was startled as she looked around. She wanted to sit in the lounger that was provided in the room instead of getting into bed. I picked her up and settled her and covered her with a warm blanket.

"You can only stay in the lounger for about half an hour since this is your first time up."

"Edward, you said that we could talk today. Why are you so important here at the hospital? I know that you are a great doctor, but so is Greg, but I don't see the other nurses and doctors treating Greg the way that you are treated. Everyone treats you as if you owned the hospital. Ha ha. They must be afraid of you. Do you have a temper that I don't know about and you yell at the nurses?"

"Britt, don't laugh because what you just said is the truth. I do own the hospital, but I don't have a temper."

"You aren't serious. I was just joking with you. Don't kid me, Edward."

"Britt, I started this hospital back twenty years ago just as a small medical clinic when I first moved to California. I started adding more doctors, and each new building we moved to, we outgrew, and so it started to grow. More doctors wanted to work for me, and now you see what we have grown to as of today, and soon we will be breaking ground for a huge addition, but that is in the future, maybe a year or two. It is one of the best medical facilities in California, and all of the Hollywood celebrities started to come to us when they heard that we had the best doctors. I only hired the best doctors in their specific fields and equipped the hospital with all the most advanced medical equipment. That's why we are always full because patients always want the best medical treatment, and I don't blame them. If it was me, I would definitely want the best doctor in his or her field."

"Do you only help people who are rich and famous?"

"No, we help anyone who needs medical attention, rich or poor. It doesn't matter what their status is in life or what their income. They are all the same to us. I have never hired a doctor who is not willing to give their best medical treatment to any patient, no matter their financial circumstances. I am just a normal medical doctor, still seeing patients every day. It just happens that I own a hospital. Last year, Greg bought into the hospital with a small share, and I was happy to do it as he is my best friend."

"I'm speechless! I just thought you were a normal medical doctor, but such a famous doctor. I don't know what to say, and you really love me though I'm not rich and famous? It is so hard to believe."

"I really and truly love you with all my heart and soul, and you are all mine forever." I smiled at her and kissed her on her lips.

"Is that why you just bought the mansion in Monterey Bay? To gloat over what you can buy with all your money and the prestige of people knowing who you are? I just want to live a quiet, normal life, and if it was my choice, I would live in a cabin in the woods. Edward, I am a very home-oriented person. I like to do my own cooking and cleaning. I am just not attuned to all this wealth. Since Monica will be marrying Greg and leaving us, I want to do all the cooking. I'm a great cook when I get the chance, and I would love to cook for my husband because when I lived in Newfoundland and there was just me, I never cooked. I always wanted to cook the fanciest meals that you ever ate."

"Britt, no one at the hospital knows that I own it except the doctors and Alicia, since she was here from the beginning. I have sworn them all to secrecy. Not even the doctor's wives know, only a few. We have our own administrator, hired by me also, and reports to me. I still oversee all the bills being paid, but it is done very discreetly. I still hire all the doctors, as I want to hire only the best in their field of medicine. I never advertise for an open position on staff, but through contact with other doctors or a chance meeting somewhere."

"We can also have you cook and clean a little if that's what you want, and when it gets to be too much, Herbert can step in or we can hire a new housekeeper to take over the cleaning. Herbert is staying with us, and when we throw parties or special dinners, Herbert will be there to oversee everything. What do you think about it all? Are you just overwhelmed, my darling?"

"So much so that I think I must be dreaming."

"Britt, the only reason that I purchased the mansion in Monterey Bay was because it's the one house that I have had my eye on for over ten years. I fell in love with it then, and I told myself that if it ever came back on the market, I would buy it. Well, every week for the last ten years, I have watched the papers, and lo and behold, there it was this week, and so without saying, anything to you, I purchased it. It has been my dream home, but this time I wanted to enjoy it with you and surprise you with a wonderful home. It has nothing to do with money, sweetheart. Money cannot buy happiness, and I have never been as happy as I am now. Money didn't have anything to do with me winning your heart. Meeting you and marrying you has been the best thing that I ever did recently. You are my whole life and my everything."

"And you are mine. I don't know what to say. You know, Edward, that I care nothing for money. It always seems to be the root of all evil. Money always gets people in trouble. I would love you even if you were as poor, as they say, as a church mouse. Can you help me get into bed now before you leave? I'm starting to feel tired, and my back is aching from sitting up so much. I have a slight headache also, but every day the headache is becoming less and less."

"Let me lift you in. You still shouldn't put too much weight on that leg until Greg says it is okay to start standing on it a little each day. I bought you something to put on instead of the hospital johnnie jacket. Open it and see the surprise. I even knew your size."

She opened the box with a smile on her face. "Edward, you shouldn't have. It is the most beautiful negligee I have owned, okay the only one I ever owned." It was the most beautiful gift I have ever received. It was sparkling as if it was covered in diamonds, covered at the neckline with sequins, and the neckline was a V-neck that showed almost all I had, but I didn't want to tell him that. I loved that he bought it for me. He was so thoughtful.

"Can you now help me to the bathroom first before putting me in bed?"

"Do you need help when you get in there, sweetheart? I'll call for the nurse to help. Wait just a second." I ran to the front desk, and Miss Ryder answered.

"Nurse, can you come to room 1005. My wife needs help in the bathroom."

"I'll be there, stat."

Nurse Ryder came and helped Britt get into her negligee and whatever else she required at that minute, and then I took over from there.

"Thank you, Nurse Ryder."

"Do you require anything else at the moment?"

"Nothing at the moment. Thank you."

I helped her get back into bed, and just before I laid her down, I couldn't help notice all the bruises that were now turning yellow on her entire body. She had been banged around so much from the fall down the cliff side, over the rocks. She was so fortunate that she wasn't hurt more. I was almost afraid to touch her. I didn't want to hurt her anymore, but they didn't seem to be hurting now. It almost made me cry to think how much she had been hurt, and I thought to myself that if it was possible, no one or anything would ever hurt Britt again. I thought that when I get her home, I might put her in a bubble. I smiled just thinking about what I was thinking, but she was my entire world, and I refused to have her hurt ever again.

She pulled me down to her and gave me a passionate kiss, and it made me want to get her home and then take her away from all this to our honeymoon hideaway, on a beach where the sun would sparkle on the ocean and the sand was white, and at night the moon would kiss the ocean.

I gave Britt her medication for her headache. It had been a long day for her. "Get some rest now, and I'll come back later and sit with you a while. Love you always, my darling."

"Thank you, my sweet husband. You are the most amazing and thoughtful husband that a wife could ever have, and I give you all my love and affection, besides you already have my heart and soul."

I gave her another passionate kiss, and I had to pull myself away from her. She kept pulling me back into bed. She wanted more than she needed right now. She swallowed the medication for her headache, but now she was on a lower dose, laid back on the pillow, and was asleep in a few minutes.

Chapter 31

I went back to my office on the top floor which is where most of the doctors' offices were located, and being in a much happier mood, I smiled and whistled as I walked. I think that I actually could have floated knowing that Britt was on the mend. I needed to get some work accomplished that I had so neglected in the last month. I answered most of my correspondence but then realized that Alicia had taken care of all my household bills and most of the bills for the medical services and supplies as they were due. She had also sent out reminders for patients to come in for their checkups after surgeries, as I had cancelled their original date and extended it a month because of Britt. Alicia also sent out bills to patients to pay their bills, especially those who could afford to pay. What would I do without her? She is my right-hand person. I depend on her for almost everything.

She had been there for Britt when she needed a friend and had sent Britt a huge bouquet of roses when my mind was not on flowers, but on Britt getting medical treatment and slowly recovering. She sent them in my name. Britt loved roses of all the other flowers, they were her favorites, but how did Alicia know? I kept thinking about how many years that Alicia had worked for me and all the work she did around the office, and realized I needed to do something special for her. She was indispensable. The special item came to me in a flash; I would do something that she could start using immediately. It would definitely help Alicia in a big way.

I pushed the intercom and asked her to come to my office. "Alicia, can you come to my office for a minute?"

"Be right there! Is there anything you need for me to bring in for you, reports or anything?"

"No, just bring yourself."

She entered Edward's office and saw him studying something on his desk. She had worked for Edward since he started the medical center almost.

"Please sit down, Alicia."

I looked at him, and he wasn't smiling, and I thought that I must have paid bills incorrectly or some other bookkeeping error. I sat down on the edge of my seat. Then he looked up and smiled the smile that we all loved to see. It gave us protection.

"Can I help you with locating something, Edward? Is there anything that you don't understand in what I did? I will be glad to explain everything. Did I make an error?"

"It's not what you can do for me, but what I can do for you."

"I don't understand. What's happening, and what do you mean?"

"Alicia, you have taken care of my office, paid all the bills that are due for my home and here at the office, sent out bills that are payment due, and also sent out checkup requests. What would I do without your loyalty to this hospital and my practice? You even sent roses for Britt's room when I wasn't thinking about anything but her getting well. Tell me, Alicia, how much do I pay you a year now, Alicia? Whatever it is, it isn't enough with all that you do for us, not just me, but I know that you sometimes help the other secretaries who work for the other doctors."

"That doesn't matter. I have the privilege of working here with a great doctor and have the best medical treatments if I ever need them."

"Alicia, please tell me?"

"I earn $40,000 a year."

"For what you do for me and the rest of the staff, you will be receiving an increase of $35,000 a year starting immediately, that will bring you to $75,000 a year. I'm embarrassed knowing that I only pay you that amount, so from henceforth that is all changed. I'll be depending on you more now since I will be moving to Monterey

Bay. It's a little longer drive, so I'll be getting in a little later and not spending so much time here as I normally did before I was married. I would always spend all my time here because I had an empty house to go back to, and as you can see, this has all changed now. Also, I will be away for a while on my honeymoon as soon as Britt is released from the hospital, so just keep paying all the bills and doing what you normally do while I am away."

I sat there with my mouth open hardly knowing what to say or do.

"Edward, I am tongue-tied and speechless. Thank you so much. I don't mind the work, in fact I enjoy it, but isn't that a rather large increase in pay. I love working for you, and all of these things that I do for you is part of my position. I love Brittney and want to help as much as possible. I try to visit her every day. I really think marrying her was the best decision you have ever made in your life. No, maybe the second. The first was starting this hospital."

"Thank you, Alicia, and I'm so happy that you're Britt's friend. She needs more friends like you right now, and that increase is nothing compared to what you do. My office would probably fall apart without your expertise in getting things accomplished."

"Anything that I can do for Brittney, please let me know, even just someone to sit with her and talk. She so loves to talk about Newfoundland, and I love to hear about this place. I think I know more about it now than you. She talks about it constantly. It sounds like a wonderful place for a vacation. I don't like to say things like this but sometimes it's nice to have a woman to talk with even though I know you are always there with her, but men don't always know what to say or understand what a woman is going through. I don't mean anything against you, Edward. You have been a sound rock for her, just like her homeland."

"I will always be there for Britt, but I do understand what you are saying."

"Thanks again for everything."

I stood up and left the office, not believing what had just happened. Edward was the most wonderful employer that I had ever had and the most gracious. I ran back to my desk knowing that I had to call my husband with this great news. We would be able to now take the wonderful vacation that we had been planning for five years now and could never get the money together to go. We wanted to go to Europe, but now I think I will try and convince my husband to take me on a trip to Newfoundland, Canada. I just couldn't pass up visiting this wonderful place.

Chapter 32

I stayed in my office for about an hour thinking about when I could arrange for our honeymoon, since I had cancelled the original, but I still wanted to take Britt to the same resort. It was a luxurious resort on the ocean, which was crystal blue and the waves with their white caps would roll upon the beach. I knew Britt wanted to be near the ocean. The water was also so warm, and it would help to heal her scars. At night, the sun looked as if it was being swallowed by the ocean, and the sky would become glorious colors. I would call the resort tomorrow, but today I called the United Moving Company to arrange with the moving of our entire household items to Monterey Bay. They would move us on the following Saturday. That was perfect. It was now Wednesday, and Britt wouldn't be released from the hospital until the following Monday. She was ready to come home, but the rest wouldn't hurt her, and I could get the house in order before she entered into our new abode.

Tomorrow was Thanksgiving, and I had much to be thankful for. Monica was cooking an entire meal for Greg and me, Herbert and herself. Everyone is included on Thanksgiving even the helper, as they were like family. She was arranging two dinners for me to carry to the hospital so Britt and myself could celebrate together. We were very thankful for everything we had, and this year, our thankfulness was very genuine while other years I don't think we really thought about being thankful. I would thank the Lord this year for His goodness to us and what we have but really didn't appreciate.

Greg would be moving into my house next Monday. Everything was running very smoothly. The transferring of the purchase funds had been taken care of by our individual lawyers, who had the authority to deal with the real estate agents. Greg had also sold his home, and Ashley was furious that she didn't get any compensation from the sale, but the house was not in her name, so she had gone crying back to her family in Los Angeles, although I had heard through the gossip grapevine that they didn't want her with them, any more than Greg did, because of her reputation in creating trouble wherever she went. They actually felt happy for Greg. They had a small house situated on their estate, so they set her up there, and they wouldn't have to see her at all.

Greg's divorce was going to be final in less than three months, and then Greg and Monica were going to have a small wedding with just Britt and myself and a few doctors on the staff at the hospital. I was so happy that they had found each other. It was like a miracle that Greg could finally have peace in his life, and especially Monica would have a very complete life with someone who would love her. She wouldn't be alone anymore.

I left the office to go home and start packing boxes that I didn't want the movers to pack, but before I left, I looked in on Britt. She was asleep. I kissed her and left. I arrived home and started in the kitchen packing. All these beautiful dishes that I had accumulated over the years had to be packed very carefully, especially the china. I thought a second time and realized we would need these dishes for tomorrow, so I decided to wait until after Thanksgiving was over. I wanted to pack all the fragile items myself. The clothes hanging in the closets would be easy, moving them on the hangers just as they were, exception being all the clothes in the dresser drawers which I would pack. I was thinking to myself that now I had to furnish six bedrooms instead of four, which means buying two additional bedroom suites. Herbert knows my taste, so I will give him full rein on what to buy. Then a thought came to me, suppose Britt ended up getting pregnant. I started to smile to myself. I guess it could happen, what about a nursery, but that will have to wait. What a wonderful thought to have crossed my mind.

Why would that suddenly cross my mind? I guess I was thinking of just being with Britt and the honeymoon that will be happening soon. We are both getting up in age, and never had we discussed starting a family. I'm not sure if Britt even wanted children, but I would love to have children running around. We are both very active. We'll have to talk about this before or maybe during the honeymoon.

I can't wait to take Britt away and spend some alone time with her on some secluded beach, and we can both forget all the misfortunes that have befallen her since she moved here to California.

Thursday and Friday went very smoothly. The dinner for Thanksgiving was magnificent, and I arrived at the hospital with a basket full of delicious food for Britt and myself. We had a most wonderful dinner, and she ate everything on her plate. She had sat up most of the day, and we talked and thanked God for who His is to us and all the doctors and nurses at the hospital, for everyone hired there were all Christians. I stayed until late, and Britt was ready to sleep after all the delicious turkey. I kissed her and then drove home to continue my mission of packing.

I took those two days off and got the remainder of the items packed that I needed to take care of myself. Britt was doing great and mostly healed, with only a very few small scratches now showing. I needed her to stay in the hospital until everything was moved into the Monterey Bay house and set up. I visited Britt every day and stayed a couple of hours with her. She wanted to know exactly what I was doing and was worried that I would overdo it. She wanted to leave the hospital as soon as possible and was getting very antsy about it.

"Darling, why are you here? You should stay home and get everything set up. You are going to be overexhausted. I want you to make sure that everything runs smoothly with the movers. There's no need for you to come and visit and then take the long drive home. I am feeling much better and want you to not be exhausted. I need you to be alert and peppy for our awaited honeymoon."

"Are you tired of having me around already?"

"I will never ever be tired of looking at you. You should know that by now. I am only thinking of you and your health."

"Okay, baby cakes, whatever you say. You're the boss, but I will definitely call you every night."

We ate dinner together in her room. Britt had chosen seafood for dinner on Friday night, and I had a nice juicy rib eye steak. We have the greatest cafeteria for a hospital with a regular chef who prepared all the meals. I kissed her passionately, then left the hospital and drove home. I was already missing her, but very soon, she would be home and in my arms once again and for always.

Chapter 33

It was now Saturday morning after Thanksgiving at 9:00 a.m., and the moving company had already arrived at the house at 6:00 a.m. Most of the large pieces of furniture were already loaded on the truck, except for two or three sofas and the master bedroom suite. I had finally finished packing all my china the night before, and Herbert was transporting all these boxes in the limousine. I didn't want any of these broken. They were given to me by my mother when I moved to America. The moving company was in the process of moving those furniture items now. I said goodbye to Monica and gave her a hug; after all, she had been with me for a lot of years and now would be a friend instead. Her eyes were full of tears, but they were tears of joy as we would see each other quite often.

Of course, I would see Greg at the hospital tomorrow when he signed the papers for Britt's release to finally come home after these two long months. Herbert was driving with me to the new house in Monterey Bay. He hadn't even seen it yet, and I was using his discretion where to place certain of the items and what extra pieces of furniture we would need to purchase. He had great taste when it came to purchasing what I needed. We were in the car and driving away from the house that I had lived in for the last fifteen years, but this time I was moving into the mansion that I had always dreamed of owning, and this time on Monday would be bringing a new wife there.

"I hope you don't mind living in Monterey Bay, Herbert?"

"No, of course, Dr. Moore. Wherever you need me is where I will go. You told me that it was a much larger home. Are you going to be hiring a new housekeeper now that Monica will no longer be with us and staying with Dr. Drew? I am so happy for both of them but will miss her."

"It's a mansion, Herbert. It has six bedrooms and bathrooms. I know it's a lot to keep clean. I wanted to hire more housekeepers, but Britt refuses to hire more and wants to do it all herself. I told her we would try it her way, and if she can't handle it, then we will hire more. She even wants to cook for me, but I think you can help her with that, especially the parties. I know that you love arranging parties for me, and I appreciate everything that you do, Herbert."

"Definitely, I'll take care of the evening meals especially. Whatever needs to be done, sir? Mrs. Moore doesn't need to concern herself with any of the work."

We talked on the drive to Monterey Bay, and I learned things about Herbert that I never knew before. He didn't talk too much, unless you spoke to him first. He told me that one time he had been engaged to be married, and just before the ceremony started, his fiancée decided that she wanted his best friend instead of him. His best friend was also his best man. Herbert was my age and still had time to find a wife. Monica did. After that, he said that he never seemed to be able to trust another woman. He thought she had been his soul mate but was very much mistaken. He said that he learned later that his so-called best friend left her because she was too demanding. He was glad in one way that she did leave him.

I felt so sorry for him, but I was going to try to help him find his one and only soul mate.

Herbert was most certainly going to be a huge help in getting everything organized in the house. When we arrived there, followed by the moving truck and everything put in their appropriate places, then we would communicate on what we needed to purchase. As far as I knew, we only needed to purchase two complete bedroom suites to furnish the two extra bedrooms, extra sheets, and anything extra for the bathroom that he thought we may need. Herbert said he would order all these items with my approval and have them delivered before Britt arrived home on Monday. I wanted the entire house set up before she set her foot inside, and Herbert agreed. I approved all the items, and Herbert said that they would be delivered that afternoon. That was fast.

I called Britt that night and apologized for not going to visit her, which is where I wanted to be, but she wanted me to stay there, and I was needed at home at that moment to arrange all the furniture set up and the delivery of the movers. That was all accomplished on time. The movers were great about the unloading and setting up of the entire household. Herbert arranged the kitchen. The extra two bedrooms were delivered on time that evening along with all the other items which we needed.

I was so tired that I could barely get undressed for bed. I had to stay awake to call Britt before she settled down for the night. "Hello, darling. How are you this evening? I'm so glad you waited for my call before settling down for the night. Are you in any pain? I think Greg was going to look in on you and sign your release papers for Monday morning. I can't wait for you to get home and see our new home. It's magnificent, darling!"

"I'm just fine, sweetheart, and my pain has completely gone. I'm even starting to walk around on my own. The cast will be coming off on Monday before I am released from here, according to Greg. He has been so wonderful. I feel bad at what has happened to him having to get a divorce and feel like it is somehow my fault but am glad that Ashley will be out of everyone's lives. I know he said that he hasn't been in love with her for a long time. I'm really excited that he has found someone else to love, and she is the complete opposite of Ashley. I can't wait until I'm finally home and we can start anew, especially on our honeymoon, which is now two months behind schedule. I pray that you didn't lose any money by having to cancel the reservations. Goodnight, dearest, I love you and will see you tomorrow bright and early."

"Goodnight, my darling wife, and don't worry about Greg. He is happier now than I have ever seen him. He is always smiling. Love you, babe."

These words sounded so wonderful. I was overjoyed that I had waited all those years and saved myself before finding that one special person who would become my wife. I had resigned myself on being a confirmed bachelor, and everyone knew it.

Chapter 34

Greg went to visit Brittney after dinner on Sunday night, and he looked so beaten down.

"What's wrong, Doctor? You don't look very happy for a man who will be getting married in a couple of months to a girl that you have loved from a distance, and she who thought you were the sunshine of her life, but could never lay a hand on, just look. It can't be me because I feel great and am looking forward to getting out of here tomorrow morning and going home to my wonderful husband."

"Brittney, I just can't seem to get over what Ashley did to you. Every time I see you, I am reminded that I should have divorced that woman years ago, and then this would never have happened. I never knew she was that conniving, especially to you, whom she didn't even know, and it seems she didn't want to get to know. Over the past few weeks, I found out that she has been doing this to other women who have very handsome husbands. She would see a beautiful woman who was single, would attach herself to that girl, and then try to set up dates for her with other women's husbands. The single women would attach themselves to that particular man, and then Ashley would tell the wives of these men that their husbands are in love with the single girl. I hope you can forgive me."

"There is nothing to forgive. You didn't do anything to receive forgiveness for, it was all Ashley, and you hadn't any idea of what was happening. She was very sneaky, and all the single women loved her for what she was doing for them. There next step was to marry a wealthy, handsome doctor, only she couldn't get Edward to cooperate with her way of thinking.

I have found a new friend in you, and I know that you are Edward's best friend. I think Ashley has a problem and needs psychiatric help. If this hadn't happened, you never would have found Monica. God kept me safe and watched over me. It had to happen that way. It was destined to happen that way. When I get out of here, I will help Monica plan a beautiful wedding for our two best friends, and then you can put all this tragedy in the past and settle down and be happy again with your true soul mate."

"Thank you, Brittney, for saying all those things. I guess I needed to hear them from you in order to move on. Monica and I appreciate everything you want to do to help us with our upcoming wedding. Getting back to your medical issue, everything looks great for your release from the hospital on tomorrow morning. I know Edward is longing to get you home to your new house, and I'm sure you want to get home to him and get a start on your honeymoon. I'll come in and remove those casts tomorrow early in the morning before you are released. Goodnight, Brittney, and thank you for being you. I can see why Edward loves you so much. He and I are two fortunate men for having found our soul mates, and from here on, I will remember that Edward and you will always be there for us, no matter what happens, and Monica and myself will be there for both of you."

Chapter 35

Brittney was very impatient the Monday morning that she was being released. She wanted to get out of there, and she felt both perfect in body and soul, except for a few bruises that were now turned yellow. Every other part of her body was entirely healed.

Edward hadn't come to visit her all weekend and here it was now Monday morning, and he would be there to pick her up at any minute to take her home. She missed being home with Edward. She thought that she might have a little fun with him, the fun being that she had a special habit that Edward didn't know anything about and it was that she could cry at will, and now she figured that today would be a great time to test it out on Edward. He didn't know that she could do this.

She heard him walking down the corridor because by now, she actually could distinguish his footsteps from others and talking to some of the nurses on duty, asking how things were going. He was always very concerned with people's health and welfare. He had a big heart. She hated to do this to him and started to think twice about it, but it was too late—the tears were already starting to come as she thought about being with him and what she had put him through in the last two months and the running away without first approaching him about what Ashley had told her. She had to try and stop being so jealous, but it was very difficult when you had a husband that looked like Edward and then a very plain wife that looked like me. She started to talk between sobs.

"Good morning, Edward. I guess you've stopped loving me. I haven't seen you for two whole days. I could be dead for all you care.

How could you abandon me like this, treating me lovingly one minute and then hating me the next? Did you have another woman over the weekend that I didn't know about?"

I started to really cry then, and these were not phony tears. Just the thought of what I had just said to my loving husband and how he was looking at me just about broke my heart. How could I do this to him? He looked at me so sad and with those gorgeous puppy dog eyes. "Britt, what did I do? Whatever it was, I definitely didn't mean it. Please forgive me for any wrong I did you. Darling, I have been fixing up our new home all weekend just for you. I called and talked to you every night and then told you that I wouldn't be there to see you, unless you were in trouble and needed me. You were the one who told me to stay at home. Did you forget? I never could stand to see a lady cry. Let me hold you, my darling. Sweetheart, I never want you out of my sight again. I love you more than my own life. I would do anything in this world for you."

"Darling, I'm so sorry. I was just doing something than I can do automatically, right on cue. I didn't mean to make you upset. Plus, I will need you always and forever."

In the corner of Edward's eyes, I saw the making of tears, and I felt so terrible for what I had done to him. He held me close to him, and we sobbed together, although my sobs had now turned to rivers. It was about that time when Greg walked into the room to remove my casts. He stopped and was ready to retreat back when I noticed him and then spoke up.

"Greg, please enter and remove these casts. I want to start walking again."

"Well, Brittney, do you feel like going home today?"

"Greg, I can't wait to get out of here. I feel like a permanent fixture here, being here for so long. Get these casts off so I can get going. I need to get going on my honeymoon as soon as possible."

"Okay, you may want to cover your ears. This saw is quite loud."

"Just please don't saw my leg and arm off. That thing looks dangerous."

The saw used to remove the casts was like a knife going through me. It gave me the shivers listening to it. The casts broke away, and there was my leg. It looked so thin and boney, and the skin was so white, and it looked as if all the muscles were dehydrated. My arm looked the same. I needed sun and fresh air to make myself look healthy again. It was so difficult to even look at myself.

While Greg was removing my casts, Edward went to the nurse's station and signed me out and signed whatever papers needed to be signed and then returned and walked around the room getting all my things together so we could leave immediately. After Greg had removed my casts, I saw Edward glance a look my way and saw the shape that my arm and leg were in, and it was then that I saw his eyes get misty.

I was so happy to be going home to a new house that Edward had bought for us. We had already been married over two months and still we had not spent one night together as husband and wife since that dreadful day that I wanted to forever put away in infinity. I was very happy to go to a different house. I prayed that I would be up to marital bliss with my husband, who at that moment looked so dynamic. He was dressed so leisurely, but his physique was beautiful, so muscular, and he still looked so suave even for a man his age. But age didn't matter. It was as if since we met, he had grown younger.

We were ready to leave, and I refused to be pushed in a wheelchair, though it was hospital policy. I walked to the car very carefully. I needed to walk and walk to get my strength back, but I knew that it wouldn't be good for my leg, and my arm felt so weak from not using either for the last two months. It was going to take some time, I guess. Edward helped me into the car, and we drove away leaving two months of our marriage back at the hospital.

"What are you thinking about, Britt?" Edward asked that question as we were driving away. I didn't want to tell him that I couldn't stop thinking about how wonderful he looked sitting in that car seat driving and that he was now all mine, but as I thought, I didn't really know my own husband. We had been married for two months, and still we had not slept together in all that time. Now we would have the remainder of our lives to sleep together. But what if he doesn't like having to share his bed with another person since all of his adult life, he hasn't had to share with another, especially a woman, at least that's what he said. He told me that he has never slept with another woman, but that was so difficult to comprehend since most men sleep around. I really hope he is okay with us sleeping together.

"I was only thinking about us and being here with you. You can't imagine what it means to be finally going home with you. I love you so much, and always have, even when I was there in the unknown, wandering around, I couldn't stop thinking about you. You were always on my mind wondering why I was so hated by you and why you did that to me. I never thought that I would ever see you again. I know of course that you didn't do this to me, and it was all Ashley. I have to get all that out of my mind and forget about her."

I reached up and kissed him on the cheek and then placed my hand on his thigh in a loving way. "Britt, I love you so much, but please don't start anything here in the car that we won't be able to take care of immediately, especially you were just released from the hospital. I think we should wait until we get to our resort for our honeymoon. I need to drive and get us home safely. You are looking very loving now, but I need to concentrate on my driving. The traffic here is very heavy. Please don't look at me like that!"

"Now I know that you must hate me. I look so sickly after being in the hospital all that time." I started to cry and it really hurt Edward. "I'm sorry Edward, I didn't mean that. You are so wonderful to me."

I smiled at Britt, and she gave me her most loving smile back. I couldn't wait to get her back home. We were almost there. I could definitely make it home now, knowing that my wife was sitting next to me, so I started to hum some songs, and Britt gradually closed her eyes. She was my princess, best friend, and most of all, my one and only soul mate.

Edward drove with both hands on the wheel, holding on tight that his fingers were turning white. I decided to relax and laid my head back and rested. I fell asleep, and when I woke, he was turning into a long circular driveway that wound around many magnificent elm trees that enveloped the long driveway like a tunnel and then opened up to a four-car garage. The driveway went to the top of a hill where this magnificent house sat overlooking the city. The house really was a mansion, and all the bedroom windows had double doors with balconies extending from each one where you could watch the sunset at evening setting below the ocean. Edward opened the garage door and drove in, and there sitting in the garage was yet another new car.

"Whose mansion is this, Edward? Are we visiting someone? I just want to get home."

"You are home, Britt. Welcome to your new home."

I opened the car door and stood there in awe not knowing what to say. Herbert came out the door to get my luggage from the trunk and welcomed me home. "Mrs. Moore, it is wonderful to have you home."

"Thank you, Herbert, and please call me Brittney. I'm so happy to be finally here, but the size of the house. I can't describe what I feel. I have never seen anything like it before."

I walked over to the new car and then realized what Edward had done. "Where did you get this car, Edward? I never saw it before at the other house. Did you have it hidden from me?"

"I kept it a secret. It's a present from me to you, my love. I know you love the Maserati, but I also know you have always wanted this car, but could never afford it, so I bought you your TESLA. Do you like it?"

"Yes, oh yes, I just absolutely love it, and of course you bought my favorite color, black, but how did you know that the TESLA was the car of my dreams? I never told you about it."

"I watched you quite a bit when we were dating, and I saw you admiring it one day, and I remembered how you spoke about it."

"You are the most loving husband that anyone could have. You are so good to me. I don't deserve such happiness. How can I ever make it up to you?"

"You don't ever need to because you are my wife and soul mate, and I love to buy you things that make you happy."

"You don't need to buy my love, Edward. I love you for being you, and you make me happy every day just being near me."

We both entered the house at Monterey Bay, Britt for the very first time, as husband and wife. I picked her up in my arms and carried her across the threshold, making it more romantic. She placed her arms around my neck and gave me the biggest hug and kissed me on my neck, so much that I almost dropped her. Britt could finally walk on her own, having finally gotten both casts off and now being completely healed. I then placed her on the hallway floor, and she stood there staring up at the gigantic circular stairway facing her. We then walked from room to room and talked with arms around each other. It took us the best part of two hours to admire all the rooms.

"There are six bedrooms and six bathrooms. I bought the extra two-bedroom suites with all the corresponding bedding for each one as per the matching colors of each suite. Do you think you will like what I have selected for each with the linens?"

"Edward, I have never known a man who had such impeccable taste. The colors are perfect. I wouldn't change a thing. I never could have selected the colors the way you have done. I'm not that coordinated."

Each of the bedroom suites had their own unique colors with matching linens and comforter. The bathrooms had matching towels, and everything was furnished down to the fancy soaps in the shape of seashells. If we were having guests, they would be trilled, and I couldn't wait for John and Joanne to return from England in another four months to stay with us for a while until they found their own family home and maybe each their own soul mate. I didn't say too much as we walked around, but just trying to read Edward's face about what he was thinking at that moment and taking it all in that this was really mine. We walked through the entire house and finally at last reached the master suite. Adjacent to the master suite were a husband-and-wife dressing room, and then adjacent to that was the master bathroom. It was so hard to absorb all this and to realize that it was all mine and Edward's, and that he bought this with thinking of what I would like to make me happy. I would be happy living in a shack as long as Edward was with me.

"Edward, I have never in my entire life seen a double shower. Just imagine taking long showers together, also all these pulsating jets in the corner of the shower. It looks so relaxing and will help especially getting rid of my stiffness in my leg and arm. It is absolutely magnificent. I have never known anyone, especially a man, with such impeccable taste as you, my sweet. You have thought of everything. Although I think you may have forgotten something about the bedrooms."

"What could I have forgotten?"

"The nursery, in case I get pregnant." I started to smile, and I may have blushed.

"We never talked about it, and I was afraid to mention it. I would love to start a family. Would you like to try and get pregnant as soon as possible? We aren't getting any younger."

"I would love to have your baby. Let's start tonight, shall we?"

"I think we should wait until you heal a little before any activity with me."

"You're the doctor, and I will obey." I was kidding with him and linked my arm with his.

"There is one room which I haven't shown you yet just off the master suite. Please open the door and enter."

I opened the door which went from the master suite through to a small bedroom that wasn't so small, and it was intended to be a nursey. There was also another room that led to the main hallway. We wouldn't set it up yet, but it was there all waiting in case we needed it.

"Edward, I just love you so much. You are the greatest husband on earth and the most thoughtful. I have never met another person who has such knowledge about decorating, and what a wife would love."

"I can't take all the credit for it. Herbert is the best decorator that I know. He picked all the colors and then asked me if I liked them."

"I will definitely thank him when I see him again. Edward, you have made my first day home such a happy one. I love you, my darling."

We kissed a long and passionate kiss.

Chapter 36

"Edward, our new home is the greatest that I have ever seen in my entire life. It is such a large home, but yet it is not too elegant or flashy, more along my line of down-to-earth, except for the master suite. Thank you for buying it. I could not have chosen a better place to live. I know that you don't want me cleaning this entire home, but Herbert can't do it by himself, and Monica is not here anymore, so are you going to hire more staff?"

"Not at the moment. We will be going on our honeymoon, and when we return, Greg and Monica will be getting married. We will close the wings of the house that we aren't using for the present, and when we need help, only then we will hire. Is that okay with you?"

"If it's okay with Herbert?"

"He is okay with the idea."

"I'm starting to feel tired, Edward, but I want to stay awake and spend more time with you. I want to snuggle against you and be with you later tonight, but before all that, I desperately want to see the gardens."

"You will absolutely love the garden area, and we actually have a pool. Let's look!"

Edward took me by the hand and fingers intertwined; we walked past his den and through the back door. What a sight to behold. The landscaping was magnificent. There was a large patio with an outdoor built in grill, also a sink for cleaning up and seating for about twelve people. There was also a huge firepit for sitting around at night with family and friends and just enjoying each other's company. I could imagine in my mind our near and dearest friends all sitting around.

We stepped off the patio and followed the path between the trees and ended up adjacent to another property that had a cobble stone walkway lined with all varieties of roses overhead. I was enthralled. As we walked back, there was also a pool at the other side of the house that was hidden from view if you weren't looking for it. I just couldn't take it all in. I could swim all day and then relax by the pool, although Edward didn't want me swimming by myself when he wasn't home in case I got a cramp.

"I really wouldn't want you swimming when I'm at work unless Herbert knows that you're going in the pool. Could you agree to that when I'm working? Otherwise, I would worry about you all day, and I do that anyway."

"I agree with that. I absolutely promise that I will not swim alone without someone knowing that I am there. I love it that you worry over me all the time. I never had anyone do that since I left home years ago. I feel so loved." He was so coddling toward me, but I didn't mind.

"Edward, this place must have cost you a fortune. It definitely cost too much. Our mortgage will break us."

"It is completely paid off. There isn't any mortgage, sweetheart. Don't you worry, you pretty little head, about money. Now that you have seen everything, I would like for you to go upstairs to the master suite and rest. We have all the time together, starting from today. I'm just so glad to have you home. I want you to continue to heal, and after today, all the walking around, it must be overwhelming for you to go from the hospital to a new home. Why don't you go and take a nap now? You'll feel more refreshed when you awaken. I'll just be happy to lie next to you and hold you in my arms. I'm not going anywhere without you for the next few weeks. By the way, do you snore? Ha ha."

"Edward, I want to stay awake and look at you as we lie together, but I can't seem to keep my eyes open. I want to see your body, but we have never even swum together at the beach or pool. I have never even seen you in a bathing suit. You have a magnificent body, and now you are all mine. Also, I do not snore."

"No other woman has ever seen me without clothes, except my mother. I am a very virile man, a very vibrant man, who would not hurt you under any circumstances. You have been hurt enough recently, and we have so much to catch up on, especially as we go on our upcoming honeymoon. Now, this is the doctors' orders, please close your eyes and rest."

"I will look forward to the joining of our bodies as one."

It was getting late in the evening, and Edward decided to go and take a shower, but Britt couldn't lift her head from the soft pillows to even think of moving from the bed at that moment, although she wanted to try out that new type of shower. There would be other times. After his shower, he returned to the bedroom, and I was already in our king-size bed fast asleep. I had slept through the entire night, and when I awoke the next morning realized that I had neglected my husband yet again. How could I keep doing this to him? He seemed to understand because of my surgeries and all the medications that were still in my system over the last two months in the hospital. My body was so full of these medications that I wondered when they would get flushed out of my entire system.

I awoke and snuggled into Edward's hairy chest as he was still asleep next to me. He turned toward me and wrapped his arms around me. I kissed him with a passionate good-morning kiss to wake him up. I loved everything about Edward's hairy chest. It made him more huggable, like a loveable teddy bear.

"Edward, can you please show me this morning how much you love me? I really need you to love me as you have never loved anyone else in your life. I need it to be special, and I think this morning is as special as it is ever going to be, our first morning together."

"I can actually say in all truth that I have never loved any other female in my life except my mother and my sister, and now you are the love of my life. I am a very gentle lover and will try not to hurt you."

We loved each other as no other, and it felt as if it was the first time for me, and he said that it was the first time for him. He became so lovingly tender and gentle. What a magnificent man! He loved me so much and cared about how I was feeling after we just lay there in each other's arms. He really did seem to have experience, yet he said that he had never been with another woman. I had to believe him even though I hadn't any proof, but it was difficult to do.

We kissed and fondled most of the morning and then loved each other all over again. What a man! We stayed in bed most of the day, but sometime in the afternoon, I needed to get some nourishment in my system to counteract these drugs. He was more man than I could handle although he never complained about my lovemaking.

We dressed and walked downstairs to get food. Herbert had already prepared cold cuts and salads, with homemade rolls and assortments of fruits. He was the best man when it came to organizing any number of kinds of food.

"My darling Britt, I never knew what I had been missing. I will love you forever."

Chapter 37

Edward and Brittney Moore

After an all-day in bed, we had dressed and went downstairs to get some nourishment after not eating for almost a whole day. I needed lots of food to gain some weight back after having lost weight from just lying around in a hospital bed.

After finishing roast beef sandwiches with a side salad that Herbert had graciously made for us, we set out for our beach resort that Edward had arranged for our honeymoon. Edward had already packed luggage for both of us and transported it to the car, and now we were ready to head out. I was so excited to be going to this or any beach resort in the Caribbean since I had never been in my life and so was going to be just the most luxurious place that I had ever visited. Any place in the Caribbean would be very supreme for my taste since I had never been to any place that was overpriced and the water green-blue. I had seen many photos on TV and in books, but never up close. This was going to be a new experience for me.

It was the end of November now, and I was so looking forward to our honeymoon and then to our first Christmas together. Christmas was my very best time of the year, although I would definitely miss the snow, so glistening white with the sun shining, that it made the snow look as if was full of stars with crystals.

We were all packed for our honeymoon, which Edward had done months ago. Herbert drove us to the airport, and I headed to check in, but Edward stopped me. He said that was not necessary. He directed me unto the tarmac where there was a smaller jet warming up. I was still scared of flying, but with Edward by my side, I could accomplish anything, and I had accomplished many ups and downs over the past two months. The jet was glorious. Edward owned his own jet, and with his own pilot waiting for us, we were flying through the beautiful blue yonder in a matter of half an hour, and so here we were on our way to the Bahamas. Edward had arranged everything. I couldn't describe in that magical moment how much I loved that man.

I fell asleep during the flight, and when I woke, we were already landing. We departed the plane, and I stood there in awe of the surroundings. I was like a person hit me over the head, and I was just staring, thinking of myself like a kid in a candy shop.

"Well, Britt, what is on your agenda to do first? Would you like to lie in the sun for a while, go swimming, or walk on the sandy beach?"

"Edward, can we just walk around the island a little? I need to get my legs strengthened. I've never been here before. I just want to drink in the beautiful surroundings, the aquamarine-colored water and then walk on the beautiful sandy white beaches and feel the sand between my toes. I need all the fresh air that I can get after being in the hospital for two months, and this is so breath-teasingly gorgeous. I still can't believe that we are actually here. I also want to see the many waterfalls. You know how much I love the ocean and any kind of water. Everything looks so magnificent. I have read of the beautiful botanical gardens where the flowers bloom year round. I would love to visit them. We may have to stay longer than two weeks, but as long as we are home by Christmas."

"We can do whatever you want. We can see it all, but relax also. You can't overdo any part of this trip."

"Thank you, Edward. I truly love and adore you, and I know that you will watch out for me, making sure I follow instructions."

We had checked in and were given the honeymoon suite on the top floor. It was bigger than any apartment I ever lived in Newfoundland.

"Have you ever been here before, Edward?"

"I hate to tell you this, Britt, but I have been here before with someone else."

"Edward, how could you bring me to a place where you brought another woman? I thought that you had never been intimate with any other woman. You lied to me. I want to leave. You have ruined my whole honeymoon, and it has just begun. I want to go somewhere that you have never been with another woman. I thought I was special and that this was going to be our special place." I started to cry and ran into the bathroom. I didn't want Edward to see how upset I was at that moment. I forgot to lock the door, and Edward came in directly behind me. He encircled his arms around me and embraced me so lovingly.

"Britt, I'm so sorry. I'm telling you the truth about not being intimate with that woman or any other woman. I always wanted to save myself for the right person, even if she never came along, but she did and that was you, Britt. Oh, many have tried, but all in vain."

"How can I ever trust you, Edward?"

"Oh, sweetheart, I would never intentionally hurt you. I love you too much."

There were tears starting to form in the corners of my eyes, and I had to turn away from her, not to see the hurt on her face. She saw me wiping the tears, and it was then that she hugged me from behind with her arms around my waist. "Britt, let's saunter down to the tiki bar and get an exotic drink."

"Okay, if you want me to. Let me fix my face first."

We walked into the tiki bar, and there were a few people there, all laughing, having a wonderful time. One was a beautiful woman with long black straight hair and who looked like a goddess who, when she saw Edward walk in, ran over to him, threw herself in his arms, gave him a huge hug, and then placed a very passionate kiss on his lips. I stood there as if in a trance with my mouth open, just staring, as all her friends were staring at her. Edward tried to push her away from him, but she clung onto him and refused to move.

"Edward, you came back to our beautiful island. We said it would be ours forever. I am so happy to have you here with me this time. Now we can do all the things that we missed the last time we were here. I see that this time you brought your maid with you, so I can move in with you and we can start enjoying ourselves together. Maybe your maid can go and get us some drinks to get us woozy, and then she can get lost."

"What are you doing here? Gloria Morgan, I would like for you to meet my wife, Brittney. Britt, this is a friend I knew years ago, Gloria."

"Edward, I think we were more than friends. I always come back once a year in an attempt that maybe you would be here. What do you mean your wife? We were supposed to get married. I wanted you and still do. Please dump her now that you have found me again."

"You wanted just the idea of having a doctor on your arm. We never meant anything to each other. I never did love you or tell you so. Gloria, Britt and I are here on our honeymoon, and I love her with all my being. She is more real than all the girls in Hollywood."

"You told me that you were destined to remain a confirmed bachelor and that you would never marry. Why didn't you marry me when I wanted you, then we would be on our honeymoon?"

"No, I didn't marry you because I wasn't in love with you, also the first time I saw Britt, I knew I had to marry her. She is my true love, my soul mate. I could never live without her. You, Gloria, are too much high-maintenance."

"What about us? You must have been so desperate to marry someone with the face of a dog and even looks like a witch if you look at her nose, very elongated, not like my perfect face. She isn't even your type. I know every inch of you. How can you get in bed with her and wake up looking at that face every day?"

"There is no us, and never will be. I don't ever want to hear you speak of my wife like that again. She is more loving that you ever could. You just wanted the idea of loving me because it gave you money and prestige. There is more, much more, to love than that, and I was the doctor that gave you that perfect face and nose. You weren't born looking as you do."

"You were intimate with me as if there were an us, also who is going to pay for my time here on the island. I used all my money on the tickets here. I think you owe me, saying we would meet here."

"Gloria, that's a lie. We were never intimate, and you know it, and I don't care who pays for your time here, but it's certainly not going to be me. Find some other sucker that you can maneuver in your claws. You are like a vulture winging your way to find the next prey. You're just trying to get back at me for not marrying you. I'm really happy that I didn't love you and do something that I would have regretted. Just get away from me. Don't ever bother me again. I will never pay for your tickets here, and why are there two tickets, brought another man here, I guess, and now he has escaped your clutches. I say that he finally came to his senses."

"Well, I had to try, and I will keep trying as long as you and the dog are on this island, especially when you see me in my new string bikini."

"I have no desire to see you in a bikini of any kind. Instead, my wife will be the one I will be watching, and she has a magnificent body, and it is not phony. She has a body that is not plastic as yours."

"You enjoyed my body when we were together, and you took me for granted, using me so that one day you could come here and humiliate me in front of my friends."

"Gloria, the only friends that you have accumulated over the friends is the ones that you have paid a price to get. Good-bye, Gloria. Do not bother my wife or I anymore, or I will have the authorities called to put a restraining order on you to stay away from us."

"You would do that to me?"

"Yes, I will."

Chapter 38

Brittney and Edward

While Edward was talking and trying to placate this gorgeous woman with explanations of why he didn't marry her and she was being as clingy as I thought, I slipped away and went back to our room and packed my bags. I started to cry and was sobbing so much, wondering why an ugly dog, as Gloria portrayed me to be, would Edward want instead of the goddess that he had recreated. I am a jealous fool, and I have yet to know why Edward married me and not her. I am always running away. Why can't I ever trust Edward, but everything he has ever told me about himself always seems like a lie. He told me that he never slept with another woman, but how could any man resist this beautiful woman that Edward had recreated. I don't care what kind of man he is, there is no way that he could, and I'm so sure of it. Gloria was this beautiful bombshell, absolutely gorgeous. I couldn't compete with someone like her, and she was going to be there the entire time trying to seduce Edward by her seductive powers. No man can prevent that for any length of time.

I took a cab to the jet, so happy that the pilot was going to spend two days on the island, and so he was still there. I asked him if he would please fly me back home. I couldn't take anymore. He wanted to know where Edward was, and I told him that he was caught up in some old business that I wanted no part of. He seemed to understand exactly what I was talking about. The tears were still streaming down my face and mixed with black mascara and eyeliner, I looked more like a wicked witch than a newly married couple.

"I know exactly what you are saying. I will be happy to fly you home." He flew me home.

Edward went back to the honeymoon suite only to find me packed and gone. He radioed the pilot, and he told him that he had just landed in California with me on board. He also told Edward that I cried all the way home. The pilot refueled the plane and then returned to the islands to pick up Edward and brought him back, which took another day. Edward called me on his cell phone, and I answered. "Hello, Edward."

"Britt, what is the problem? Gloria meant nothing to me. If she had, I would have married her years ago."

"You took me to her island as she so plainly said. It was sort of both of yours. I just couldn't compete for you with her. She was all over you, and I was so jealous. I couldn't take it that you were letting her touch you as she did."

I couldn't take that sweet voice anymore and started to cry. He was still in the air flying back. "Britt darling, no more crying. It is you that I love, and there is no one else worthy of that love. I want to spend the rest of our lives together and give you beautiful children."

"How does that saying go, keep me pregnant and barefoot and then you can run around with your other women? How many women have you had, Edward? You are so suave, muscular, and handsome. I don't see how you could fall in love with me. She called me your maid and having the face of a dog, and I think that is how I look, at least to myself. Goodbye, Edward."

I hung up the phone and decided that I was going to leave again. It seems all I know how to do is run away so I don't have to face him or get hurt again. I am a coward at heart and an even bigger fool for letting this happen again. My phone kept ringing, but I refused to answer any of Edward's calls.

This time running away, I didn't take a suitcase. I pretended I did by putting it in my closet behind some boxes that were yet to be opened. Then I left the house before Edward returned, and as the phone was ringing in the house, which I knew Herbert would answer. I figured that it was Edward calling Herbert to question him about what I was doing and if I had left the house again.

I returned back to the beach, only this was a different beach than before. It was midafternoon. I threw my new phone that Edward had recently bought me in the ocean so I wouldn't have to answer any of Edward's calls. I dressed only in a T-shirt, jeans, and a pair of grubby sneakers. I walked and walked until I came upon a beautiful flat rock that was quite large in the middle of the sandy beach. I was about a couple of miles from the house, so I decided to lay there and rest before I started walking again. I still got tired very easily. The sun was hot, and it made me tired and sweaty. I must have dozed off because I knew nothing until Edward was there shaking me awake. I was startled and jumped up punching, thinking it was a mugger.

"Get away from me. I want nothing to do with you."

"Britt, you are not running away from me this time. I had Herbert watch you because I thought you might run. We're going to sit and talk even if it takes all night. This is the perfect spot."

"Sorry, Edward. I thought you were a mugger."

I started crying, and Edward put his arms around me, and there were tears in his eyes also. "Britt, you really don't get it through that pretty little head of yours how much I love you. Yes, I have had lots of dates, none ever being intimate, although many have tried, but none have ever succeeded. Mostly they were dates that Ashley set me up with, thinking that eventually I would marry them and she would have the satisfaction of saying that she put us together. I must admit that Gloria is beautiful, but only because I made her that way, she was a patient. That is my handiwork. You should have seen her before the surgery. She was the dog face, only she would never admit it. She never had any manners and was very self-conscious about how she looked. I operated on her, and then she became that beast that you witnessed seeing yesterday. Before the surgery, she was a very quiet girl.

"Britt, you have always had a very quiet nature and very beautiful. You have never had a beast within you come out, even when you are crying and upset. You have a pure soul."

I stopped crying a little, and Edward wiped the tears from my eyes. "Are you planning to make me into one of your plastic ladies also, since I am so plain? That would be quite a challenge, Edward. I have had only one man, Anthony Carter was his name, in my whole life, and that ended up in divorce. I am not beautiful, but it seems as if I can't hold onto even one man."

"You are beautiful to me. You don't need plastic surgery to be beautiful. I love everything about you, especially being as plain, as you say, but you are not plain. You have a beautiful soul. You will definitely hold onto me. I will not let you go. Britt, do you mind answering me a question? Why did you get a divorce, if you don't mind talking about it? You never did tell me."

"I didn't want the divorce, he wanted it. He said that in bed, I was as frigid as being adrift on an iceberg in the North Atlantic Ocean."

"Have you had any other suitors since you're divorced?"

"No, when he told me that, I believed him because I didn't have any confidence in myself, and I didn't ever want to go through the same thing ever again. I started to dive into my work more so as to never get hurt by friends or just plain anybody. I think that was when people started to stay away from me because I took my anger out in my stories. You're the only man that I have been with since my divorce. That's why I don't understand why you want the quote 'iceberg' in bed with you."

"Britt, you are not an iceberg, and I don't ever want to hear you say that about yourself again. You are loving in bed and out, and I have the proof."

"Edward, you are a very compassionate lover. I don't understand how you haven't had other women in bed with the way that you are intimate with me. You seemed to be very experienced."

"I'm a doctor, Britt, and I know how things happen and how other things are supposed to work. I studied it in medical school. Things are supposed to happen naturally. You don't need experience to love someone. You're the only person that I want to love and to have a family with. Britt, I think your ex-husband wanted a divorce for either another woman or maybe he was the one frigid and that the only way he could get away from you was to make up a lie that you were frigid in bed. Those are fighting works in divorce trials."

"Let's go, Britt, and walk back home with me now. It's starting to get dark."

"Do you realize that this is the most that we have talked since the first night we met in Newfoundland?"

"I love talking to you. I love your British accent."

Chapter 39

Brittney and Edward

We walked back home arm in arm, and for the next two weeks, everything went along as smooth as a pancake. Edward returned to work for three days a week, and the house was kept neat and cleaned by Herbert and me. I was truly happy and enjoyed taking care of my husband. We kissed and loved each other passionately every night until we would finally fall asleep in each other's arms. I loved to cook for Edward whenever I got the chance. I could cook, but in Newfoundland, I never really got the chance since it was only me eating dinner. I cleaned around the house even though it was always spotless, not a speck of dust anywhere to be found. Herbert was so used to caring for Edward by himself that I barely got a chance, and as he told me, it kept him busy. He sometimes went out during the day, not sure where, but it gave me the house to myself.

Finally, it was time to decorate for Christmas, and I was excited, just like a little kid. Edward has so many decorations, and Herbert and I put ornaments everywhere. The railings going upstairs had garland wrapped with red bows and beautiful white lights. Finally, it was time for the tree, and Herbert went to the tree lot and bought the most humongous tree that I had ever seen. The tree was placed in the middle of the huge living room and a smaller one at the bottom of the circular stairway. I wondered where we would get enough decorations to put on it, but when Herbert entered the house, he carried armloads of boxes. It was a never-ending supply, and they were carried by men from the tree lot. I had found out from Herbert that normally the tree was decorated by these men. I was so saddened by this. This was my best time of the year, and I was so looking forward to decorating the tree. I ran upstairs and fell across the bed sobbing. Everything about Christmas was being spoiled. I remembered the family gatherings around the tree when my parents were still alive and how we had so much fun together decorating. I wanted that time again with Edward and Herbert.

Edward finally came home from work and came upstairs and found me upset. This happened quite often these days, but at Christmas time I should be excited, but I wasn't.

"Britt, what's wrong? Did I promise something that I didn't actually do? If I did, just let me know, and I will correct it. I hate seeing you so sad."

"I wanted to decorate the tree, and you had men come here today to decorate it. This is my favorite thing to do at Christmas, and I wasn't allowed to touch it. I felt so left out in my own home."

"I'm sorry, my darling. You should have told me, and I would have cancelled the workers. I engage these men every year, but this year you get to entertain at our Christmas party here at the house. We usually have about 150 people during the night passing through. These are people from the hospital. You can help Herbert with the menu. We are going to be extravagant this year because I want to show you off, and normally, I only have a few intimate friends in, but this year I want to entertain the hospital employees and thank them for all their hard work during the past year."

"That sounds so wonderful. I love parties. I'm sorry for being such a child and complaining about everything that doesn't go my way. I'm such a brat. You must think of me as a spoiled child."

"Every one of the nurses and doctors will be receiving bonuses, and I usually put them under the tree with their names, and I have hired a Santa to give them out. By the way, what would you like for Christmas this year?"

"I think that is the most wonderful thing to do for the employees. This year, I have all I need, right here within my reach. Darling, you have given me so much that I really don't need anything. All I need is for you to constantly be by my side and be there when I'm sad, and I know that you will. When is the party to be?"

"It will be next week on the eve of Christmas. The menu is all arranged, and the bonuses all written. Everything will be catered. We are going to be the host and hostess."

The next week came fast, and everything was being set up by the caterers for tonight. I was upstairs getting ready, after having taken a shower and now applying makeup and my jewelry, earrings and a diamond necklace, the one that Edward had given me when we were married. Edward was already dressed in his tuxedo, and I had a long red flowing gown. We entered downstairs just as Greg and Monica entered. They looked so happy and in love and would be married in a few weeks after Christmas. I hugged our new best friends, and Greg warned us about maybe if Ashley heard of the party that she would try to crash it. It wasn't advertised, so I didn't think she would know, but I was always on my guard where Ashley was concerned. I wanted tonight to be the best ever.

Finally, all the guests were there, and Britt and I wished everyone a very Merry Christmas, and Edward made a toast. Britt somehow didn't seem to be herself. I would have to question her later to see if she was okay. "Everyone, as you know, the hospital has been doing very well, and so this year I would like for everyone to receive bonuses. Please step up to the tree and receive them. You all have gone beyond your normal duties, and I am so grateful."

Everyone was so stunned by the announcement of receiving bonuses. I saw Alicia and Cliff there at the party, and I went to her and hugged her for being so helpful when I needed it and thankful that she did call Edward, even when I said no.

The party went on for hours and hours, and the last people were leaving except for Greg and Monica. They were just about to leave when Ashley came running through the door and ran to hug Greg. "My darling, where have you been? I missed you so much. Please let's go home."

"Ashley, get away from me. We are no longer married. I am engaged to another and will be married in a few weeks. We have been divorced for about two months already."

"No. You are mine for all time. Never again will I leave you. I am your wife, a paper cannot separate us. Why would you want to marry a person who looks like a dog, when I am so beautiful and I'm already yours to do with what you want?"

"We are divorced, Ashley. The courts have said so. I will be married to someone who truly loves me, not just my money. Monica is the most beautiful woman in the world to me, now get lost."

"Greg, I'm lost without you. I need you."

"I hate you, Ashley. Never again as long as I live would I need you."

As Greg was trying to get rid of Ashley, Edward called the police to come and get her. She was supposed to be in confinement, but here she was trying to get Greg back. Monica was startled and stood there with her hand over her mouth, almost in tears. I moved to her and hugged her. Finally, the police arrived and carried her off in handcuffs.

"I am so sorry, Monica. This is not your fault. I love you. I haven't any feelings for her anymore."

Edward went to the bar and returned with a brandy for Monica as she was shaking and Greg holding her to calm her.

"I know you don't, but it's so sad to see her like this. I hate seeing her do this to you. I love you and don't want to see anyone hurt you, ever again."

"Edward and Brittney, you are the best friends that we could ever have in this world. Thank you so much for everything."

They then walked out and drove back to our old house, and we walked up the stairs, tired and sleepy. I still didn't know what Edward had bought me for Christmas. I would find out tomorrow, Christmas Day. The party was grand, and everyone had a most wonderful time, but I missed the snow and ice and all the things connected with the Christmas celebration, especially the tradition of Mummers, which is to go around to people's homes all dressed in crazy costumes carrying many kinds of musical instruments and then you dance and drink and everyone would try to guess who you were. Then on the day after Christmas, we would go to the top of the highest peak to celebrate Guy Fawkes night and set the biggest bonfire after stealing everything that wasn't nailed down, and sometimes things that were nailed down and carried them to the top of the peak and burn them. All these memories to look back on made me sad, but we have to grow up eventually, I guess.

"Britt, you look so sad. Didn't you have a good time?"

I sat on the bed and explained to him all the celebrations that I had over the years and how I missed them. I now have a great husband, and so I would try not to dwell on the past things that was so childlike, but meant so much to me all these years ago.

"My greatest Christmases were when I was a child. As I grew older all my friends despised me, and they weren't friends anymore. All during high school, I didn't have any friends, and so my last year in high school, I went to St. John's to Bishops College and then stayed in the city and never returned back home except for a weekend here and there." I went to the dressing room to dress for bed, and when I returned to the bedroom, I found Edward in tears. "What is wrong?'

"That is the most sorrowful story of childhood I have ever heard. I am so sorrowful that growing up was so miserable for you. I will make your married life the best that I can make it. Now I really understand why you cry when I do something wrong like taking you to that resort. You have no confidence, and you have never had any real close friends to rely on. Britt, I will always be your best friend, along with husband and lover. Do you believe me, sweetheart?"

Chapter 40

Edward was very intimate, nothing like my ex-husband. I never knew what I had been missing all these years. Edward was very caring, and during the day, I looked after our home. I felt so useful, which I hadn't felt in years. The following week, Edward returned home after a long day's work with a wonderful surprise for me.

"Here is your Christmas gift, sweetheart, at least part of it."

Edward handed me a beautiful wrapped jewelry case with the most beautiful necklace inside, a diamond pendant surrounded by rubies on a most gorgeous gold chain, and when I examined it, I saw something extraordinary. It was in the shape of Newfoundland. I was stunned knowing that this was made especially for me and no one else.

"Edward, this is the most wonderful gift I have ever received. It is the most loving gift to keep reminding me of where I have come from and my roots. I love you, darling, and not because of the gift. You are the most precious gift I have ever received in my lifetime. What is the other part of the gift? I can't wait. Please tell."

"Britt, I am taking you away this time for a honeymoon to a place where the beaches are beautiful and where neither one of us have ever been before. We are going to Costa Rica for two full glorious weeks in the sun of relaxation and love. Would you like that?"

"Oh yes. I would love a trip like that since we still haven't had a honeymoon, and Costa Rica sounds fabulous. Thank you, Edward. When can we leave? I love you so much. You treat me as if I were a queen. I don't deserve someone like you after all the trouble that I've caused you over the last three months."

"I'm just an ordinary man with ordinary wants and desires, and you are the only one who fills both requisites every day. You can start packing immediately because we are leaving in the morning. I think we need to get away from here, just the two of us for a while."

"Can you be away from the hospital for so long a period?"

"Greg will look after everything, also Alicia runs most of the day work, and they can always get in touch with me by phone. Let's get a good night's sleep so we can start out early tomorrow morning."

Chapter 41

The next morning, I was ready having packed the night before. I wanted to make sure that we wouldn't miss the flight, but then I realized that we were being flown in our own plane. Edward was putting the luggage in the car. Herbert was driving us to the airport, and the jet was all fueled up for the flight. Everything was in readiness.

As I was in the bathroom making a last pit stop before leaving the house, I started to feel stomach sick and, before I knew it, was rushing to the toilet and was throwing up. I thought to myself, not today, I didn't want this to be happening. I wanted to go away with Edward. Why was something always happening when we are about to go somewhere? It seemed as if it wasn't meant to be.

Herbert had been listening outside the bathroom door when he came to announce that we were all ready to leave. He heard me throwing up and ran to tell Edward, although I didn't want Edward to know. I didn't want to disappoint my husband by getting sick today.

Herbert ran to the car to inform Edward of what he heard through the door of the bedroom.

"Edward, I think Brittney is sick. I went to the bedroom to tell her we were ready to depart for the airport, and as I approached the bedroom door, I heard her in the bathroom, and it sure sounded as if she was throwing up."

"Thank you, Herbert. I'll run and check on her immediately." He ran up the steps two at a time, being very concerned. She had never been sick before.

"Britt, are you okay in there? I hear you throwing up. Please open the door and let me enter, so I can check on you."

"I'm okay, Edward. I will be right out."

Before I had a chance to open the door, I threw up again. What was happening to me? Not today, of all days.

"You don't sound okay. Please open the door. Britt, I'm the doctor here, darling. Let me help."

I opened the door, and he immediately got a washcloth, wetted it and placed it on my forehead.

"Edward, I don't know why I'm sick. It came on very suddenly, so maybe it will go away just as quickly. I didn't eat anything different than what you ate. I just feel queasy, not really stomach sick as if I ate something bad."

"I think I may know why you're sick, but I need to do a test to be sure. It doesn't seem likely so fast. Just a second, darling. I have a test in my medical bag. Stay where you are. I'll be back in a flash."

He returned to the bathroom with a pregnancy test. I started to laugh so much that I was ready to roll on the floor. He really wanted to do a pregnancy test on me; surely he jests.

"Edward. Dearest, how could I be pregnant this quick? By the way, why would you have a pregnancy test in your medical bag? Are you expecting a miracle from me?"

"It doesn't take much to get pregnant, and we have been very intimate with each other the last two months every day and night. I picked up one at the hospital pharmacy knowing that we might need it in the next few months."

I took the test from Edward and followed all the instructions. Edward waited in the bedroom so I could test myself in private. In a few minutes, the answer came back. It turned blue which meant positive and that I was pregnant. I called Edward in the bathroom, and when he viewed the results, he was all smiles. I have never seen a man so happy. He was jumping for joy. "Britt, we are going to be parents. We are having a little baby. Britt, I love you so much. You couldn't have made me any happier. This is the happiest day of my life except the days that I met you and married you. Are you truly happy, sweetheart? Did you want a baby so soon, Britt?"

"I'm in shock, but I'm also very happy. But how did it happen? It must be a mistake. I didn't tell you this, but I was told a long time ago by another doctor that I could never have children. I didn't want to tell you because I wanted children so much, especially your children, sweetheart. I thought now that I must be too old."

"You know how these things happen, Britt. Did you ever think that it was your ex-husband who had the problem? Did they ever test him? The old doctors always think that it's the woman that is defective, as they say. You are a very virile woman, my sweet, as I think I must be very powerful in that area also. The tests that you just used are usually 99 percent accurate. I can't wait to tell our friends."

"Edward, you mean all those years, I thought it was me. What a wasted life, but it wasn't really wasted because I had to wait for you to enter into it. Can we still go on our trip to Costa Rica?"

"Now more than ever. We have a tremendous amount of celebrating to do and more intimate moments to share and catch up on."

"Is it still okay to be so intimate together?"

"Of course, we can darling. It doesn't hurt the baby. When we return from our honeymoon, I'll get you an appointment with a colleague of mine, Dr. Carl Lester, the Head of Obstetrics at the hospital who will take excellent care of you during the entire pregnancy."

"Can't you be my doctor?"

"If there's an emergency, I can help. Also, I can deliver the baby if we can't get you to the hospital in time, but otherwise it's not a good idea for the husband to tend on his wife. Most of the time, he is just in the way and tends to tell the other doctor what to do. I'll be there for all of your doctor appointments and be there at the birth. I will not allow you to go through any of it alone, sweetheart. I was there at the beginning, so I will be there at the end. Are you okay with that?"

"Thank you, Edward, for making me feel perfect for you. I wouldn't have it any other way."

Edward called Greg at his former home to let him and Monica know that we were leaving town on our honeymoon for a glorious two weeks in Costa Rica.

Chapter 42

"Good Morning, Greg. I haven't awakened you, have I? I called you this early because I wanted to let you know that Britt and I are finally embarking on our honeymoon, traveling to Costa Rica for two weeks, which should have taken place four and a half months ago, but finally better late than never. I was wondering if you could check on a few patients of mine that are scheduled for surgery when I return, unless there is an emergency. You can get their patient records from Alicia. I wouldn't expect anything from them since they are just routine surgeries and can wait until I return. Also, Greg, I have a surprise for you and Monica, so are you sitting down or still in bed lying down?"

"What's the problem? Is Brittney okay? Any type of complications? Also, I will be glad to check on those patients for you. I haven't much in the way of appointments this week. I may take Monica on a few outings this week just like you requested that we do."

"No problem. It's just the opposite. Everything couldn't be going any better than if I had planned it this way. Britt is pregnant."

"How do you know? Did you do a home pregnancy test, and why would you suspect that she is pregnant so soon?"

"I bought a pregnancy test a few weeks ago at the hospital pharmacy just in case and had it in my medical bag thinking that being so intimate together, she may get pregnant. This morning as we were getting ready to depart for the airport, she was in the bathroom throwing up. She tried to hide it because she wanted this trip so much and thought that she might have food poisoning. I smiled at her and got the test from my bag. She took it, and sure enough,

I was correct. It came back positive. She didn't think she could get pregnant so fast and still has a hard time believing it."

"That's perfect, Edward. I'm so happy for both of you. Now you have everything that a man could ever want. Congratulations to you both. I'll tell Monica for you. I know Monica really would like children, and I do also. We are going to start trying as soon as we are married."

"Greg, I hate to bring this sore subject up when you are so happy, but why didn't you have any children when you were married to Ashley? I would have thought you would have wanted them then."

"I did want children, but after we said I do, Ashley decided those children would ruin her perfect figure and that mainly they would be in the way. We also slept in separate beds, which I don't think you ever knew about. Children to Ashley were a nuisance because she was more interested in partying and being on the arm of an important surgeon. What a crock of beans! I wish that I had ended it back then, but I'm not going back and rehash that, even when I think back I shouldn't have married her. I never had feelings for her the way that I have for Monica. Now I truly know what love feels like. I'm so much happier at the moment with Monica. By the way, I don't want to forget to tell you that when you return from your honeymoon, we'll be getting married the following Saturday. The divorce came through faster than we anticipated with no hitches."

"Perfect! We'll talk when we get back. But in the meantime, if you need to contact me about anything, just call me on my cell phone. I'll have it with me at all times."

"Have a great honeymoon to both of you."

"Thanks. See you when we return."

"Again, congratulations to you both."

"We have so much to celebrate, I'm overcome with excitement. This is all I've ever wanted, a wonderful wife and a family."

Chapter 43

The luggage was all in the car, and I was feeling much better after drinking a ginger ale and eating a few saltine crackers. I put the box of crackers in my suitcase. Herbert drove us to the airport where the jet was waiting, fully fueled. Edward keeps a pilot on standby at all times. The pilot is on the hospital payroll in case of an emergency; all the doctors on staff have the use of the jet. We had a wonderful flight with me sleeping most of the trip.

Edward rented a car, and he drove immediately to the resort. It was a Sandals Resort, and Edward had arranged for us to have the best suite in the place, which of course was the honeymoon suite on the top floor, which was the entire top floor. I always dreamed about vacationing at a Sandals Resort but never had the resources to travel there. It was as if Edward could read my mind.

We went to our room where the bellhop already had deposited our luggage. I unpacked and put everything in its proper place since we were vacationing here for two whole weeks. I didn't want to live out of the suitcases. After that, I went to the window and looked out at the pool below and the glorious beach with the white sand that glistened like crystals with the sun shining on the sand, and it looked as if the beach was full of jewels. What a sight to behold! I wondered if Edward had ever been here before even though he said he hadn't, but still all these thoughts were going through my head. Just as fast, I forgot them.

This time we were just going to relax in the sun, swim, and take long walks. Just have fun like all the other couples here. Many couples here were at the resort with their families, and I thought and smiled to myself how we could be doing the same when our child was old enough to come here in a few years. I touched my belly, and I could tell that I was starting to get a little bigger, just enough for me to notice, but not anyone else. It was hard to fantasize that we were going to be parents in approximately six and a half months if I calculated correctly, although I wasn't exactly sure when I actually got pregnant. I was just guessing.

I didn't want any special treatment while here, just some fun in the sun with my new husband, and long romantic walks on the sandy beach just like we did when we first dated in Newfoundland. I still missed my beloved island every day, but when I touched my pendant, there it was, my Newfoundland. Edward was ever so thoughtful about getting me this piece of the rock. Every time I touched it, I felt a longing that I was back there.

We talked together and decided that we would first take a walk on the sandy beach to find our way around and know where everything was located. I changed into shorts for walking to get some fresh air, and of course, I couldn't resist walking in the aquamarine-colored water. I never saw water look so colorful or beautiful, and it was actually hot. It was like something from a movie set that I had walked on. I just absolutely love the ocean. The sand between my toes felt so wonderful. I felt just like a kid again running through the water.

"Edward, sweetheart, this place is just perfect."

I kissed him passionately, and he reciprocated. "I knew it when I saw the brochure that it was the perfect place for us to enjoy two glorious weeks of relaxation. The water is so relaxing. Are you happy, sweetheart? I mean do you regret marrying me and leaving Newfoundland?"

"I'm as giddy as a schoolgirl having her first crush. I don't know what I did to deserve such a wonderful husband as you, especially the way you look. You could be a model with the way your body looks. I'm afraid that all the women here will be admiring you. I get so jealous of all the other women that are looking at your handsome, suave, tall, and muscular body. Sometimes I think that their eyes are going to pop out of their sockets looking at you and gawking. I know that I shouldn't be jealous because that's a sin, and you did marry me, not them. I will never regret marrying you, but I would be lying if I said that I didn't miss Newfoundland, although when you take me places like this, it helps these feelings. I don't feel so lonely for it, but I guess I always will in a certain way. Even though I was always treated so badly, I still loved it because it was my home. Sweetheart, would you like to go swimming? That's one thing that we haven't done together."

"Britt, you are making me blush saying all these things, but I only have eyes for you, my sweet. You know I try to stay in shape with exercise. Because of my age, I need to exercise more so I won't start to look like an old man. I feel like a new man having you as my wife. Have you ever thought about me as being an old man and wondering about the difference in our ages? Okay, let's forget all this talk and let's go swimming at the pool. You need to get some sun, especially on your leg and arm after all that time in a cast, and by the time we go home, you will be tanned."

"You are not vain, are you? I love you just the way you are, and I wouldn't want it any other way."

"I'm definitely not vain. That would be a sin. I just want to remain healthy, and fitness keeps me that way. Let's stop talking about bodies, otherwise we will get intimate and go back to the room for the remainder of the day instead of enjoying these beautiful surroundings. Are you ready for swimming?"

"I only have a bikini under these shorts. I hope that is okay for this place. I don't think that it will fit in a few months because already it's starting to feel tight, but I think the size is incorrect on the label. I was thinking that I would have a few more months before my clothes felt tight."

"Maybe it's from Herbert's cooking. We have been eating very rich foods. Your bikini looks great. Now I know that I was the man who loved you so much that you became pregnant. I've wanted a family for so long, I had almost given up, but I found the right person in you who eventually became my wife. Of course, we did it the right way, you became my wife first, and then you became pregnant. I found you as my soul mate. Are you happy that you are pregnant, sweetheart? Do you think that it was too soon? Maybe you think that we should have waited longer and be able to spend more time together doing different things and traveling to exotic places more because once you start getting big, it may be difficult to get around."

"Oh yes, sweetheart, but only if you are happy also. Just the thought that I'm carrying a part of you inside me makes me want you more and more every day. It's hard to fathom that there is a little person growing inside me and that we created him or her with the love that we have for each other."

We returned to our room and gathered towels and suntan lotion and then walked down to the glorious outdoor pool. The pool was the largest that I had ever seen, and you could walk in for a few hundred feet before it got deep, and then there were steps going all the distance around with a tiki bar at each end where you could swim up and get drinks and sit on benches in the water. The water was glistening and shimmering. We jumped in and swam for almost an hour. Edward was a great swimmer, much more powerful in the water than I was ever.

After swimming, we found two lounge chairs facing the sun and relaxed. Edward coated me with suntan lotion, as I have a tendency to burn, and I wasn't sure how my skin would react to the tropical sun. Edward already had a tan from living in California, and that made his body more irresistible.

"Would you like a nice tall cold tropical fruit drink from the bar, sweetheart?"

"Oh yes, Edward, that sounds so refreshing."

"I'll be back as fast as you can wink an eye."

While Edward went to get our drinks, another couple who seemed to be approximately our own ages, came over and sat down next to where we were. Edward came back with our drinks, and they got up and introduced themselves to us. They were from Los Angeles, California.

"Excuse us, but you seem to be about our ages and probably the only other couple that we don't feel out of place next to, with everyone here tending to be very young with children. I'm Kristen Conway, and this is my husband, Alfred."

"I know what you mean about the ages. Please sit with us. I am Brittney Moore, and this is my husband, Edward. We are from Monterey Bay, California."

"Alfred is a doctor, and I am a stay-at-home mom with a new-born daughter, Amelia Ann."

"Edward is a doctor also, and I'm pregnant with our first child, only about two and a half months along."

Edward and Alfred got along excellent, talking about medicine. They moved over one table and let the ladies relax in peace. Kristen and I talked about children. I told her that we were a newly married and just found out that I was pregnant. They were newly married also, just over a year. He was fifty-two years old, and she was forty-three. We seemed to get along perfect together and spent time talking together. The men ordered lunch, and we ate there beside the pool, eating lobster, clams, and shrimp. I didn't eat too much, unsure whether this rich food would agree with my digestion now that I was pregnant, although I was starving and this was my selection of food. We all seemed to have the same things in common. After lunch was finished, Edward came over and spoke to me.

"Britt, do you mind if I spend the afternoon with Al? He may be looking to move to Van Nuys or Monterey Bay and is looking for a new place to practice medicine. I really would like to find out more about him to see if he would fit in with our services at the hospital and our way of treating our patients. He is an orthopedic surgeon for children, and we have been searching for some time for such a doctor to fill that slot as chief of orthopedic surgery. He doesn't know who I really am yet, so please don't say anything to Kristen."

"That'll be fine, sweetheart. Kristen and I are going to lounge around here in the sun and then swim a little. I won't be able to do this in a couple of months dressed as I am now. Are you okay with me staying here by the pool? You're not afraid that some man will come along and eye me?"

"Just let one try."

"Will you get jealous if I fall madly in love with someone else before you get back? Edward, I promise that you are more man than

I can handle. I love you, sweetheart, and the baby loves you also." I was laughing as I said it.

"You best not fall for any other man or have your eyes on any other man while I'm away from you. You know that I hate to be away from you any length of time. I love you so much, and I get very jealous when I see any other man looking at you."

"I love hearing you talk like this."

He stood up to leave, and I grabbed him with a very passionate kiss, and he returned the same.

"If you do not let me go and stop kissing me like that, I will not leave at all, and then I will have to drag you back to the room and be intimate and spend the afternoon in bed. I just can't deny you anything. I am very jealous of you. I love you so much that sometimes it hurts when I am away from you, especially when I am at the hospital all day and then the long drive home."

"I love you, sweetheart. Now go. Kristen will be here with me, so I won't have a chance of finding someone else, and why would I really when I have the most romantic man close by at all times?"

I smiled, and he left. In the meantime, Alfred went over to Kristen to explain what Edward and he were doing together.

"Kristen, I'm going to talk to Edward about the hospital that he works at, and then maybe he can get me a foot in the door there. Are you okay staying here?"

"Al, that sounds wonderful. I'll pray that he can help us get out of Los Angeles. That place is starting to be so dangerous, and I really hate having our daughter grow up there amid all the violence and garbage, especially when you are working, I really get scared. Love you, darling."

"Why haven't you said something sooner?"

"I didn't want to rush you. I knew that sooner or later, the Lord would hear our prayers. Maybe it was this specific time and place that we met this couple. I will keep having good thoughts about all this. Love you, Al."

I smiled again at Edward, and he winked at me. Then he and Alfred walked off together toward the beach.

Chapter 44

"Al, how about we take a walk on the beach, so we can talk and not be disturbed. We can maybe find a log to sit and talk. I would very much like to know about your practice that you have in Los Angeles. If you're looking to move to the Van Nuys or Monterey Bay area, I may be able to help you. Have you ever heard of the Van Nuys Medical Center?"

"Have I ever heard of that hospital? Are you kidding me? Who hasn't heard of that hospital? They are the most prestigious hospital around and have hired the best doctors in their perspective fields. I was thinking about sending my resume there after we returned home from our vacation, but I heard that you have to know someone who works there to even get near that place. I would probably have a better chance if I did."

"We have been trying to find a children's orthopedic surgeon for about two years. I hate to tell you this, but they wouldn't even take a second look at your resume. You need to be recommended by a doctor who is on staff at the hospital. If you are really serious and want to be Chief of Orthopedic Surgery, I can help you. This will be your interview. You see, Al, I am the owner of the Van Nuys Medical Center, and everyone has to go through me if they want to work there. I run the medical center where we help the rich and the poor, no matter their circumstance in life. We absolutely do not turn anyone away regardless of their ability to pay. We will not discriminate for any reason. That is our policy. I need to know if you have any problem with living up to this kind of policy."

"No, absolutely no problem with living up to that kind of policy because I have always followed that same policy. Since my patients are children, sometimes the parents don't always have the money to pay up front because most of these surgeries are emergencies and due to some sports injury. I have never had a problem with payment. They always do pay later. I have never had a problem with any patient refusing to pay, and I never force the patient for payment. I give them extra time for payment if they need it or put them on a payment plan if that is better for them. If you want to see my resume, I do have one back at the hotel room if you think I have the qualifications for the position."

"I would very much like to go over it, and I always keep my doctor's resumes on file at the hospital. How about we walk back to our wives, and then we can have dinner later tonight and talk about it. You can mention the job to Kristen, but please don't tell her about me owning the hospital, not until you both agree that you want to move there. Okay?"

"I just thank you for the chance at this position. If you have any more questions, please don't hesitate. Just ask anything. I have never met the owner of a hospital before and never in my wildest dreams did I ever think I would meet the owner of the Van Nuys Medical Center where I have always wanted to work. I have dreamed of this day. We have prayed about this for so long that we could find the right person to talk with to try to get my foot in the door, as a doctor, not a patient."

"Well, Al, I started this hospital as a small medical clinic twenty years ago, and more and more doctors wanted to join our staff, so I created what we have today. I am very proud of our medical center and all our doctors. They are the best in their respective fields. We all share the same ideals, which is why I asked those questions when I told you who I was. Now that we have all this settled, please don't give me away to Kristen, at least, not yet?"

"Let's go back and join the girls."

"Thank you, Edward. I will keep it quiet until dinner tonight."

Chapter 45

Kristen and Brittney were lounging at the pool with fruit juices and talking about children and where they were each living.

"Kristen, how is it having a baby at an older age? I am so scared of having a baby now. I thought at this time in my life that I would be close to being a grandmother and ready to spoil them, but things don't always work out the way you want, but I had always wanted a great husband, and when I met Edward, it was like it was meant to be. I'm sure the Lord had his hands in our meeting from the very beginning."

"I was scared, but each time I felt her move, all I could think of was having a little person to take care of each day while Al was at work. I hired a nanny, but she mainly takes care of Amelia when I need a change or if we are going to a party. It will all come to you naturally. Don't be scared. It looks as if you have a very attentive husband who will be by your side continuously. I know that we were blessed with Amelia from the Lord as well. She is so special to us. I couldn't ask for a most blessed child."

"I know I'm so fortunate. I thought that I would have been married years ago and had a grown family already, but it wasn't meant to be. I'm so much happier this way though. I wouldn't have it any other way. Edward has made me the happiest woman that I have ever been in my entire life."

"Brittney, I'm also older, and like you, I thought I would be married years ago. I love my daughter so much. She is my whole world. She surrounds my days with so much happiness when Al is at the hospital. I love staying at home with her, and this way I get to watch her grow up and see all her accomplishments every day. We want to move to Monterey Bay or Van Nuys soon to a larger home if Al can get a position at a hospital in that area. He has always admired the Van Nuys Medical Center and what these doctors accomplish there and the way they give of their time and the awards they have received for their dedication and commitment for helping those without money. He has a big heart for helping the children in the same way. That's all he talks about putting in his resume. I pray every day that something will work out soon for him. We need to move from Los Angeles. Everything there is so busy and not a place to raise a child. We are looking for a place where there is green grass and a yard for Amelia to play. Do you think I'm dreaming way too big?"

"Maybe Edward will be able to help him, Kristen. Everything will work out for the good of those who trust in the Lord. Are you and Alfred soul mates? When you work together, all seems to go according to the plan. It is always good to dream because sometimes these dreams do come true, and I don't think your dreams are too big when you are thinking of your family. Just keep praying and who knows!"

"Al and I are definitely soul mates. That is how we met. I do believe what you said, and everything will work out at the perfect time, but only in God's appointed timing. We must not complain, and we mustn't rush. You are such a great friend that I would love to live near you. We are so alike. I have no friends in Los Angeles."

"Thank you, Kristen. I think so too."

Chapter 46

As we were talking and drinking our fruit juices, I noticed that there were two men on the other side of the pool that kept staring at us. In one way, it was a little eerie, but still I guess I still can attract men even at my age. I wasn't afraid of them because there were many people around, and if we screamed, I'm sure someone would truly come to our rescue, at least I hoped so.

"Kristen, don't look now, but it looks like we are being admired by two gentlemen across the pool, and they're starting to come our way, and it isn't Edward or Alfred. Have you seen them here before we came? Do you think that we should let them talk to us and then see if our husbands come to our rescue, because I see that Edward and Alfred are just coming up the path from the beach?"

"Brittney, I haven't seen them here at the pool before now, but I'm game if you are to make our husbands jealous. I haven't done anything like that in years, not since I started dating Al years ago. First, let's take a swim and get all wet. That will make us more irresistible by being all shiny from the water and also give our husbands time to walk over here faster if they see these guys."

"Kristen, I'm game. Let's go. You think like me, girl. Let's go."

We arose from our comfortable lounge chairs and jumped in the pool and swam for a few minutes and then returned to our loungers where the two guys were standing as we came from the water, and it seemed, waiting for us. They introduced themselves to us saying that their names were Tony and Cliff from California here on vacation to find some honeys and liked the look of us, especially all wet.

Kristen and I saw Edward and Alfred getting closer and still talking, but were staring at the two men talking to us. They started walking toward us faster.

"Bree, is that you? I never imagined that I would find you here of all places."

"I recognize your voice, but not your face. You can't be Anthony. What are you doing here? I don't want you here or anywhere near me or know why you are here."

"Bree, I saw you across the pool and couldn't believe my eyes that it was actually my wife. I had plastic surgery on my face after an accident last year."

"Anthony, I am no longer your wife, and don't call me that. You were the one who wanted a divorce and I gave you one, so we have nothing to say to each other anymore." I started to get hot under my collar as they say. I wanted him gone.

"How about dinner tonight, please, Bree? I need to talk to you. You can bring your friend here."

Edward heard me getting angry and came running. He placed his hand on my shoulder to let me know that he would fight for me and that no one would ever hurt me again.

"Hello, Dr. Moore, that's really you. You seem to know my wife. What are you doing here? I thought I told you about vacationing in Newfoundland, but never thought that you would meet my wife there. Did you bring my wife here with you?"

"Hello, Anthony. Are you bothering these ladies? Are you ladies being bothered by these so-called gentlemen?"

"I just wanted to talk to my wife. I was trying to arrange having dinner with both of these women for tonight."

"Anthony, I am no longer your wife and haven't been for years. Edward is now my husband."

"You are remarried and to my plastic surgeon. You didn't even wait for the ink to dry before jumping in bed with another man, I see."

"Anthony, we have been divorced for ten years, and I didn't jump in bed with Edward. How dare you say such things to me? You are the most vulgar person I know, and I am so glad that you wanted to divorce me because you were never my soul mate, but Edward is."

Edward then spoke up and started yelling at the two men to get away from their wives; otherwise, he would report them to the resort for badgering their wives. "If the two of you don't leave our sight, I will report you both for harassment. I don't think you want to be thrown out of the resort, and I can do it. Now get away from us, and I don't want to see your faces around our wives.

Al then spoke up. He couldn't take it any longer, and I didn't blame him. We all had enough of this bantering. "These wonderful ladies are our wives, and the only persons that they will be eating with tonight are Edward and I and every night after that."

"Dr. Moore. I need to talk to Bree in private for a few minutes if that's okay with you and her, and then we will leave you in peace. I'm so sorry that we interrupted your time together here at the resort, but since she is here, I need to explain something to her that I should have told her years ago, and I think she now needs to know the truth."

"Only if Britt wants to talk to you. Do you, sweetheart? I don't see any harm, but if he makes you cry, I will be on him in a second."

"Okay, I don't mind talking to him, but, Anthony, please stop calling me Bree. That is not your privilege anymore. We'll talk on the other side of the pool this minute because I don't have time for this. We are on our honeymoon." We walked to the other side of the pool and sat in the chairs. Edward was watching to assure me that he was onto him if he hurt me. Edward made me feel so safe.

"What do you want, Anthony?"

"I wanted to let you know the real reason why I divorced you. It wasn't because you were an iceberg, as I stated. You were never an iceberg. I'm so sorry for saying that and hurting you. It was mean, but I wanted children so much, and you weren't getting pregnant. I'm sorry that I didn't tell you that before. Does Dr. Moore know that you can't produce any children for him?"

I started laughing and laughing, and Edward couldn't figure out what was happening or what he had just told me. I then smiled and spoke. "Anthony, it isn't me who can't produce children because you see I'm pregnant with Edward's baby at this very minute. I think you may have to get a checkup for yourself and get tested."

"I think you're lying. You just want to hurt me."

"Anthony, I haven't any reason to hurt you now, especially in that way. I have a great husband and a great life, and since you were the person that told Edward to go to Newfoundland on vacation, I want to truly thank you. If I hadn't met Edward, I probably would still be there feeling sorry for myself."

"You can't be pregnant. You are the one who is impotent, not me. I should have left you years ago, and I was also the person who told lies about you in Newfoundland to pay you back." Anthony started to get angry, raising his voice, and Edward didn't like what he was viewing across the pool.

"I'll call Edward over here, and he can tell you the truth. How could you have hated me that much to let all these lies go through the city and get me in so much trouble?"

"Edward, can you come over here, please?" Edward came running over, thinking that Anthony was hurting me. "Edward, please tell Anthony about my pregnancy."

"That's true, old boy. She got pregnant the first time we were intimate. There is not a thing wrong with Britt, but I think that you may want to have yourself checked out by a specialist when you return home."

"You are not just making up these lies? Can you do it and check me out, Dr. Moore?"

"I can, but under the circumstances, of Britt being your ex-wife, I don't think it would be wise. We do have other doctors at the medical center that you can make an appointment with, who are excellent in that field."

"I understand. Please forgive me for barging in on your honeymoon, Dr. Moore."

"Try and have a good life, Anthony."

"You did come to our rescue. Kristen and I saw you and Al across the pool and wondered if you both were our knights in shining armor? I love you so much. In a way, I feel sorry for Anthony, but all these years, I thought that I couldn't have children and was an iceberg. I lived a life being angry and never enjoying myself, but now that I think back when we met, it was supposed to happen that way.

I never would have met you if you hadn't operated on Anthony and if he hadn't told you where to go on vacation. I feel so loved. Edward, you are the best husband that a girl could ever have."

Edward leaned down toward me and gave me a kiss.

We walked back to Alfred and Kristen arm in arm, smiling at each other. Edward bent down and kissed me. I just absolutely adored this man.

"Kristen, now that Edward and Brittney have returned to the table, allow me to go to the room and get my resume for Edward. I refuse to allow you to sit here alone and maybe get hit on again. I'll be right back."

Al returned with his resume and gave it to Edward, and then Edward and I returned to our room to relax a bit before dinner. He wanted me to rest and take a nap after all day in the sun and also all the swimming I did, but the exercise was very good for me.

Chapter 47

"Edward, how about we all meet tonight for dinner in the main dining room about 8:00 p.m.? I'll make reservations for the four of us."

"That sounds fine with us. We'll meet you both in the main dining room."

We said our "see you later" and returned to our room as Edward wanted me to take a rest after spending all day at the pool. Kristen and Al left to call Kristen's parents to see how their little daughter was doing without her mommy and daddy. Just the thought that before we knew what happened and where the time went, we would be having a little one of our very own. I wondered who he or she would look like. I hoped Edward because he was so handsome, whereas I was very plain.

"Edward, I have a feeling that Al and Kristen are soul mates."

"I think so also. I plan on hiring him at the hospital to be the chief of orthopedic surgery. I'll tell him tonight at dinner. This way he can have a great vacation and not have to worry about whether he got the position or not. He carries the same principles as all the other doctors on staff."

"That's great, sweetheart. How about telling them also about the house next door to us that's for sale? They wanted a bigger home, and that would be perfect, of course, only if they want to move to Monterey Bay. The house is not quite as large as ours, but it's large to what they have now. It's a beautiful home, and I think Kristen would love the area, and I would have a great friend next door when you are working. We got along great together. I wouldn't feel so lonely."

"Oh, sweetheart, I never ever thought about you being home all day and being lonely when I bought the house. I was probably just thinking about myself. I'm so sorry, sweetheart, that you feel that way. Would you rather that we move to a different area closer to the hospital? I was just so wrapped up in buying my dream home that I didn't even consider your feelings. I wanted to surprise you."

"No. I love our home, and now I can spend time decorating a nursey, and that will keep me very busy in the next few months. If Kristen and Al buy that home, then I will have a great new friend."

Soon after that, I fell asleep and slept until it was almost time to meet the Conway's for dinner. Edward came over to the bed and nudged me, and I immediately woke up. Edward had spent the time on his computer and did some reading in a few medical books that he had brought with him. He e-mailed Greg to tell him the good news of hiring the new surgeon to fill the position of chief of orthopedics, and that he would be joining the staff in approximately two weeks.

"Are you okay, Britt? You slept quite a long time."

"I feel fine, but why do I feel even more tired now after taking a nap? I know that the fresh air always makes me tired, especially I'm not used to all this sunshine and heat."

"I need to go to the drug store and buy you some prenatal vitamin supplements that could enhance your system. I'll write a prescription and then go to the pharmacy and get it filled."

"I'm afraid of taking medication that may hurt the baby. Are you sure it's okay?"

"I know you are worrying about the baby, but they won't harm our child. It feels so wonderful to hear that word."

"Say what word?"

"Our child! Are you sure that you still want to go to dinner with Al and Kristen? I know that they would understand if you are too tired after all day at the pool."

"I'm just fine, sweetheart. Let's get dressed."

We dressed for dinner and walked to the main dining room arm in arm. We met the Conway's as they were just being seated at a table away from the crowd, which was perfect as I wanted to tell Al the good news. Everyone looked fabulous although the dress that

Edward had bought me recently was already starting to feel slightly tight around my stomach. I didn't think that it would feel so tight so soon. It was too early for that phase pf pregnancy, but what did I know? I guessed that I was about close to three months pregnant, but I could be actually four and close to four and a half. It had been now two months since being released from the hospital.

We ordered dinner, and I felt famished, but of course I was now eating for two. We all ordered steaks, lobsters, and baked potatoes with a nice tossed salad. While we were waiting for our meals, Edward decided to tell Al about the position.

Chapter 48

"Al, I have something to tell you that I think is going to make a perfect ending to a perfect day. I would like to offer you the position of chief of orthopedic surgery at the Van Nuys Medical Center. You can start as soon as you are able to get everything cleared up in Los Angeles from your practice there. What do you say?"

"Edward, I am tongue-tied. I want to thank you for this great opportunity to work with the greatest surgeons at the best hospital in California. Now the only thing that we need to do is to find a house to buy."

"Do you have to sell your house in Los Angeles because if you wanted to live in Monterey Bay Britt came up with the most perfect solution? Go ahead and tell them, sweetheart."

"We live in Monterey Bay close to the ocean, and next door to us is the most beautiful home. Not quite as big as ours, but big with five bedrooms. The same style as ours and absolutely magnificent. It's great for entertaining and, Kristen, you would have a ready-made friend next door. What do you say? I know you would want to see it before buying."

Kristen just sat there looking stunned as Edward was telling Al about the position and that he was being offered exactly what he wanted for years, and now it was being placed in his hands. She looked at Al in awe. Finally, she spoke. "Everything sounds too good to be true. Is it true, or am I dreaming? I can hardly believe our great fortune in meeting both of you here. A ready friend, Al. I think that it would be perfect, and it wouldn't take any time to sell our home in Los Angeles. Homes are selling as soon as they hit the market. Al, how could you be accepted to such a high position in just an afternoon at walking on the beach with another surgeon?"

"Kristen, when we get back to the room, I'll call our real estate agent and put our house on the market. It should sell before we leave the tropics. Well, Edward, I am very excited about joining you and the other surgeons at the Medical Center in about two weeks if that's okay with you, since you are the boss."

"What do you mean, Al? The boss."

"Is it okay with you to tell Kristen?"

"Sure."

"Well, Kris, Edward owns the Medical Center that I have always dreamed of working and always bragged about where I wanted to practice medicine if I ever received the chance to be so fortunate. He has for twenty years. It's as if I needed to meet him at this resort to be able to get into that hospital. Kristen, we were praying so much for this opportunity that when we had planned on spending time at the other resort and everything fell through, and then this is why. It was meant to be. The Lord works in mysterious ways, His wonders to perform."

"Al, honey. I am so happy. Can we go dancing tonight to celebrate our fortune in meeting our new friends and your new position as a dream come through? Will you join us?"

"Not tonight. I want Britt to rest. It's been a long day for her."

"Edward, I would love to go dancing with you. I won't be able in a few months."

"Are you sure? I don't want you to get over tired."

"Please? Other women have babies and do everything like dancing and even running."

"Okay. We'll come with you."

We finished up our delicious dinner with some tropical fruit for dessert. The food was perfect. After dinner, we went next door to the tiki bar and danced for about two hours. It was so wonderful to be dancing with Edward. He was such a great dancer and just resting my head on his chest and swaying with the music, I felt like I was floating on a cloud. Nothing could have felt better than this. After that, we said our good nights and returned to our suite.

Chapter 49

We went to bed so happy after having a great day with our new friends.

The next morning and for the remainder of the two weeks, we spent the time with Al and Kristen. We visited the Bahia Ballena, which is shaped like a whale's tail, and visited the popular beach of Whale Bay to watch the whales. Costa Rica is also a birdwatcher's paradise and saw the most beautiful birds in my entire life. We went to a small town of Heredia, which is the city of flowers. The most fascinating that I have ever seen in my life were the pink flamingos. I could not get all the beauty out of my mind and thanked Edward so much for bringing us here. It was a glorious honeymoon. We were ever so thankful for this great world that we lived in and the entire splendor that it beheld. What a wonderful Creator we had!

We arrived back at the room one afternoon after taking in glorious surroundings, and I was feeling tired after all day walking, eating dinner, and then dancing. Taking the elevator up to our honeymoon suite, I had to hold Edward's arm to steady myself. Edward held on to me tight with his arm around my waist. He wanted to carry me, but I refused.

"Britt, are you okay? I knew we shouldn't have gone dancing tonight. It was too much for you. You are starting to worry me that this pregnancy is going to be too hard on you. I'll have to watch you very carefully."

"Edward, you're scaring me. What's wrong with me?"

"In the morning, we'll take a trip to the hospital to have you checked out. This way we can enjoy our honeymoon without worrying. You are getting too tired so early in your pregnancy. At least, you shouldn't be this tired. I don't have equipment here to check you out myself, and I don't think that Al would have brought any either."

I knew that Britt was worried. She tossed and turned most of the night, then I felt her get up and go to the window seat, and then I heard the tears and the sobbing. I knew that women cry more when they are pregnant due to their hormones, but I didn't think that was what was wrong or bothering her. I got out of bed and went to try to comfort her and get her to talk to me.

"Darling, please don't cry. We'll go to the hospital in the morning, which is only a few hours away. Please try to lie down and get some sleep."

"Suppose there's something wrong and I lose the baby. I couldn't live with myself. I need to go now. Please take me."

"Okay, if that's what you want, sweetheart, I'll take you."

We dressed quickly, and Edward drove to the hospital after getting directions from the desk clerk at the hotel. We drove directly to the emergency. It was very quiet there. We entered, and Edward explained what was happening. He gave them his name and explained all the symptoms. They had heard of Edward even as far away as Costa Rica, but I didn't want any privileges. The emergency department wasn't busy when we arrived, so I was ushered immediately in to an empty room.

They took Britt immediately and did an ultrasound test on her while I waited outside. The ER doctor, Dr. Cortez, came out and asked me to come in since he wanted to tell us whatever it was at the same time instead of retelling it over twice.

"What's the situation, Doctor?"

The doctor started to smile.

"Britt sweetheart, are you feeling okay?"

"Well, Dr. Moore and Mrs. Moore, you are definitely pregnant. No mistaken that, as you are starting to show already. You are four months pregnant. There is something that you should know from the ultrasound test that I don't think you did know, and it's causing you to be so tired."

Both Edward and I had the look of alarm on our faces, and we held hands. The doctor smiled.

"Don't worry, nothing is wrong that you need to worry, except that you are having triplets, not just one little one as you thought, but three."

"Triplets, how can that be? Doesn't it usually follow in the family blood line? I don't have any twin or triplets in my family."

"You're a doctor, Dr. Moore. It doesn't always happen that way."

"How about you, Britt?"

"I hate to tell you this, Edward, but my family had twins all over the blood line, but not directly in my family blood line, only distant cousins. I should have told you, but I always thought I couldn't have children, according to the doctor in Newfoundland, so I didn't think that there was any need to bring it up as I assumed we would never have any children. I never ever questioned his diagnosis."

"It doesn't matter now. I wanted children, just that. I didn't think we would have them all at once. How are we going to cope with three babies? Dr. Cortez, can you tell the sex of the babies?"

"Yes, as far as I can tell from these images, there is a boy and two girls."

"Thank you, Doctor; for all your information and the help here tonight. I'll make sure that she has more rest as required."

"I will give you a prescription for vitamin supplements to take that will help you to enjoy the remainder of your time here."

"Thank you."

"You are free to leave now, Mrs. Moore, and you can get the prescription filled on the way out at the pharmacy."

Chapter 50

We filled the prescription, left the hospital, and returned to the resort. Now I thought I would be able to get some sleep, but Edward hadn't spoken all the way back. I guessed that he was mad about the family blood line situation even though he said that he wanted children and not just a child. When we arrived back at the resort, I decided that I would say something when we got to the room. It was not like him to be so quiet, so I knew that he must have been so mad and what was going through his mind. I was almost scared of what he would say or do. I had never ever seen him get mad before, and so he scared me a little.

"Edward, I'm so sorry that I didn't tell you about the twins in my family's blood line. I didn't think that it would matter since not one woman in my immediate blood line has ever had twins. Does it bother you that much? You haven't said a single word to me since you found out, and you're scaring me. It almost sounds like you don't want them and that it's my fault. I guess you would have thought twice about marrying me if you had known."

"Okay, it's quite a shock to say the least. A ready-made family in one night of passion, and it seems like it happened the very first night home from the hospital. I'll just have to stay away from you, otherwise we may end up with a dozen."

Edward was getting even angrier and yelling, which he had never ever done since I met him. His voice was getting even higher with every passing minute. What was going through his mind? I wanted and needed to get away from him.

"Please go to bed, Edward? I'm going to sit up for a while. You need to get your rest as much as possible. Don't worry your head about that or anything else concerning myself or the babies from here on. I'll take care of us."

"What are you talking about?"

"When we get back home, I'll be moving out and have the babies on my own, and you can go on with your life without us to bother you, since you don't seem to want these children."

"Britt, you are talking crazy. They're my children too. It's just been a huge shock to take all this in, thinking that we were going to have one little child, but now I'm stunned and you getting pregnant so soon. I'm really wondering if you knew all along that you could get pregnant, but according to Anthony yesterday at the pool, I guess you were telling the truth that you thought that you couldn't have children."

"So now, I'm also a liar in your eyes. I'm starting not to know you or like anymore. You are not the man I married. You don't seem to want anything to do with two of these children. Other families have triplets and don't think of not having them. We can even afford to have them. We aren't poor, and the house is definitely big enough. I'll have them and return to Newfoundland to raise them in quiet surroundings with all the love and help that comes from growing up in a beautiful country. I wouldn't want to stay here in your house as intruders on your lifestyle and then have you only love one and the other two be ignored. You are being a hypocrite."

I started to cry and ran to the bathroom, and while I was sitting there, I got these horrible pains in my stomach. They were so bad that I couldn't take the pain, and I can tolerate most pain. I was screaming so badly that Edward came running thinking that I was hurting myself or the babies. He looked at me crumbled up on the floor, and then he saw the blood. All that I could think about was that I was losing my babies. Edward ran back to the bedroom and dialed 911 for an ambulance.

"Oh darling, this is my entire fault. I am so sorry for what I was thinking and the words coming from my mouth. Can you ever forgive me? How could I have been so insensitive? I want these babies, but now it looks as if we are going to lose them. The ambulance will be here ASAP."

Tears were starting to run down Edward's face, and I was already crying from all the pain. It was hurting so bad that I thought that I would pass out, and I finally did with Edward holding my head up off the floor.

The ambulance arrived and rushed me back to the same hospital that I had been examined at only a few hours ago. Edward followed in the car behind the ambulance. He had to wait outside the ER, and so he paced the floor and prayed that the babies and I would be fine. The same doctor saw us again.

While Britt was being examined, I started to pray. I truly believed that I was being punished for what I had thought and the words that I had spoken to Britt in anger. "I pray, Lord, that everything will be as it was when we found out that Britt was pregnant. I know you only let us endure as much as we can. You gave us the three babies, I know now because we are both getting up there in age and maybe Britt may not be able to get pregnant anymore. I ask for your forgiveness for all my sinful thoughts and ways. I pray that Britt will we fine and that the babies are fine. I know that you know what is best for us. Thank you. Amen."

I was pacing the floor back and forth in the ER waiting on news of Britt. Even though I'm a doctor, I couldn't be in the room with her, so here I am just waiting. I was just like any nervous husband and father. I wonder if I will be this way when the children arrive. I was on a steady path when after an hour of pacing, I was called in and the doctor told me that Britt was feeling much better, but the bad news was that she had lost one of the babies, the boy. Britt reached out to me for support, and we hugged and cried over the loss of one baby that we would never get to see and hold. I now knew that this little baby boy was with the Lord and some day we would see him. Britt had stopped bleeding by this time but needed plenty of rest.

"Don't overdo it with the rest though. You need to exercise. Just go about your regular routine day by day."

"Thank you, Doctor."

"I'm so sorry, Britt. The Lord knew how much we could endure, and he took one from us. I really did want all three of these babies, Britt. They are part of us, the best part. We can hire a nanny to take care of them when they're born."

"No, Edward. I'll raise our children without the help of a nanny. I don't want strangers raising our children. I want to spend my life raising them. That will be my goal."

"What about looking after me?"

"You can help me raise them, so that's when we can spend time together. I'm tired, Edward. I just want to get some sleep. Please go back to the resort and let the Conways know what has happened. I can't stop thinking about our baby boy that will never be."

It was then that the tears started to flow down Britt's face. She turned her head from me, and I know that in a way she was still blaming me for the loss of the baby.

Chapter 51

B ritt stayed in the hospital overnight for observation. I returned to the resort and left a message at the front desk for Al and Kristen Conway about everything that had happened the night before. I prayed that night that everything would be okay concerning Britt, and I really did want the babies, now more than ever, realizing that a part of me died that night with a part of Britt. I did want them even at my age. I knew that I could handle it; I just had to for Britt's sake. It would be hard on Britt because of her age, carrying triplets, but now there were only the two girls. I felt so bad that we wouldn't have the little boy, and I wept in our room alone, but then I knew that everything happened for a reason.

The next morning, I returned to the hospital to bring Britt back to the resort, and as I entered the hospital, there were our two new friends waiting to see how Britt was feeling. Kristen hugged me and was so sympathetic about all that had happened. These two new friends made me feel so loved and that we were not alone in this travesty. How wonderful to have found them. It was so comforting to have them there that they wanted to share this with us and comfort us. They were both in tears as we hugged. We had just met them almost two weeks ago, and yet they were so concerned about Britt. That what you call a true friend!

"Edward, we are so sorry that you lost one of the babies. You didn't know that Brittney was having triplets? That must have been quite a surprise to you both. We both want you to know that we feel your loss. We loss three babies before we had our precious Amelia, but not all at the same time. I can definitely feel what you are going through. We can't have any more children, so Amelia is our little miracle."

"Edward, I blamed everything on Kristen every time we loss a child, so I also know what it feels like to not be in control. Being a doctor, you need to be in control of everything that happens, especially where your family is concerned. I think the Lord was in control of this pregnancy. We're here if either of you need anything."

All three of us then entered Britt's room to see her. She was already dressed and ready to return home to Monterey Bay, as I thought. The room was nothing like the rooms at the Medical Center in Van Nuys, and I knew she wanted out of there. Even Al looked around, and the look on his face just said it all. The room was dull and gray, and if you had to stay there for any length of time, I was thinking that you would walk away sicker than when you went in there. The doctors and nurses could only do so much. They didn't have the resources, although they took very good care of Britt. To repay them for their care, I knew that when I returned home, I would pack up a shipment of supplies and send back here to help with their medical needs. I was ever so grateful for any help that Britt had received.

Britt begged to stay the remainder of the two weeks, and I just couldn't say no to her request, also I thought that she would get more rest here than at home where she would be running all over the house organizing things and redecorating for the nursery. We had only been at the resort for ten days, so we still had the remainder of the two weeks left to bathe in the tropical sun. Al and Kristen were also there for the exact same dates we were and so since we met them, we spent every minute together walking, swimming, and just hanging out. During the last evening together, we went to the main dining room for a fabulous dinner, and Al and Kristen entered all smiles as we were already seated at the same table that we had reserved for the entire two weeks.

"You two seem so happy tonight looking at the smiles on both your faces."

"Well, we have some great news, actually it's overwhelming news. We just bought the house next to you in Monterey Bay, sight unseen. We trust both of your instincts when you say that it's a great house, and then it must be great. We did see pictures and liked very much what we saw. We arranged everything through our attorney, sold our house in Los Angeles, selling it almost as soon as it hit the real estate market. It only took overnight, transferring all the funds and everything is in completion. We just have to return, pack everything, and hire the movers."

"Al, you know that your move there will be paid for by the Medical Center?"

"I didn't realize that. Thank you."

"That's wonderful news. Both Britt and myself are overjoyed at having you both next door. Thank you for your support and for being there for us."

We had a great meal together here on our last night together and enjoyed great conversation with our two new friends. It was now the end of two great weeks. We packed our luggage, and at the same time the Conways were also packing to return to Los Angeles. At the last minute, Britt came up with a great plan and met the Conways to ask them what they thought.

"Al and Kristen, why don't you fly back to Monterey Bay with us and look at your new home and then fly from there to Los Angeles. Don't you think that would be a great plan, Edward?"

"Britt, that's an excellent idea. What do you think, Al? Would you both like to fly back with us?"

"Our tickets are for direct flights to Los Angeles."

"Cash them in at the ticket counter. Edward has his own jet that seats eight, and so we have plenty of room. It won't cost you a cent. The pilot is standing by. You can stay with us while you are in Monterey Bay and then spend the remainder of your time looking at your new home and going over how you'll plan to decorate."

Kristen then spoke up. "How could we have made such wonderful friends on a trip to Costa Rica, I'll never understand, but it was as if it had all been arranged beforehand. I really think it was by a power bigger than any human. We are soul mates forever, my darling Al. Let's go and cash these tickets in, we can use the money to rent a car to drive from Monterey Bay to Los Angeles. It's only about 275 miles. I already checked. It won't take us anytime, and the way I am feeling at this moment, I could fly there under my own power."

"Slow down, my love, or we will be packing for the entire time when we return and you will have me worn out completely."

They returned to the ticket counter and cashed in their tickets, holding hands and smiling as no other married couple could ever be.

Chapter 52

We had checked out of the resort after two weeks of the most heavenly bliss and relaxation, after a few minor difficulties concerning Britt's health that neither of us would ever forget and had never expected. We had spent the time in the sun lounging and a little walking for Britt, but she wasn't going to overdo it if I had any say in the matter.

We arrived at the airport, where I had arranged for my pilot to meet us on the tarmac and to let him know that we would have two friends traveling back with us. They had already cashed in their tickets to Los Angeles without any complications.

"Well, everyone, here we are. The jet is fueled and ready for takeoff as soon as we are all on-board. I hope you are not scared of flying in small planes?"

"Edward, this is flying in luxury and comfort. This is definitely not small, at least by my standards. What kind of jet is it?"

"This is a Gulfstream G100/G150/IAI Astro SPX Series. I like it because it can fly long distances, and the seating is beautifully arranged that you can talk and also stretch out if you are tired after a long day. As a doctor now with the Medical Center, you do have the use of it, especially where you need a patient transported to our hospital from somewhere that emergency help is needed immediately. The pilot is always on standby. Please meet out pilot. Brian, this is our newest doctor at the Medical Center, Dr. Alfred Conway."

"I'm pleased to meet you, sir. I'm sure you will enjoy it at the Medical Center. Are we all ready for takeoff? Please buckle your seatbelts for takeoff." Brian returned to his seat, and soon we were airborne.

"Everything is going so perfect that I think sometimes I'm going to wake up and it will all be a big joke. If everything keeps going the way it has, I see no reason why I definitely will be able to start in two weeks or maybe sooner."

"That's going to be great, Al. We've needed the right doctor in the orthopedic department for so long that I almost had given up hope of finding one with the right qualifications. As you can see, we never advertise with any openings, not even the nurses, just word of mouth, the same way that I located you, and sometimes that is a tiresome process. Just talking to people at parties seems to be the only way sometimes."

"Edward, I spoke to the right mouth at the right time by sitting together at the resort when I realized that we were about the same ages, and it would be nice to know someone at the resort."

We all laughed together.

The flight home to Monterey Bay was wonderful, smooth all the way with Britt resting as much as possible with her feet up and talking to Kristen. We all talked about being neighbors with only our circular driveway between us. Our lawns abutted each other, and there was a walkway at the back of our houses that was probably built there by the former owners. This would definitely come in great for visiting each other. The walkway was surrounded on both sides by varieties of roses, which was Britt's favorite flower, and Kristen adored roses.

We arrived home in record time with Herbert meeting us at the airport with the limousine on the tarmac. I had already contacted him to arrange with him that we were having two extra guests flying back with us and that they would be staying for a couple of days after having bought the home next door. We all climbed in with plenty of room and returned to our house with Al and Kristen staying the night with us before returning to Los Angeles the following day. They couldn't wait to walk through their new home.

As Herbert drove up our driveway, Kristen couldn't help staring at our home. "Your house is a mansion, absolutely breathtaking,

201

especially with all these balconies. If our new home is anything like this, I'm going to just love it here. The neighborhood looks so luxurious and seems to be the perfect place to raise children and take them on long walks. I didn't realize the water was so close to the house. This is beyond words and what a view being up here on the hill. Oh, Al, do you think you will be happy here? Edward and Brittney, you have great tastes, and I'm so happy we met you."

She turned to Brittney and hugged her as tenderly as only true friends could. I was so happy that Britt was happy with her new friends, always smiling and holding Kristen's hand.

"I won't be home much, but if you love it, then that is the only thing that really matters. This is your home to decorate and enjoy as your heart desires."

We all went inside together. Al and Kristen were staring at the giant circular staircase.

"I had admired this home for years, but it never went on the market, and when it finally did, I grabbed it in a flash. I would look in the real estate guides every week and was disappointed when I didn't see it, so about four months ago, I drove here and saw the 'for sale' sign and called the real estate agency and bought it immediately without even walking through it."

"It was sort of the way you bought the house next door. Sight unseen!"

I wanted Britt to take a nap after the trip, even though she rested on the flight, but she never slept. She had already gone upstairs to show Kristen their suite for the night. "Do you mind if I make Britt comfortable in bed and that she takes a short nap before dinner? She has a habit of going upstairs and then finding things to do. Herbert will take your luggage up and put them in your suite. Just make yourself at home. We're not formal here."

I ran upstairs taking two steps at a time and found Britt lying across the bed asleep. I took her shoes off and covered her with a warm blanket. I then lovingly planted a kiss on her forehead, and before I knew what was happening, she opened her eyes and reciprocated by kissing me on the lips with very passionate kisses and trying to pull me in bed with her.

"Darling, I would love to so much, but we do have guests downstairs. You are still so very sexy-looking even being pregnant."

"I need to get up and go downstairs and do some entertaining. We can't neglect them. What will they think?"

"Britt, our new friends understand. You just went through an emotional trauma to your body. You rest, and I'll wake you for dinner. Herbert is already starting to cook for tonight. We are having a lavish spread of chicken, new small red potatoes, and green vegetables with a nice tossed salad with shrimp. In the meantime, I'm going to take Al and Kristen over to their new home to look around. Herbert somehow got the key for them from the real estate agent that was selling the house. You rest for a couple of hours, and I'll let you know when dinner is being served."

"Edward, I want to spend some romantic time with you. I want to kiss you until you can't take it anymore and, then the best part, be intimate with you all night."

"Sweetheart, we just had two weeks of romance and resting in a very romantic setting with the glorious orange-and-red sunsets glowing into our suite. It was like balls of fire that shone so bright amid the glories of the heavens. Britt, it was spectacular! You are going to wear me out. There won't be anything remaining of me when you get finished. Just a shell of a once-former vibrant man!"

"I need to spend all this time with you now because next week you'll be starting back at the hospital, and I'll not get to see you until late into the night. I guess I could seduce Herbert."

"Now, you see here, my darling wife, I'll not have any of that talk. Are you trying to make me jealous? Because if you are, you're doing a very good job of it. I'm a very jealous man when it pertains to you, and I'm not afraid to admit it. If I ever lost you again, I couldn't take it. I love you so much, Britt, that it hurts when I'm away from you, and now the babies also. I really can't wait to actually get to meet them."

"Sweetheart, you are my pride and joy. You mean everything to me. I pray that these baby girls have your looks, be tall and beautiful like their dear daddy."

"Britt, I need to get downstairs, otherwise I will jump in that bed with you. I want my baby girls to look just like their mommy—beautiful, down-to-earth, and not plastic looking, wearing all kinds of makeup. I'm leaving now and going to the Conway's new home with them. They're so excited to see it, especially Kristen."

"I wanted to see their house also, Edward. Can't I come with you all?"

"You'll get a chance to see it tomorrow, sweetheart."

"Okay, sweetheart. I'll have her show it to me later tonight after dinner. Please let me know when dinner is ready."

"I will, darling. Just rest now."

I left and she closed her eyes and was asleep almost as soon as her head hit the pillow.

Chapter 53

After Edward left the room, I dozed for a couple of hours. When I tried to wake up, I had a hard time trying to open my eyes. I couldn't get my eyes to stay open; my head felt like it weighed a ton, and I felt like I was in the midst of a furnace. It was so hot. I thought that the house must be on fire. I remember Herbert coming into the room to check on me and let me know that dinner was ready, but his voice seemed to be in a distance, and it sounded echoing. He spoke, looked at me, put his hand on my forehead, and just knew I was burning up with a fever. I had felt I was in a twilight zone, drifting in and out of consciousness. I could hear voices, but couldn't open my eyes. What was happening to me this time?

"Mrs. Moore, dinner is almost ready. Are you coming down now? You really don't look so good, and your forehead is so hot. You are burning with a fever. I've got to get Dr. Moore immediately. Be back in a flash, Mrs. Moore. Please hold on."

Herbert ran like lightning to the Conway's new home, calling Edward as he ran. "Edward, can you hear me? You must come at once. Something is terribly wrong with Mrs. Moore. I went to check on her and tell her that dinner would be ready in thirty minutes, and she was sweating. The water was pouring off her. I felt her forehead, and she's burning up with fever. I couldn't get her to awaken. I really think she is unconscious."

"Oh no. she must have an infection of some kind. If we don't get her stable, it could affect the babies."

Edward, Al, and Kristen ran back to the house. Edward took the staircase two steps at a time. He had to get to her fast. They all entered the master suite. Edward and Al both checked her out.

"We don't have time to get her to the hospital. I'll need to administer an antibiotic here. Herbert, can you go to my office and bring me my medical bag? I have some antibiotics that I keep on hand for emergencies. I carry them all the time, and they won't hurt the babies, but I pray it will bring her fever down fast."

While they were standing around waiting for Herbert with Edward's medical bag, Kristen ran into the bathroom and got a towel, went to the kitchen and grabbed ice, wrapped them in the towel and then went back upstairs and started applying the cold towels to Brittney's head to help with the fever.

Herbert returned with the medical bag, while Al then administered the mild antibiotic, as Edward was shaking and Al saw and took the needle from him. He administered it as a shot instead of a pill which wouldn't have been so effective, as she needed it to start taking effect immediately.

"I'm giving her erythromycin in the smallest dose possible that won't hurt the babies but will reduce her fever."

After about a half hour, her breathing seemed calmer, and she was starting to cool down between the ice and the medicine.

"I'll stay with her for a while and keep applying the compresses."

She soon woke up and was feeling much better. She wanted to go to the bathroom, and as she did, started bleeding again. She was screaming, and I knew that something was up.

"Edward, I can't take the pain. Am I losing another baby? I can't, I just can't. I was feeling fine until I stood up. Please help me."

I started to cry fountains of tears, not knowing what was happening to me and the babies. I kept thinking that I wasn't meant to have any children. I dialed 911 and called for the ambulance service, and it came in a matter of fifteen minutes. We rushed her to the Medical Center. Al and Kristen drove behind with Herbert at the wheel. Everyone was very concerned. This time I called the chief of obstetrics, Dr. Carl Lester, who was going to be Britt's obstetrician, to

SOUL MATE

check on her and the babies. I explained what had happened to Britt while on our honeymoon to let him know ahead of time.

We arrived at the ER, and Britt was rushed into the ER room where Carl was waiting for us. I had called ahead and asked that he be there when we brought Britt in. I waited outside in the lobby pacing back and forth with Al and Kristen while Carl examined her and the answer came back.

While we waited in the lobby, Kristen suggested that we hold hands and pray. "Dear Heavenly Father, you are our great Creator, and you know all things and also allow us to endure only what we can. Please be with Brittney tonight and also with the doctor attending her. She has gone through so much in the last couple of weeks that we lift her up to you. We ask that you watch over her and Edward and allow them to keep their dear babies, and your dear children. We ask for guidance in everything that we do in our everyday life for our families. We ask all these things, in your name, amen."

"Kristen, thank you so much. You are both special friends. I'm so glad that we have found you. I really needed that prayer tonight. I sometimes forget what our Savior can do for us and what He does every day of our lives."

Carl returned in a few minutes, and we were allowed to see Britt.

"Brittney, you didn't lose the babies. They are quite active in there, moving around. It was a mild bleeding which sometimes happens. I want you to come back and see me in a month unless you need to see me before, but everything should be fine from here on."

"Britt, sweetheart, how are you feeling?"

"I feel like an inadequate person, first losing the baby boy. It must have been my entire fault. What am I doing, Dr. Lester, that I shouldn't? Other people have babies and don't go through what I have gone through in the last two weeks."

"You are no different than other patients that I see from time to time. Some women can never carry babies and then some have no problems, and then there are a few that have similar problems like you. Everyone is different. Just go home, Brittney, and enjoy being pregnant. I don't foresee anything else happening."

207

"Thank you, Dr. Lester. Please let's go home, Edward. I'm starved."

"That's a good sign."

"Thank you, Carl, for being there. I knew I hired you for a special reason."

"Carl, while I have you here, I would like to introduce you to the latest member of our team here at the hospital. Dr. Al Conway, meet Dr. Carl Lester. Al will be the Chief of Children's Orthopedic Surgery."

"Great to meet you, Al. Welcome aboard. It's the greatest place to work, and the boss is a delightful person."

"Thank you, and I've found that out just by spending time with him and his lovely wife the last two weeks. I'm really looking forward to the change."

Britt was crying again for the one baby that she lost. She hadn't cried too much before. She was mainly in shock. Now it was starting to sink in that maybe she would lose the other two. I joined her, holding her, and we both felt like our family was disappearing before our very eyes.

Carl had told us that it was probably the infection that had caused this bleeding. The infection could have been from the hospital in Costa Rica. It didn't seem too sanitary there. They are not as concerned about things being as sterile as we are in the United States and Canada. Girl babies are stronger, so it did not affect them as much.

Chapter 54

$\{\infty\}$

Four weeks had passed since we had arrived back from our honeymoon in Costa Rica, and now it was getting close to the wedding day of Dr. Greg Drew and his lovely fiancée, Monica. They were getting married in two days, and all the arrangements were being made by Dr. Edward Moore and his wife, Brittney. She was doing most of the telephoning, as she did most everything she could these days sitting down. Edward would barely allow her to do any exercise especially if she had to stand or walk to get it accomplished, but of course when Edward was not at home, she would walk almost every day down the driveway because it was slanted, and it gave her great exercise. She needed the exercise, otherwise the belly fat would never go away after the babies were born. Edward had been treating her like an invalid, but what he didn't know wouldn't hurt him in the least, and Herbert wasn't telling. Edward loved her so much that he couldn't think of anything happening to his beloved Britt. Sometimes Herbert watched to keep track of how she was doing.

She had arranged for the caterers, the flowers and had sent out all and the invitations. It was to be a small wedding with mainly people that Greg worked with at the hospital. These were the only people that Greg was closely related to day after day. Monica didn't have any close relations. She was alone, but she had Edward and Brittney. They were being married at the Van Nuys Country Club, and the reception was planned for there also. There was an announcement put in the paper, but no one knew who put it there, certainly not Edward or Britt, which is something that Greg didn't want because Ashley, his former wife, would find out. He didn't need any trouble, and she could cause much, and she had a mind for it. She was good at things like that.

The RSVPs had all been returned, and now Brittney was scanning through them to make sure that they had the correct guest head count for the seating arrangements. As she was counting, the phone rang. Thinking it was one of the caterers about the food, she answered on the first ring. "Hello, Brittney Moore here. May I help you? Who is calling please?"

"I think you have helped enough and have gone beyond what any person should do, and you know who I am. Everyone blaming me for everything that concerned Edward. Well, I can still say that we were having an affair and still I see him at least twice a week. He still loves me so much. When I see him, he wonders why he ever married you. He visits me whenever he can get away from you. He says you keep him on a leash and feels like you are strangling him. Now that you are pregnant, he has to get away from you more. He also said that these babies should be mine and maybe they will be as soon as we can get rid of you. We have the most wonderful romantic love affair that anyone has ever known. Now I see that you have gone behind my back and set my husband up with a mere housekeeper. Is she even human? She looks like a dog. I will be at that wedding, and I will stop it. Greg will never have a chance to remarry anyone as long as I am around. I am still his wife and always will be. Divorce is not a word in my vocabulary. He may have divorced me, but he is still mine. He still loves me. He told me so yesterday when I called him. We were and married for life.

"I will get back at you, just wait and see. Sometimes when you're not looking, so you better hide. I see you daily walking in the driveway. Maybe I will just get your babies instead, since they should be mine and Edward's, not yours. I will stop this wedding, and I'll say again that I will be there. No one will stop me. Greg wouldn't give me any babies as I wanted. I have lots of connections out there still. My friends still love me since I set up all kinds of dates for them with gorgeous women. Just you wait and see, missy. Ha ha."

Ashley hung up the phone, and I screamed. "Nooooooooooooo ooooooooooooooooo. Edward, where are you? Please help me!"

I hung up the phone on her, and Edward came running. My hands were shaking as I tried to put the phone down. I actually dropped it. He thought that I was bleeding again. He saw the look on my face. I was white with terror. All the blood had drained from my face, and I was shaking. I told him exactly what Ashley had said and since he records all calls coming in, he also listened to the words on the tape recorder. I was scared. She had been watching our every move. She must follow us wherever we go. I immediately started crying after hearing the words again. I finally had to tell Edward about my walking down the driveway since she had mentioned on the recording that she saw me.

"I promise that I won't walk down the driveway anymore in case she is watching. Oh, Edward, what are we going to do? I am so scared of her and her accusations about both of you together. I know you haven't been with her because we have been together at all times. I trust you, darling."

Edward called Greg and told him to come to the house immediately telling him it was an emergency. As soon as he arrived, Edward replayed the tape for him, and he was astonished. "Edward, Brittney must be terrified. I need to stop this now. I'm calling her psychiatrist and have him commit her somewhere. She has gone off the deep end and has turned into a complete maniac. I really don't trust her anymore being out there. She could really harm Brittney and now Monica, especially after we are married. I don't want Monica to know about this tape. She may get too scared to get married fearing for me. I haven't talked to Ashley, and she can't call me, especially since I changed all the phone numbers, and they are all unlisted."

"I think you are doing the right thing, Greg, for Monica's sake and sanity."

Greg called Ashley's psychiatrist, and he fully agreed with Greg. He called back within an hour and told Greg that they had committed her to a hospital for the mentally impaired that afternoon before she had a chance to go anywhere. She went kicking and screaming. She needed help. She is a very manipulative person.

In the meantime, Edward had been calming Britt down telling her that everything was all lies, except for the part about seeing her walking. From now until the babies were born, she would walk in the backyard and swim in the pool.

"Britt, don't worry your sweet head. Greg has called her psychiatrist and her family, and at this very minute, she is being committed to a mental institution for an indefinite period of time. I love you, sweetheart, and would never allow anyone to get that close to you to hurt you ever again, especially Ashley. Please don't believe anything that she has told you. She is lying to get back at me. I would never do anything to hurt you or our precious babies. You must believe that. I truly love you more than my life."

"Thank you, honey. I needed to just hear it from you. I love you. Now you can allow me to get back to work here or there won't be a wedding."

Chapter 55

The day of Greg and Monica's wedding was finally here, and I was as excited as they were, as if Edward and I was getting married all over again. I just loved weddings, especially for two people who truly love each other and are soul mates. There are couples who are destined to be together, like Greg and Monica, and then there are some couples who are never meant to be together and never should, and that was definitely Greg and Ashley.

Edward had bought me a new dress for the wedding that would fit me perfectly, especially for my growing stomach. I looked like a beached whale, at least to me. Edward on the other hand still looked his suave and debonair self in his black tuxedo. I wanted to attack him with kisses. He was so handsome. I still had a hard time thinking that he was all mine. How could he love someone like me, a nobody from a backwoods town, as Ashley put it? How could I think of her today, but in a way I felt sorry for her? She had had so much and lost it all, even her mind. She lost a great man because of her manipulating, yet I was so happy that Greg found a person who will love him unconditionally for the remainder of their lives.

The wedding was beautiful, and they had the same pastor that we were married by. Monica looked gorgeous in a long white gown, low on the shoulders and a long train in the back. Her veil was long and draped over a crown of crystals. They sparkled in the sun as it streamed in through the windows as if telling them that everything today was right in their world. Even at her age, she looked like a princess.

"Greg Drew, please hold your bride's hands. Do you, Greg Drew, take Monica Mason to be your wife? Do you promise to love, honor, cherish and protect her, forsaking all others and holding only unto her as long as you both shall live?"

"I, Greg Drew, take thee Monica Mason, to be my wife. To have and to hold from this day forward, in sickness and in health, for richer or for poorer, to love and to cherish, till death do us part, according to God's holy ordinance, and thereto I pledge thee my faith and abiding love. With this ring, I thee wed, all my love, I do thee give."

"Monica Mason, please hold your groom's hands. Do you, Monica Mason, take Greg Drew to be your husband? Do you promise to love, honor, cherish, and protect him, forsaking all others and holding only unto him as long as you both shall live?"

"I, Monica Mason, take thee, Greg Drew, to be my husband. To have and to hold from this day forward, in sickness and in health, for richer or for poorer, to love and to cherish, till death do us part, according to God's holy ordinance, and thereto I pledge thee my faith and abiding love. With this ring, I thee wed, all my love, I do thee give."

"I now present to the entire crowd gathered here today Mr. and Mrs. Greg Drew."

All of a sudden, in the back of the room, came this very distinct voice that spoke up. The person was dressed in black and had a veil over her face.

"You cannot marry that lowdown person because you are still married to me. I am your wife. I don't care what the divorce papers specify about us. I love you, Greg, and always will. I will haunt you and that cheap dog of a person continuously. You may never know when or where I will pop up like today. Please get away from my husband, you manipulating person. He is mine, all mine and forever will be."

She started to walk to the front of the aisle to confront the pastor about marrying someone who was already married, but as she did was confronted by Edward and some other men. The hospital was contacted, and they had been trying to find her all day, and they realized that her ex-husband was getting remarried today and made a dash for the ceremony to nab her. According to the doctor, she would be confined to a cell for a long time, and the person whom she manipulated to let her go to a wedding today had already been fired. She was given a sedative and then led away.

"I am so sorry, Monica. This is your day, and this happened to spoil it. I love you so much and will always. You mean the world to me, and I will never let anything come between us."

"Greg, you are so wonderful. I don't blame you for what happened today. You put her away for her own safety and didn't know that she would find a way to get out. She didn't spoil anything. The best is yet to come. I love you, sweetheart, and always will."

The wedding continued as if nothing happened with all the festivities.

Monica had never been married before and looked beautiful, all smiles, but underneath was a mass of jelly, so nervous. Greg looked as nervous as if this was his first marriage, but here they were, finally married to each other, soul mates together. Greg had told Edward that he never felt so nervous in all his life. After the celebration with their friends, they were flying to Paris for a month on their honeymoon. Greg and Monica loved each other with all their heart and soul, and as Greg told it, he wanted Monica to have the very best and then told us that he hoped that Monica would be pregnant by the time they arrived back to the United States.

Chapter 56

I was beginning to get bigger and bigger with each new passing day. The nine months would be here before I knew it, but not soon enough for me. It seemed like I had been pregnant for a year. Time just dragged. I started to get irritable and started yelling at Edward for no apparent reason whatsoever. I just couldn't seem to stop myself. I would blame him for everything, even the shape I was in.

Al and Kristen had finally moved into their new home about four months ago, and so I had a new friend next door that I confided in daily when I needed help controlling my temper.

Edward had decided that he was not going to work such long hours until after the babies were born. Things were happening to Britt, which he needed to be around her to supply her with all the love he could give her. He wanted to go through all this with her himself.

Every time that Edward went to work, I found it difficult not to be jealous. Why was I like this? He loved me, he told me so, but these were only words, and the tongue is like a two-edged sword. I still got a knot in my stomach when he left, and I still acted like a jealous fool whenever I imagined him examining all these gorgeous plastic women, slim and curvy. Three days a week he worked the longest hours and would never arrive back home until almost midnight. I was so upset that I would cry myself to sleep, and instead of sleeping in our king-size bed in our suite, I would go to one of the guest rooms and sleep. What was happening to me? Why was I like this?

"Britt, you need to start sleeping in our bedroom. I'm finding it very difficult carrying you to our bed every night, even with all my muscles. Why do you do it?"

"I'm so jealous, and when you are at the hospital and away from me, all I can think about are those plastic girls that you are examining, lying there on the examination table, mostly half clothed. You keep telling me that you love me, but I can't seem to get it through my head that you really do, especially now with the way I look. Also, Edward, why am I getting so huge? I have seen pregnant ladies before, and they are not as huge as I'm getting. The doctor says that I'm fine, but I'll never be able to lose all this extra weight after delivery. I should maybe stop eating, don't you think?"

"No, you shouldn't, but maybe a healthier diet for the next few weeks, maybe more salads and plenty of fruit."

"I have an appointment with Dr. Lester again this afternoon, and he'll tell me if I'm ready for the delivery of these babies. I feel so unsexy. You must hate the way I look, even I don't like me for looking this fat. I love these babies, but everything else makes me uncomfortable and not the way I should look for my husband."

"I'm going to your appointment with you this afternoon. I want to know how everything is with our baby girls. I think you are even sexier knowing that you are carrying a part of each of us that we have created out of our love for one another. Please believe me, I love you more and more every day that I spend with you. As I look back on my prior years, I can't imagine what I did without you in my life."

"That's just talk. You love the babies now and not me. They're the most important things in your life right now. You wanted a nice warm body to lie with who could give you a family. I'm nothing but a human baby machine, that's all I am. Oh, Edward, what did I just accuse you of, what is wrong with me? I didn't mean any of those things. I'm so sorry, Edward. Please forgive me."

I started to cry, and Edward came to me and surrounded me in his most loving arms that I love so much. "There is nothing to forgive. Your hormones are going crazy in your body, especially now that you are getting near to the delivery date."

After having a variety of salads for lunch, they packed up and drove to the Van Nuys Medical Center for Brittney's appointment with Dr. Carl Lester. They arrived there in plenty of time to see the doctor, and he was waiting for them with smiles.

"How are we all feeling today, Moore family?"

"How does everything look, Carl?"

"Everything looks great, Edward. We're planning another ultrasound to check the babies before sending you home."

"Brittney, you started out with three, and as of this moment, you still have the two baby girls. I'm sorry about the baby boy, but it was all for a reason that it happened. We don't know why, but we will know when you get to meet him in heaven. I didn't want to tell you before in case something happened, but you are now ready to have them any day now. The second lot of bleeding was just what I told you, minor bleeding, which sometimes happens. You didn't lose another baby. There are definitely two girls in there from what we can see, and they are very lively and fairly big from what I see."

"This is just great, Britt. We now need to go home and order another crib and all the necessities. They will be daddy's little girls. I'm so happy, Britt. Are you happy, sweetheart?"

Chapter 57

We walked out of Dr. Lester's office at the Medical Center. He helped me into my seat and even buckled my seat belt for me. With Edward at the wheel, we drove home happy. Edward was all smiles, and I couldn't help smiling myself. Edward decided to stay home for the next week in case I went into labor.

When we arrived home, I went into Edward's office and telephoned the baby store and ordered another crib and made sure that the entire order of two cribs would be delivered that same afternoon. I wanted to be able to have both cribs set up while Edward was home with me and to be able to make the room cute, particularly for baby girls. Both cribs that I ordered were white, one with pink borders and the other with purple borders. Everything had to match. Edward said he wanted to be involved, so he would put the cribs together. I also ordered all the linens with both cribs to have firm mattresses. The cribs also converted into toddler beds and then junior beds, which was cheaper in the long run than having to buy all these different size beds. The two beds would represent the two girls having their own individual identity.

"Britt, we have forgotten something which I think we should sit down and decide upon."

"What is that, my love? I think we have everything."

"We haven't decided on names for the girls."

"How careless of me! We don't want to call them baby one and baby two. Okay, let's decide right this minute. Edward, you name one, and I'll name one. Agreed?"

"Agreed."

"I have been thinking about names now for a couple of weeks, and I think I have set my sights on a great name."

"What is it? Please tell me."

"I would like to call one Kiera Morgan. What do you think? Do you like it? It's partly Celtic."

"I just love it. A beautiful name for a beautiful girl. I would like the other name Kasey Moira. Do you love that name? I think we can accommodate them being a twin by giving them each a different name because they will have different personalities."

"I never thought of that, but I think that is absolutely the perfect solution. You are so smart. So now we have another hurdle accomplished. Both names are beautiful, and I'm sure as they grow up, they will like them also. Most kids hate their names as they get to be teenagers."

Chapter 58

Edward was in his study working on some hospital paperwork as he usually was these days and keeping communications going between himself and some of the other doctors at the hospital, knowing that he would be home for a while with me.

I started to feel out of sorts in my stomach, not aching or any pain, but just a little queasiness. I didn't say anything to Edward as I felt that it might upset him, and he would then try to talk me into going back to the hospital, although I probably should. I really didn't want to bother him about every little ache and pain. I didn't want to complain anymore to Edward especially also he needed some peace and quiet for an hour or two. He hadn't gotten much sleep in the last month, although he never complained. Since he owned the Medical Center, he seemed to have more work than some of the other staff doctors, even the administrator. Besides the day-to-day patients, he was still involved in the daily routine of the hospital functions with Alicia's help. I don't know what Edward would do without her taking care of day-to-day activity in the office. Alicia was a big asset for Edward at the hospital, and she never complained about the work. She seemed to enjoy it.

Herbert had prepared lunch for both of us at noon, turkey sandwiches with a tall glass of milk. I just couldn't bring myself to eat not even a morsel. I wasn't sick, just really felt strange, and of course, Edward noticed immediately that I wasn't eating, and so he wanted to know why I hadn't touched my sandwich. I just sat there staring at the food, whereas before I was pregnant, I would have devoured everything on my plate.

"Britt, you have to eat something to keep up your strength. You will need all your strength to deliver two babies."

Chapter 59

"I didn't want to upset you, but I feel a little weird, Edward, in my stomach, maybe just because I had an internal examination today."

"What kind of weird?"

"It's hard to describe, not like being sick, but an incredible amount of movement and almost like swishing around. It's just not what I have been feeling before. This is completely different, almost like the babies are getting ready for their journey into this world."

"I would have to say that you are starting the labor process, my darling. You probably have quite a few hours yet to go before it gets to be really hard labor, but I will be by your side the entire time, sweetheart."

"I don't want to go back to the Medical Center immediately. Can I wait for a while?"

"We can wait a little while, but if the pain starts to increase in intensity, then I will put you in the car, and we drive. Okay? The first babies usually take a few hours, and since you are delivering two, it may take longer."

"Why can't I stay at home and have them, Edward? Can't you deliver them? I really don't like being in the hospital. I have spent so much time in the hospital this year that I feel every time when I enter, something bad happens."

"Because Carl is at the hospital, and I don't think he will drive out here to deliver them. I can deliver them, but it has been many years since I have delivered a baby, and you are talking about delivering two. I don't have the necessary equipment that I might need, and it is not ethical for a husband to deliver his own babies, unless if there was an emergency, and we couldn't make it to the hospital. Is that your wish, Britt?"

"I really want you to deliver your children. It would mean the world to me. You participated in the start, and I would like for you to participate in the end." I was smiling, and Edward's face turned beet red. "Don't be embarrassed, Edward. There is nothing to be embarrassed about. You are a doctor, and you know how babies are created." I was laughing when I had finished saying these words. It was so funny to see Edward get so embarrassed.

"All right, my darling wife. I can get all the equipment I need from the hospital. I will make a list and send Herbert to the hospital and talk to Carl, whom I will call beforehand. I will do it immediately, this way he will be back in plenty of time."

Edward made out the list, and then Herbert headed out the door to the hospital, and as he did, he stood there for a second and stared at us both, shaking his head and smiling. "I guess you really do want to deliver the babies if you would do this for me. I love you, sweetheart. You are going to make the best dad to our dear daughters."

"I really do want to deliver them, only I didn't want to tell you."

A couple of intense hours went by, and then I heard Herbert pulling up in the driveway with everything that Edward had requested from Carl at the Medical Center. While Edward had Herbert help him with all the items, Edward requested something of me. "Britt, I need for you to walk around as much as you can. It will help to bring on labor, and the exercise will do you good. Maybe walk around outdoors and walk over and see Kristen for a while. Maybe she will walk with you."

I thought that was a great idea so that I could take my mind off the pain, and Kristen had already gone through a delivery, so she knew what I was going through at the moment. I walked over to her house along the walkway between our homes. It was wonderful having a best friend so close. She was delighted to go walking outside, while her nanny watched after her baby girl, Amelia.

We left Kristen's home, and she grabbed her phone, in case of an emergency, as we were going out the door. We walked about thirty minutes when I thought I was about to drop something. I stopped and held onto my stomach.

"Are you in more pain, Brittney? I think we should start back home."

"Kristen, I think I need to get back home as soon as possible. The pain is getting harder. I need Edward. I feel as if I need to use the bathroom."

"We need to time the contractions on the way back. I'm calling Edward. It's a good thing I remembered to take my phone with us. Brittney, just don't push, or you'll be having the baby here on the sidewalk."

"Edward, it's Kristen. Brittney's in hard labor. You need to come immediately and pick us up. Just a second, she's having another contraction. Let me time it."

"Now, Edward. I need you now."

"Brittney, breathe through it. Little puffs."

"It's over."

"Edward, they're coming every two minutes. We better get her home as soon as possible."

"I'll be there in a minute, I'm on the way. Are you on Oak Street?"

"Yes. Hurry!"

Edward rushed to us in record time and got Brittney in the car, then quickly drove back to the house. "Britt, I need to get you upstairs in bed. We'll put you in the small guest room for this undertaking. Kristen, can you stay? I may need some help."

"I can be here as long as you need me. I'll call the nanny to let her know, and then she can convey to Al what is happening when he gets home and where I am."

Edward picked Britt up in his arms as if she were as light as a feather. He was so strong, but his adrenaline was flowing on high. He carried her up the winding staircase, into the small guest bedroom, which wasn't as small as anyone would consider small, and laid her in the bed. Kristen removed her clothes and draped her with a plain white sheet. Britt was so hot and was perspiring profusely. Kristen put the blood pressure cuff on her to monitor whether her pressure was being elevated too high. The pains were coming closer and closer together now, and Brittney couldn't help but scream. She was still sweating profusely and getting so tired.

Kristen went to the bathroom and wetted some towels to keep Brittney cool. She kept wiping her forehead and kept talking to her to keep her awake. Since the time that Edward carried her upstairs, two hours had passed. It was hard to believe. Time was just flying by.

Brittney wanted medication, but Edward told her that she was too far along for any medication to work, and he needed her to be wide awake. Kristen kept soothing her as she knew what Brittney was going through, since she had gone through the same thing only a short time ago, and how it was when she delivered her daughter only a while ago. Kristen also kept brushing Brittney's hairs back with her hand to soothe her and calm her.

"Edward, how long is it going to take? I am so tired. I want to sleep. It's already been hours."

"It shouldn't be that much longer now, Britt. Please hold on. Try not to close your eyes. I need you awake to push."

"Breathe, Brittney, little puffs. I remember what it was like. I'll stay with you, and you can squeeze my hand with every contraction. It really helps. Scream as much as you want. It helps, believe me. No man really can understand the pain that women go through having a baby."

"Thank you, Kristen. I'm so glad you're my dearest friend."

There were so many tears falling down the sides of her face. She was in so much pain. I was probably the only person in the room that understood her pain, but then I looked at Edward, and I could see the tears on his face. He felt so horrible that only Britt was going through this, but it was almost like he could feel her pain, and he sympathized with her, knowing that she was his wife. Edward checked Brittney out again and said that the head was crowning.

"Okay, Britt, this is it. On your next contraction, start pushing. Again, now. Here comes our first baby girl. Kristen, can you take her and weigh her before the next one enters this world?"

Kristen took the baby and wrapped her in a blanket and put her in the bassinette under a warm heat lamp. She had already weighed her, and her eyes couldn't believe the weight.

"She's 7 lbs. 14 ozs. Quite a big girl."

"Thanks, Kristen. Britt, on the next contraction, start pushing again. Okay, Britt, push again now."

"I'm so tired, Edward. I can't do it. I just want to sleep."

This baby was being stubborn. She didn't want to be born. Britt was too tired to push, and she seemed like she hadn't any life left in her.

"Britt, darling, you have to push when I tell you, only one more push. Now! Here she is! Our other baby girl. Let's get her weighed."

"Edward, she's 7 lbs. 12 ozs. What big girls. No wonder, Brittney, that you were so big. They look very healthy. You fed them really well."

"Are you feeling okay, Britt?"

"Just sooooooooooooooooooooo tired." With those few words, she fell asleep.

Edward and Kristen cleaned Brittney up, and Edward stitched her as she had torn some from the big girls. Edward then went downstairs and called the ambulance to get them to come and transport all three of them to the Medical Center to be checked out and for much-needed rest for Brittney. The babies were beautiful with full heads of hair.

"Thank you, Kristen, for being here today. I couldn't have done it alone. You are such a great friend, and I know Britt really appreciated your being here." Edward was so tired. He sat there with his head in his hands.

"You look exhausted, Edward. You did a great job, especially being the husband. I can't imagine Al doing what you did here today. I'm so very glad I could be here for both of you."

"The ambulance will be here in a few minutes, and we'll take her and the babies to the Medical Center for a few days. I'm exhausted, but I will grab a ride back with Al, if you can call him for me."

"I'll be glad to. I'm so glad to have been here for you both. You're two of our closest and dearest friends.

Chapter 60

The ambulance arrived within the hour, and Britt and the girls were loaded aboard to be transported to the Van Nuys Medical Center to be examined by Dr. Lester and then to stay for a few days for rest.

I drove in the ambulance with them being so exhausted, but my adrenalin was so high I could have stayed awake for another few hours. I wanted to be sure that Britt and the girls were feeling fine before getting a ride back home with Al, who now was a great friend and doctor living next door. No way was this a coincidence, but the Lord was working in all of this from the time we arrived at Costa Rica and met them.

Chapter 61

B ritt was put in a private room on the OB-GYN floor. The girls were put in the nursey until Britt received a lot of rest after what she had just gone through. She was exhausted, and then the girls would be put in the room with her.

I heard Britt crying as I neared her room.

"Britt, what's wrong sweetheart? Are you in any pain? Carl checked you out and said that you're healthy and that we have two wonderful, beautiful and healthy girls."

"I was just thinking about our baby boy who didn't survive. I feel as if I did something wrong. How could I have brought two baby girls into this world, but not him? You must hate me because he was the only boy and usually a man would like a son to carry on his name. Now you will hate me for the remainder of my life. You may not say so, but I'm sure in the back of your mind you really do."

"Britt, I wouldn't mind having ten girls if they were all like you. Just so everyone is healthy. It just wasn't meant to be. I could never hate you; you are the love of my life. It wasn't in God's hand to give us a son at this particular time. I told you that they would be daddy's little girls. I love the thought of being called daddy. What do you think mommy?"

"Whatever!"

"Sweetheart, I'm leaving for a while to get some rest and you need your rest. I know you must be exhausted. I'll be back in about four hours. Get a little sleep before they bring them in the room, and you have to nurse them."

I kissed Britt and then left. I stopped by the nursery to visit my darling daughters. The nurses were approaching me and congratulating me on the arrival of the girls. The girls were the image of Britt. They had full heads of hair, and their skin was so soft and they smelled so wonderful. I held each one, and it was so perfect. My children! I was so proud of them and of having Britt as my wife and giving me such great babies.

After I left the nursery, I returned to my office to wait for Al to end his shift. I needed sleep because from now until they were grown, I guessed I would never have any, always worrying about them, where they were and who they were with.

After a few hours, I went back to see Britt, and the nurses had moved the girls already into her room. We were a family now. Britt woke up and was starting to learn how to nurse them.

"When can we take them home?"

"In a couple of days, sweetheart. Please get some rest first because when you get home, you won't get much rest after taking care of the girls and also a husband who just adores you. I have never loved anyone as much as I love you at this very moment being here together with my family. Britt, we are a family now. Also, I wanted to let you know that before you come home, I need to trade in the Maserati and get a family car that can hold two car seats in the back. I'm thinking of getting a Mercedes or Lincoln SUV. They have to be safe vehicles to carry my family."

"Please don't trade-in your car. Take mine and trade it in. It has never been driven. I think the Mercedes SUV will be just perfect for our family. You can still use the Maserati to drive back and forth to the hospital, and I can drive the SUV. How about buying a black one with a beige interior?"

Chapter 62

"Britt, you will be able to go home in a couple of days after the healing process. I need to go and buy two car seats, the car to put them in, and also a double stroller for taking long walks along the shoreline. I don't know why I've waited for so long in doing these things. I should have bought those months ago. I can't wait to take walks on the beach with all of us together. I can show off my accomplishments."

"What do you mean your accomplishments? I guess I had nothing to do with this pregnancy. Were you the one who carried these big girls for nine months? Did you go through all the labor pains?"

Britt was starting to get upset. She was yelling at me for no apparent reason. I had never seen her ever before raise her voice in all the time that I have known her. What was the matter with her? Was she upset because now she had babies to look after? I guessed she was so tired after the delivery, and it would take her a few days to return to normal.

"Darling, for a man saying this, you must know what I mean. Men make it a huge accomplishment especially since I produced two beautiful girls. They'll say that I'm very virile. I never ever thought that I would have a wife, let alone a family."

"You produced these girls. There you go again. It is all about you, what you have accomplished. Maybe I won't ever want to come home, at least with you since you are such a braggart."

Here, Britt was yelling again. I was afraid to speak in case of saying the wrong things. Then all of a sudden, she was back to her old self.

"I know you are very virile. I can't wait to get you home again and be with my wonderful husband. How I've missed you since I was too big to have any kind of relations with you, but you better watch out now since I am ready and able."

"How I love you, my darling. You have made me all my dreams come true. I never thought I would ever have a wife who fulfills all my desires and happiness and now have given me, not one but two beautiful children, especially at my age, and here I have always told everyone that I would always be a confirmed bachelor."

"And I also, my sweet husband, after having been told years ago that I could never have children and then to be given two at once. I couldn't have asked for anything more precious than this. Edward, we have been truly blessed indeed."

Chapter 63

It was now three days since Britt had given birth to our two beautiful daughters, and now all four of us were headed home to Monterey Bay. A new Mercedes SUV, black of course, had been purchased, and now the twins were in their new car seats in the back seat. Edward couldn't wait to be home caring for his new family. He had taken a couple of weeks off from work to spend with Britt and the girls to help with the everyday routine.

It was a true miracle for him, not ever thinking that he would find a soul mate, especially when he wasn't even looking at the time, but had stumbled across her on a cliff overlooking the raging waters of the Atlantic Ocean thinking that she was going to jump in and commit suicide, whereas she was only enjoying the beautiful surroundings of her homeland.

Here he was, a confirmed bachelor, now married with a family. He was driving very cautiously down the highway toward home, smiling to himself and so aesthetically happy thinking that here he was married to the most beautiful, wonderful woman and now with a family. How could he have so much love poured out onto him in the last year? God was certainly looking down upon him, and from here on, he would give Him thanks for all the blessings received.

Britt was very quiet in the seat beside him. Almost too quiet. Why wasn't she bubbling over with joy as him? He was thinking to himself if maybe he should have left her in the hospital for another couple of days with the trauma of delivering two large babies. Usually, all mothers were overjoyed with having a baby.

"Britt, darling, are you feeling up to going home? You're so quiet, not at all like you were when you were in the hospital and you wanted to go home. Maybe I should have left you there for a few more days of rest. You won't receive much rest at home with the two girls to feed, change, and look after and also look after me."

"I'm fine! I should be back to my old self, whoever that is, in two or three days."

"What are you talking about, Britt? You know who you are. You are starting to scare me, sweetheart. You're my wife and now a mother with not one but two new babies. I love all three of you more than anything in this world. I pray that, you know that."

"I guess I am who you say I am, although I won't be getting much loving from you in the near future because now I have to share you with two other girls."

"Britt, are you telling me that you are jealous of your very own daughters? How can you even speak those words? They are little replicas of both of us. We have a great deal of love for each other, at least I do for you. No one can ever replace you. I have more love to go around than I ever knew I could produce."

Britt started to cry, just sitting there in the car, for no apparent reason. They were sobs that turned into rivers of tears, just streaming down her face. The girls were asleep in the back, and here Britt was like a baby crying her eyes out, as if her whole world was about to end. I reached across the armrest to soothe her, and she immediately pulled away from me. That was something that she had never done before as long as we had been married, whereas before, she couldn't get enough of me being with her. What was happening?

"Let's get you home for a little rest. I've hired a nanny to look after the girls until you get back on your feet enough to care for them. I know you never wanted a nanny, but I definitely think under the circumstances, it is the perfect idea in the long run. Kristen and Al have a nanny, and it seems to be working out fine for them."

"Thank you, Edward. Whatever you decide will be fine with me. You make the decisions."

The remaining leg of the ride home, Britt slept as well as the girls. On arriving home, she immediately went to bed. She didn't even bother with helping me carry the girls into the house, so I took each of them and carried them up to the nursery where the nanny, Mrs. Carrier, was waiting for them. She had arranged each of the cribs perfectly with the colors of a purple and a pink.

"Mrs. Carrier, at the moment, my wife is resting. When the girls are each ready for their individual feeding, which should be soon, just let me know."

"Of course, sir. I will tap on your door."

I needed rest myself, so I entered Britt's and my bedroom and lay on the bed beside her. I thought that she was asleep, but as soon as I lay down, she reached over and pulled herself nearer to me. She wanted to start something, and I refused, which started her getting mad at me, yelling and screaming.

"Britt, the nanny may enter in any moment, and she may find us in a very compromising position if you don't stop it."

"Why will she enter in here? She hasn't any reason to enter our bedroom. Let her stay in the nursery where she belongs. I will demand that she stay there. I want you, Edward, and I mean now."

"Britt, you have to feed the girls as soon as they awaken. You've been nursing them in the hospital, haven't you?"

"Yes, I have. Now I think I will buy formula for them. It's too much trouble to nurse two babies, and I will start to look like an old cow. This way, the nanny can feed them or maybe you can. This way, I'm completely out of the picture, and I can take care of my body to get it back in shape."

I jumped out of bed and went to my study. I was so mad that I could have had steam coming out of my ears. I was so upset with Britt with what she had just said and that I witnessed her saying. I couldn't believe it. She was like a completely different person. I had to talk to someone, so I called Greg. He was my best friend, and I could tell him anything. I called him and explained how Britt was acting and what she was saying about the girls. I was ready to break down and cry.

"Greg, please help me. I know I'm a doctor, but right at this moment, I can't think straight."

"Edward, it sounds to me like she may be on the verge of post-partum depression or postpartum psychosis. She just delivered two babies, and then the trauma of losing the one before. It may just be catching up with her. Her mind can't adjust to the entire trauma."

"She's been completely ignoring the girls and doesn't even want to nurse them anymore. She's very moody and has become very jealous of the girls taking me away from her. I know all the symptoms of both postpartum depression and postpartum psychosis. I guess I never thought that Britt would have them."

"I think being so close to Britt is making it hard for you to think that she could have either one of these, but now that you think about it, Edward, I would get her to see Carl as soon as possible. He is her doctor, correct? That is why we normally shouldn't diagnose any one from our family. We are just too close to them and would never think that they could have something wrong."

"Yes. I don't think she'll go to see him, but I may get him to come out here to just watch and observe her. Maybe he can then prescribe something to help her. Well, enough about us, Greg, how was your honeymoon in Paris?"

"Edward, I now understand the way you felt. It was like something from a fairy tale. What a difference being with Monica than being with Ashley. I never knew how great love can be when you're with the right person. I made the correct decision, and I want to truly thank you for being there and making me talk to her when I did, otherwise I would have missed out on the greatest experience and would still be alone with no one to love."

Chapter 64

I immediately called Carl and invited him and his wife to dinner for the following evening. I explained what I needed, and he agreed that he could do it very discreetly without Britt really knowing. I also invited Greg and Monica, and Al and Kristen. Everyone accepted without reservation. I thought Britt would like to see Greg and Monica and hear all about their glorious honeymoon to Paris. Herbert was committed to start cooking the day before as a surprise for Britt. It was going to be one of her most delicious meals of various seafood and varieties of salads.

I went back upstairs to tell Britt about the party the following evening. It was nothing formal, just a get-together with colleagues and old friends. "Britt, I've invited some friends for a dinner party tomorrow evening. There will be only Al and Kristen next door and then Greg and Monica, since we haven't seen them since their wedding, and then Carl Lester and his wife, Bridgette. I thought that it would be good for you to be around friends, and everyone is longing to see the girls. You have always enjoyed being with Greg and Monica. What do you think, sweetheart?"

"I think that would be a great idea, although you could have asked me first. I don't like surprises thrown at me on a moment's notice."

"Britt, you have always loved surprises, especially when I surprised you with where we would go on our honeymoon and then meeting Al and Kristen. Didn't you enjoy yourself?"

"I was pregnant. How did you think I could enjoy myself and then losing my son?"

"I lose our son also. Did you not think that I was hurting inside? Did you even think of me back then?"

I had to get up and walk away before I said something I would regret. I loved Britt and always would, but she was getting worse. Carl was bringing some medication with him tomorrow night as he knew exactly what was happening to Britt. I sat in my office and sobbed, knowing that was not the Britt I had married eleven months ago.

Britt had followed me downstairs and saw the tears. "Edward, what is wrong? Did I say something that I shouldn't have said? I love you and the girls more than anything. I would never want to hurt you or them in anyway, but I feel I have wronged you, otherwise why are you there crying?" I went to Edward's side and put my arms around him and hugged him.

"Edward, the weather is so warm, and I need some sun, so I thought I would like to take the girls out in the stroller for a pleasant walk along the beach. Do you think that would be okay with you?"

"I think that would be a great idea. Do you want me to come with you? We could walk as a family."

"No, you stay here and get some work done. I know I have been so much trouble lately. I want to spend some time with the girls alone as I seem to be neglecting them. Before you know it, they'll be gone."

"They're just babies. It'll be a few years before they'll be off to college. We'll have them around for at least another eighteen years and maybe longer."

"You never know what can happen, Edward."

I started to get scared of the things that she was saying. Nothing she said made any sense. I ran to my study and called Kristen next door praying that she was home and that she could maybe help. I explained what I thought was happening to Britt.

"Edward, this same thing happened to me until Al got me to a doctor, who gave me medication. I know exactly how she feels and not knowing sometimes that she is saying and doing things that are not normal. They seem normal to her, but she doesn't realize that she is saying all these hurtful things."

"Kristen, do you think you could go walking with Britt just to have someone looking out for her?"

"I will be there immediately to see if Brittney wants to go walking along the beach with us."

Almost immediately, Kristen was at the back door. I opened the door to her knock. "Hi, Kristen. What are you up to today? This is a surprise, and you've brought Amelia with you. Come in, please. Britt is in the living room getting the girls ready to go for a walk. It's a beautiful day outside."

"I thought I would go walking, and I immediately thought about Brittney and wondered if she would like to go also."

She entered in the living room and hugged Brittney. "Kristen, have you been out walking?"

"Not yet. I thought maybe you would like to walk along the beach with us. Would you like to go walking together? It's a beautiful day outside, and maybe after the walk, we can have lunch at the wharf."

"I really wanted to go by myself. I haven't spent much time with the girls, and I feel like I have been neglecting them."

"Okay, if that's what you want."

"Thank you, Kristen. Another day maybe."

Kristen hurried toward the back door and slipped into Edward's office unnoticed from Brittney. She closed the door behind her so Brittney could not hear the exchange of words concerning her.

"Kristen, aren't you going walking with Britt?"

"Edward, she actually told me not to go with her. I recognize all the symptoms from myself, and she is in bad shape, especially her mental condition. I'm thinking of following her without her noticing me. I will keep you informed of where she is headed and what she is doing or thinking of doing. What do you think?"

"That sounds perfect. I'll keep my phone next to me. Please call me immediately if anything at all seems out of the normal. In the meantime, I'm calling Carl Lester, her obstetrician, to get him to call in a prescription for her to start taking immediately."

"I will. I need to get moving because Brittney has already left the house. I'll call you if I see anything out of the ordinary. Everything will get better, Edward, don't worry. With all of us looking out for her, she is well-loved."

I left Edward and Brittney's house and kept a good pace behind Brittney. She was walking normally and sounded as if she was talking to the girls. I couldn't hear what she was talking to them about, but as long as I stayed closed by, I could keep her under surveillance for Edward. She made a turn toward the wharf, and I knew immediately she was headed to the edge of the pier. I called Edward ASAP, and he immediately picked up.

"Edward, Brittney is walking out to the edge of the pier. I'm scared. I don't know what to do. I don't want to scare her, and there isn't any place for her to sit down there."

"Don't worry. I'm almost there."

Almost as fast as I hung up the phone with Edward, he was there. Brittney was lifting on of the girls and walking to the pier's edge, and she held the baby out over the water. Edward ran and grabbed her and the baby before she knew what was happening.

"What are you doing, Britt?"

"The girls wanted to go swimming. They love the water so much, and the weather is so perfect."

"Britt, they're only babies, they can't swim."

"Edward, they're eighteen. I was going to go swimming with them."

"Let's go home, Britt. I called Carl, and he called in a prescription for you, and we'll stop at the pharmacy on our way home. You will be back to normal in no time."

We drove to the pharmacy and picked up the prescription. I then took Britt home and put her to bed after giving her the medication. Mrs. Carrier took the girls to the nursery and gave each of them a bottle of formula. What a day! Now I knew that she would start to be normal again.

Chapter 65

The following afternoon, Britt was getting dressed and came up behind me as I was putting on my tuxedo, placed her arms around me, and hugged me lovingly, the way she used to do before all this happened.

"Edward, why is this a formal dinner? I thought this was just a get-together with our closest friends? But here you are in a tuxedo and me with a long red gown."

"I thought about it and then realized that we haven't gone anywhere recently to get dressed up, and so when I mentioned it to everyone, they all agreed to get dressed up also."

"Edward, can you tell me something, please? I have a feeling deep down inside that I did something evil yesterday. I can't remember what, but I think it had something to do with the girls. Please tell me what I did. Please don't try to keep things from me. It's like putting me in a plastic bubble to protect me. I can take it."

"You have been sick and very depressed over having the babies and then losing the baby boy that you went to the pier yesterday to take yourself and the girls swimming. I asked Kristen to follow you, and she kept an eye on you and called me the minute that she realized that something was definitely wrong. Carl called in a prescription to the pharmacy for you, and now you will be on the mend. You shouldn't need it for very long as soon as your body adjusts to the entire trauma that it has been through. We got the medication for you in time."

"Edward, the girls can't swim. They are only babies. Why would I do such a thing to my precious little girls? I'm scared, Edward.

Suppose it happens again. I'm almost afraid to touch them as I might hurt them. I love them so much."

Britt started to cry, and I held her while she nuzzled her face into my chest. She was devastated at what she had almost accomplished in doing to her precious babies. She was crying uncontrollably, and before we knew what was happening, we were hugging and kissing as we used to before she got pregnant.

It was sensational to be loved by Britt again, back to her old self, my soul mate. All our friends were joining us for dinner, even my brother and sister, John and Joanne, who had moved to Monterey Bay a few months ago. This was the very first formal dinner party at our new home here in Monterey Bay.

Chapter 66

The guests arrived promptly at seven. It was so great to see everyone away from the work environment, especially Greg and Monica, who had been through so many hassles with Ashley but now looked so happily married.

Herbert had prepared a wonderful full-course dinner laid out in the dining room, but first, cocktails were being served in the living room.

"Would everyone like a cocktail before dinner?"

"Of course, Edward. That's why we came, to drink all your expensive alcohol, but right at this moment, we would like champagne to congratulate both of you on producing not one but two beautiful children."

"Thank you, Carl." He was teasing. He barely drank anything.

"Men, could you get drinks for the ladies? Everything you need is in the bar. Britt darling, why don't we go upstairs and get the girls. Everyone would love to see them, and I want to show them off. They've grown even bigger than when we brought them home."

"I'm right behind you, sweetheart."

We went upstairs, and they were both dressed in blue matching dresses with yellow butterflies in a taffeta overlay. They were looking beautiful, both having dark hair which was thick and long.

"Britt, I'll take Keira. What's wrong?"

Britt was staring down at Kasey as if she was afraid of something.

"You're better, Britt. Don't be afraid. Go ahead and pick her up."

"Suppose I drop her on purpose. I never remember when it happens or when I do something crazy. You don't realize how horrible I feel knowing that I almost drowned them."

"Britt, you have your medication now, and it seems to be working, and in a few weeks, you probably won't need to take it anymore according to Carl."

"I guess both you and Carl are right."

Britt picked up Kasey, and I could tell that it was so comforting for her to hold her. She snuggled into her. They both smelled so wonderful, all these baby smells. We carried them downstairs, and our guests went crazy over them. Everyone each received a turn of holding them and then acting like pure idiots talking baby talk to them.

"Edward, I never would have believed you, had it in you to produce such beautiful children. Put it this way, I never thought you would ever get married, nor much less have children."

"Well, Carl, I never thought so either until I met Britt on that glorious afternoon high on the cliff overlooking the ocean. We are truly soul mates and have been truly blessed."

"A toast to Edward and Brittney. It couldn't have happened to two better friends and family. We all love you."

"Thank you so much, John. The best part with having so many friends is also having my family, John and Joanne, now here and working with us. Now before we get all teary-eyed, let's go into dinner. I know Herbert has put out a special spread for everyone. Let me first take the girls back to the nursery. I will be back immediately."

Everyone entered the dining room for a sumptuous dinner. Herbert had outdone himself with the layout of the food. The beef was succulent, and then there were the new red potatoes in garlic sauce, toasted asparagus and mushrooms, tossed salad, and to top everything off, lobster newburg. There were also varieties of clams, oysters, shrimp and lobsters. We would eat dessert later with coffee. Everyone ate until full. They all marveled at the many kinds of food, and everyone wanted to hire Herbert full time.

I pulled Carl to the side and told him that the medicine he prescribed for Britt seemed to be working, and that now he didn't seem to need to watch her constantly, and he agreed.

"Everyone! Could I have your attention? I would like for us to lift our glasses and propose a toast to Greg and Monica on being such good friends and finally getting together after all these years, finding each other and being soul mates, as Edward and I are soul mates. I wish you many happy years of wedded bliss and many children."

"Britt, that was a wonderful toast, and I truly agree."

Everyone raised their glasses and shouted, "Here, here."

Edward was looking around, and he saw Greg and Monica smile at each other, and then Greg spoke up. "Thank you for that great toast, Brittney, because if it wasn't for Edward and you, we never would have spoken to each other about our long-forbidden feelings that were there lingering and, therefore, might never have been spoken to each other. We may have never known that we were meant for each other. Together we have some glorious news which we want to share with all you, our special friends. Monica is pregnant. Carl, do you think you can handle yet another patient?"

"I would gladly. I'm overjoyed to take care of Monica."

'Everyone was all over them with many congratulations and hugging all around. It turned out to be the most wonderful party ever."

Epilogue

We are in our home in Monterey Bay, and Kiera and Kasey are now six months old. They are a pleasure to watch as they try to move around. I have never seen Edward so ecstatically happy. He spends most of his time at home, working only three days a week. He doesn't want to miss out on any accomplishments of the growing up years of the girls.

It's as if he was never happy until I came into his life, and he also into mine. He is still as sexy as ever, suave, debonair and handsome. I will never tire of looking at him, but still get a little jealous at times when I see a beautiful lady eyeing him. He is and will always be my soul mate.

John and Joanne, Edward's brother and sister, have been here in Monterey Bay for almost a year now. John bought a house not far from us, and at the moment, Joanne lives with him and takes care of the house and is also working at the Van Nuys Medical Center hospital as a Registered Nurse. John is a Doctor there. Edward is even happier having his family close by here. More about them in the next novel of the series *My Soul Mate*.

I have more exciting news about Edward and I coming up that he doesn't even know about. More about that to come.

A soul mate is a person with whom one has a feeling of deep or natural affinity. This may involve similarity, love, romance, friendship, intimacy, sexuality, sexual activity, spirituality, or compatibility and trust.

About the Author

Audrey Ennis is a Newfoundlander, Canadian, and for the past twenty-five years an American citizen. She is living in Tennessee with her husband Orville. Her children are now grown-up, married, and living for the Lord.

She is a Christian author. She loves to sing in the choir with a beautiful soprano voice.

CPSIA information can be obtained
at www.ICGtesting.com
Printed in the USA
LVHW021702200221
679520LV00004B/380